A Chance in a Million

T.A. Williams lives in Devon with his Italian wife. He was born in England of a Scottish mother and Welsh father. After a degree in modern languages at Nottingham University, he lived and worked in Switzerland, France and Italy, before returning to run one of the best-known language schools in the UK. He's taught Arab princes, Brazilian beauty queens and Italian billionaires. He speaks a number of languages and has travelled extensively. He has eaten snake, still-alive fish, and alligator. A Spanish dog, a Russian bug and a Korean parasite have done their best to eat him in return. His hobby is long-distance cycling, but his passion is writing.

Also by T.A. Williams

Chasing Shadows
Dreaming of Venice
Dreaming of Florence
Dreaming of St-Tropez
Dreaming of Christmas
Dreaming of Tuscany
Dreaming of Rome
Dreaming of Verona
Dreaming of Italy

Escape to Tuscany

Under a Siena Sun
Second Chances in Chianti
Secrets on the Italian Island

Love from Italy

A Little Piece of Paradise
An Escape to Remember
A Chance in a Million

T.A. WILLIAMS

A Chance in a Million

CANELO

First published in the United Kingdom in 2022 by

Canelo
Unit 9, 5th Floor
Cargo Works, 1–2 Hatfields
London, SE1 9PG
United Kingdom

A CIP catalogue record for this book is available from the British Library.

Print ISBN 978 1 80032 768 9
Ebook ISBN 978 1 80032 384 1

Look for more great books at www.canelo.co

Printed and bound in Great Britain by Clays Ltd, Elcograf S.p.A.

1

To my wife, Mariangela, and Christina, my daughter, but, above all, to my new granddaughter, Iris. I look forward to taking her to the magical city of Venice some time in the future.

Prologue

It was the silence that so often brought it back to her.

She was lying on her bed, gazing unseeingly at the ceiling. All sound disappeared and the only thing she could hear was the pounding of her own heart. She was awake enough to know she wasn't quite asleep but her subconscious was yet again taking her down memory lane and she was powerless to stop it. The bedroom around her disappeared, to be replaced by bright sunshine and the all-too familiar vision of dust and devastation that had once been the quiet suburbs of Fallujah.

The events of that afternoon once more took shape in her head. She could actually feel her fingers returning to the shallow depression in the sandy earth that she had been painstakingly excavating, spoonful by spoonful, for what seemed like an age. Lying out here in the baking sun she was bathed in sweat, but she knew from experience she would have been sweating from the tension even if the ground below her had been frozen.

She inched her fingertips into the soft soil again until they landed on the unmistakable feel of electrical wires and confirmed that she had found what she had been looking for. Turning her head gingerly to the left, she called over to Mark who was dealing with an unexploded bomb in a crater twenty yards away from her.

'I've got it, Mark. It's definitely an IED.' She tried to keep her voice as low as possible to avoid startling him.

She saw his face emerge from the crater, his cheeks bright red and running with sweat.

'Need a hand?'

She shook her head. 'I'm all right. Just thought you should know.'

'Okey dokey.'

He didn't wish her luck because that was something they never did. This was their job and, if they did it right, there would be no need for luck. That was what they had been taught and they respected the tradition, but both of them knew it wasn't true. In this line of business, they needed all the luck they could get. He just gave her a smile and a little wave before ducking back down into the crater as she returned her attention to the landmine in front of her.

With infinite caution she continued to remove the earth, scoop by scoop, until the top of the device was clearly visible. As with so many improvised explosive devices, at first sight it looked mundane, little more than harmless builders' refuse. But by now she knew that this sort of home-made landmine was anything but harmless. She had seen the horrific results so many times already here in war-torn Iraq as people struggled to rebuild their lives after the bitter fighting had finally moved away, while the menace of unexploded ordinance remained an ever-present threat beneath their feet.

Inching herself forward on her elbows, she took a good look at the IED. Drops of sweat ran down her face and dripped into the dust beneath her but she didn't dare move her arm to wipe herself dry for fear of sparking a detonation. After blinking to clear her eyes, she saw that the cable had been stripped at one end and the positive and negative wires were fastened to two harmless-looking pieces of wood, while the other end disappeared into an ordinary five litre paint can, the trademark on the lid still clear to see. From experience born of months of active service, she felt sure that this was no longer filled with paint but with home-made explosive laced with lumps of shrapnel, capable of destroying everything and everybody in the vicinity if it went off – starting with her.

She lay there and studied the problem now facing her. Under normal circumstances she would simply have retreated with infinite caution and then detonated it remotely and harmlessly, but in this instance she knew that was impossible. First there was Mark and his unexploded bomb to her left, while less than three metres away to the right was the wall of one of the last functioning hospitals in Fallujah.

She knew she had two choices. One was to crawl slowly backwards away from the landmine and take shelter while Mark finished defusing his bomb. She could radio for help, hoping the vibrations of heavy trucks on the nearby road wouldn't trigger an explosion while they waited for the rest of their team to arrive. The other was to attempt to defuse it right here and now with the limited resources at her disposal. However, a sideways glance at the wall of the hospital, behind which she knew were helpless people, confirmed the fact that she didn't really have any choice at all.

Taking a deep breath and moving deliberately and carefully, she stretched out her right hand towards the upper-most of the pieces of wood. Red electrical tape showed where the contact had been strapped to this primitive trigger, only separated from the other piece of bare copper wire by a matter of millimetres. The slightest tremor on her part and the device could explode with devastating results. She lay there for a full minute, doing her best to calm herself, before her training kicked in and she could almost hear her instructor's voice in her ear.

'You know what you've got to do, so don't take all day. Just do it, Reed.'

As delicately as she could, she caught hold of the piece of wood and lifted it up and away from the other half. She set it down very carefully and then, with her free hand, lifted the plastic lid off the paint can and saw the other end of the cable disappear into the amorphous beige mush that could cause so much carnage. Resolutely, she gritted her teeth and began to pull on the wire until she saw the detonator gradually emerge – an unremarkable little black package with an ordinary Duracell battery taped to the side of it. She disconnected the battery and tossed it away, laid the now disarmed detonator onto the ground alongside her and finally allowed herself to breathe again. She was just rolling over to give Mark the good news when she heard him scream, the sound now forever burned into her memory.

Almost simultaneously a massive explosion picked her up and threw her against the wall of the hospital, cracking her skull and spraying her with shrapnel. She found out later that this tore a vicious gouge across her right thigh, just missing the main artery. The blast also broke most of her ribs and punctured her lung. They told her that only the fact that the bomb had been buried in the crater had saved her from instant death.

Mark didn't stand a chance. The dust slowly began to settle around her and she lay there, barely conscious, staring in disbelief at the huge hole in the ground where he had been only moments before. Her hands, rock-steady up to now, suddenly began to shake.

A car in the street outside her window hooted its horn and the noise broke the spell, tearing her away from her recurring nightmare, but as she opened her eyes her hands were still shaking. It took her a few moments to get her bearings and realise that she was no longer in Iraq, but safely back home in the UK.

It took much longer before the all-too familiar shaking stopped.

Chapter 1

'Your name is Jane Reed, Captain Jane Victoria Reed?'

'Yes, sir.'

'And you are twenty-nine years old?' Mr Gordon Russell, of Barnett and Russell Solicitors in Temple Chambers, London, rattled off the questions and she answered equally formally.

'Yes, sir.'

'You used to be in the army?'

'Yes, sir.'

For the first time he looked up from the file on his desk. 'Captain Reed, you have an impressive CV. First degree in mechanical engineering, six years in the army, including two tours of active service. What regiment were you in?'

'The Sappers, sir, the Royal Engineers.'

'What? Bridge-building and so on?'

'I was in bomb disposal and mine clearance, mainly training local troops in how to go about it.'

'Remarkable.' His bushy eyebrows arched upwards. 'That sounds like a very demanding job. And now you've obtained a Masters in Creative Writing from the University of Cambridge.'

'That's correct, sir.' She wasn't sure whether she really needed to keep calling him 'sir', but some habits were hard to break.

'Can I ask why you decided to leave the army?'

6

'A combination of things. I was involved in an incident that resulted in my being injured, but most of all I needed a change, and I've always wanted to write.' There was so much more she could have told him about weeks in hospital, followed by long months of convalescence, Post-Traumatic Stress Disorder, and of course her broken heart, but he didn't need to hear any of that. That was nobody else's business but hers.

'I see. So why do you feel you would be suited for this position?'

Jane had been preparing for this question ever since reading the advert.

'The advertisement mentioned a famous author looking for a PA. I love writing and can't imagine anything better than being able to work alongside a successful writer. I believe my military background makes me a very organised person, and I must confess that the idea of moving to Italy has considerable appeal.'

He leant forward on his elbows. 'How well do you speak the language? That is fairly fundamental.'

'Quite fluently really. My mother's originally from near Milan and she usually speaks Italian to me and my sister. I'm maybe a bit rusty now but it'll soon come back.'

'I see. And your command of the written language?' He selected a sheet of paper from the file and handed it across to her. 'Can you give me a translation of this, for example?'

She took it from him and studied it. It was an official-looking document granting permission for the renovation of a dilapidated oak door dating back five hundred years. Interestingly, the document was on City of Venice headed paper and she felt an immediate surge of excitement. The advert had only mentioned Italy, not a specific place. After giving him a quick oral translation – it wasn't particularly complicated – she queried the document's provenance. Venice would be amazing. Her spirits leapt as he confirmed it.

'You will have noticed that the position would involve you working principally in Venice. This is a residential position and you'd find yourself living right in the heart of the city. Might that pose any problems for you?'

She shook her head emphatically. 'None whatsoever. In fact, it sounds wonderful.'

'Do you know the city?' Seeing her shake her head. Mr Russell allowed a little smile to spread across his august features. 'Then you will have a treat, a thousand treats, in store.'

She noted with interest his use of the future, rather than conditional tense. Might this mean he was going to offer her the job? She concentrated hard as the interview continued for almost another half an hour and when he finally drew it to a close, she saw him sit back and utter the words she had been dying to hear.

'Captain Reed, I'm pleased to say that I'm convinced you are the best candidate for this position and on behalf of my client I would like to make you a formal offer of employment.' The smile reappeared on his face. 'Do you feel able to accept or would you like time to think about it?'

'Thank you so much, Mr Russell. I would be delighted to accept although I do have a few questions.'

The smile didn't leave his face. If anything, it broadened. 'Excellent and, yes, I've been expecting you to ask quite a few questions. I imagine top of the list is the identity of your new employer.'

'Indeed. Can I assume she is a household name?' All it had said in the advertisement had been *world-renowned author*.

'Yes, indeed. Her name is Lady Veronica Cooper. She instructed me that she didn't want to broadcast her name until I'd found the best candidate for the position.'

'Veronica Cooper...?' Jane had to stop and think. She was a voracious reader and she felt pretty sure she would have recognised a *world-famous* name. Maybe this lady wasn't as famous as she thought she was. She glanced up at the solicitor and saw him positively grinning now.

'Unfamiliar with the name, Captain Reed? Then how about her nom de plume: Veronica Leonard?'

'Wow!' Jane had been expecting a reasonably famous name, but Veronica Leonard was one of the best-known romance writers of all time. Her numerous books had been translated into dozens of languages all over the globe and she had enjoyed celebrity status – and no doubt income – for many years now. 'I had no idea of her real name.'

'She was married to General Sir Peter Cooper.'

'*Was* married?'

'Sir Peter died two years ago.'

'I see. And she lives in Venice?'

'Yes, indeed. Now, what other questions can I answer for you?'

Jane produced a number of questions about pay and conditions as well as asking for more details regarding the exact nature of her duties. The solicitor was able to answer most without trouble and she was pleasantly surprised by the generous nature of the package, particularly as it would include free accommodation in one of the most expensive cities in the world. Her last question about exactly what the job would entail, however, was evidently not so easy for him to answer.

'As for your duties, I'm afraid I can't give you much detail. I asked my client to draw up a job description, but all she managed to produce was this.' He reached for another sheet from the file. Although Jane couldn't read it upside down, she could see that it was far from lengthy. He read it out to her.

'*Secretarial duties, including routine typing, mail, answering the phone, emails and other messages. General assistance with day-to-day life. Representation of VL at functions.*' He dropped the sheet back on the desk and caught Jane's eye. 'I'm afraid that's all I managed to get out of her.'

'I see.' Jane smiled back at him. 'So it sounds like I'm in for a voyage of discovery.'

'Indeed. What I can tell you is that Veronica is a very honest, straightforward person. You can trust her implicitly. I've known her for almost forty years now and I have nothing but the highest regard for her.' She saw him hesitate. 'There is just one thing, though. I don't think I'll be infringing client confidentiality if I add that her husband's death two years ago came as a massive blow to her and, entre nous, I imagine a good part of your job will be to help cheer her up, to provide support and encouragement. Do you think you can do that?'

Jane very nearly told him she could do with a bit of support and encouragement herself, but she decided not to say anything. The fact was that this would involve revealing much about her recent past that she was keen to keep to herself. Instead, she took a deep breath and did her best to reply in positive tones.

'I promise I'll try as hard as I can.'

'Excellent, excellent. Now, as you know, this is a residential position. Could I ask if you'll be alone or accompanied?'

'On my own, sir. I have no partner.' She almost added the word 'now', but stopped herself.

'And when might you be available to begin?'

'Whenever I'm required. Whenever it suits Lady Veronica... or should that be Lady Cooper?'

'The correct appellation is Lady Cooper, but Veronica was never interested in her title. She's a very down to earth sort of person, you'll see. Now, I know she's keen for you to start as soon as feasible. Would you be able to start early next month, maybe even as soon as next week? Monday will be the first of June or would you like more time?'

'Next week would be fine. I'm back living with my parents at the moment so I don't have any complications with tenancies or anything like that.'

'Excellent. So, Captain Reed, can I take it that you accept the position?'

'Yes, sir, I'm very happy to accept. Thank you.'

'Like I said, Veronica hasn't been herself recently, so you may have to tread a careful path.' He shot her a little smile. 'But after your experience in mine clearance that shouldn't be a problem for you.'

'Certainly, sir, and thank you again.'

They both stood up and shook hands again. 'Good luck, Captain Reed.'

She almost saluted him, but just managed to restrain the instinctive response in the nick of time.

Chapter 2

Venice was unlike anywhere Jane had ever been before. She travelled in from Marco Polo airport in a vaporetto, one of the ubiquitous waterbuses that plied to and fro around the Venetian lagoon just like normal buses in an ordinary city. This dropped her at a landing stage just past the imposing arch of the Rialto bridge and from there she had to walk the rest of the way through the pedestrians-only area. The address she had been given wasn't easy to find. All she had was Palazzo Morea, Calle dell'Asino, and the fact that it wasn't far from the Rialto Bridge. Fortunately she had managed to locate the tiny alleyway on Google Earth the night before and put her military training to good use as she wheeled her suitcase across the flagstones, using glimpses of the sun between the buildings to maintain her bearings.

Everywhere she went, the narrow streets were packed with tourists and the temperature was high, the air almost as humid as the Tropics. By the time she finally reached the door she was perspiring, and she was initially disappointed with what she found. With a name like *palazzo*, she had been expecting a grand entrance, but all she was faced with was an admittedly rather fine – and recently renovated – oak door, but it was set in a fairly scruffy wall on one side of an unprepossessing alley little wider than a single bed, at the end of which there was just the grey-green water of the Grand Canal. The plaster had come off the base of the wall, revealing centuries-old red bricks, worn and weathered by the passing of the years, and vandals had even sprayed one spot with graffiti. Incongruously, this was in basic – and questionable – English, rather than Italian, and read *Pinck Floyd Sux*. Clearly this was no medieval relic.

An impressive brass door knocker in the shape of a lion took pride of place on the door and gleamed in the dying rays of the sun. Evidently somebody was looking after the door and the knocker, if not the plaster. She reached out and gave it a hefty thump, hearing the sound echo up the high walls of the alley and, no doubt, around the palazzo inside, and she hoped she hadn't offended the inhabitants. A few seconds later there was a rattling sound and the door was pulled open to reveal a mature lady dressed in black. Jane gave her a smile.

'Lady Cooper?'

The lady shook her head and replied in Italian. 'I'm afraid she isn't available at the moment. Can I help?'

'My name's Jane Reed. I'm here to start my new job as Lady Cooper's personal assistant.' She was pleased to hear her Italian sounding pretty fluent. She saw the expression on the lady's face soften.

'Do come in, Signora Reed. We've been expecting you.' She stepped to one side and ushered Jane into a shadowy hallway where it was blissfully cool after the stuffy heat outside. Shutting the door behind her she turned, wiping her hand on a cloth, before holding it out. 'My name's Maria. I'm the housekeeper.' She gave Jane an appraising look. 'You're so much younger than I was expecting.' A smile spread across her face. 'That's rather good. We need some fresh young blood here in the house.'

'No other younger people here?'

'No, not now. They're all grown up and have fled the nest.' Maria suddenly took in the fact that Jane had brought a suitcase. 'Have you come from the airport? You should have called. Alvise would have been happy to come and pick you up. He's my husband. He looks after the launch and the cars.'

'Cars, here?' Jane knew full well that the whole of the *centro storico* that wasn't under water was a pedestrian zone.

'They're kept in a garage near the station and the launch is moored right outside the main entrance of this palazzo.'

Jane indicated the door behind her. 'So this isn't the main entrance?'

'Goodness, no. Come and I'll show you around. Leave your bag. Alvise will take it up to your room for you.'

'Shouldn't I go and see Lady Cooper first? Or is she too busy?'

Maria shook her head. 'To be honest, she was feeling a bit tired so she's having a little nap.' She glanced at her watch. 'Six o'clock. She should be stirring pretty soon. Come along in.'

Jane followed her through a doorway into a far larger hallway, barely a few feet above the level of the waters of the Grand Canal, which was immediately on the other side of a series of glazed arches. This huge open room, punctuated by hefty brick pillars, was flooded with dappled light as the sun's rays reflected on the water outside, making it look as if the ceiling was alive. The floor was a complex mosaic composed of swirls made up of squares, triangles and other geometric shapes of marble, stone and ceramic tiles in various colours and ranging in size from an open palm to the smallest fingernail. The overall impression was of looking at the most splendid giant Persian carpet. It was breathtakingly beautiful.

Jane walked across to the windows and looked out. A handful of steps led down to a wooden jetty supported on hefty posts sunk into the bed of the lagoon, the tops painted in rings of red, white and blue, almost like old barber's poles. She stood there, taking it all in, watching a gondolier scull expertly across the canal, narrowly avoiding a vaporetto and a police launch as he did so. On the other side of the canal were delightful ornate palazzi, one more charming than the other, no two the same, and all in different states of preservation. Alongside freshly decorated façades were weathered buildings, painted in sun-bleached pinks and creams, the plaster ravaged by the passage of the centuries and the elements, but all of them combining to produce the incomparable spectacle that is Venice. It was a wonderful view.

'Is this your first visit to Venice?' Maria must have noticed the awed look on Jane's face.

'Yes, and it's absolutely amazing. This palazzo, is it very old?'

'They say it was built in 1603.'

Jane caught her breath. So this place was over four hundred years old. The idea of living in such an ancient – and exquisite – building as this was an enchanting prospect.

'Come on up to the living room and let me get you something to drink. Some tea, maybe? I know you English like to drink tea in the afternoon.' Jane followed her across to a sweeping marble staircase that led them up to the main living area, no doubt safely above the levels of the infamous *acqua alta* floods that had plagued the city for centuries.

Nice as a cup of tea sounded, Jane knew that an ice-cold beer would have been even more appealing, but she was quick to accept. The first floor, or *piano nobile* as Maria told her they called it here, had much higher ceilings, supported by hefty wooden beams which had been highlighted in intricate patterns of red and gold paint. Maria left her in a huge room with arched windows similar to the hall below and with enormous four tier chandeliers hanging from the ceiling, sparkling in the evening sunlight. Jane stood and gazed out over the busy scene that opened up in front of her. It was like stepping back in time and she could imagine beautiful ladies in ornate dresses and wigs, accompanied by handsome men wearing tights and carrying swords, being ferried about on the Grand Canal.

After a few minutes, her musings were interrupted by, of all things, a cold wet nose prodding her wrist. She looked down to see a fine-looking black Labrador at her side, tail wagging in greeting. She was stroking his ears when she heard a voice.

'Good afternoon. You must be Captain Reed. Truffaldino, leave the girl alone.'

Jane whirled round and found herself confronted by a tall lady with grey hair. She was probably in her mid to late sixties and she looked weary. There was what might have been an attempt at a smile on her face but even from distance Jane could see dark rings under her eyes that indicated that she maybe didn't do too much smiling or sleeping. She remembered what Mr Russell had said about the effect the death of her husband had had on her and Jane immediately felt a common bond with the older woman.

'Lady Cooper? I'm really pleased to meet you.'

They shook hands and Jane studied her more closely. Her new employer was wearing a seriously rumpled cotton dress and her hair was loosely tied behind her head in an untidy ponytail. Jane's first impression was of a person who looked run-down and careless about her appearance, and it saddened her. Their eyes met and Jane couldn't miss the fact that she was being closely observed in her turn.

'Please don't call me Lady Cooper. I'd prefer it if you used my pen name and, before you ask, Leonard is my maiden name. Seeing as you'll be principally looking after my alter ego, it's probably just as well if you try to think of me as Veronica Leonard. I value my privacy, so the fewer people who might associate the two names the better. Besides, the title's not really mine anyway. It belonged to my husband. I'm just an impostor.'

'I hardly think so...' Jane hesitated, wondering how to address her new boss before settling for 'Miss Leonard'. There was no negative reaction so she decided to stick with it. 'I'm very excited to have the opportunity to work for such a household name as you, Miss Leonard. I've read so many of your books and I love them all.' She caught her eye. 'They made for a wonderful bit of escapism when I was on active service.'

'Ah, yes, you used to be in the army. My husband and my son used to be in the British Army.' Jane filed this snippet of information away while Miss Leonard continued. 'Army life was probably a bit different from this, I imagine.' She nodded her head vaguely towards the spectacle outside the windows before changing tack. 'You're very pretty.' She delivered the compliment deadpan, as if making a simple observation, and Jane didn't even find herself blushing. 'Gordon told me he chose you because of your qualifications and experience, but he's always had a soft spot for a pretty face.'

Jane thought she could hear a note of disapproval and was quick to set the record straight. 'I'm sure my looks didn't come into it. At least, I hope not. I'd like to think I got the job on my merits alone.'

Miss Leonard held up her hand wearily. 'All right, all right, no need to come over all feminist on me. I was just stating a fact.'

Jane felt herself bristle but, fortunately, at that moment Maria reappeared, carrying a silver tray with teapot, cups and saucers and some delicious-looking little cakes. She set it down on a low table and stepped back. Miss Leonard caught Jane's eye.

'Sure it's tea you want? It's so hot I fancy a glass of something cold.'

'I'd love something cold but I said yes to Maria's offer of tea so I feel duty bound to drink it.'

'Well, you do what you think you must do. I'm having a G&T.' She glanced over at Maria who was standing by the door. '*Il solito, Maria, per favore.*' Her Italian accent sounded almost perfect and even a bit Venetian.

Jane noted that she had just asked for her 'usual'. Could it be that the grieving widow had chosen alcohol as her coping mechanism? Jane hoped not. One of her colleagues in the Sappers had started hitting the bottle heavily – to combat the stress of the job – and had been drummed out of the service as a result. Booze could change lives.

They settled down on comfortable leather sofas facing each other and Jane leant forward to pour herself a cup of tea. As she did so, the dog appeared at her right hand and sat primly beside her, looking as if butter wouldn't melt in his mouth, his eyes trained unerringly not on her, but on the cakes. Miss Leonard was quick to remind him of his manners.

'Dino, no! No cakes for dogs. You'll just get fat and then David will tell me off again.'

'Isn't he your dog?'

'No, he belongs to my son, David. He's away for the whole month so Dino's been left with me. He's a lovely dog but, given half a chance, he'd eat himself to death.' Jane was pleased to see her employer's expression soften a fraction as she glanced down at the dog.

Jane stroked Dino's head and did her best to keep the conversation light. 'We used to have a lab and he was the same. I think it's the way they're made.' She glanced out of the window at the waters of the Grand Canal. 'Where does he go for wal… W – A – L – K – S, or does he only understand Italian?'

'When it's a matter of food or exercise he's bilingual. Alvise looks after him mostly. You'd better ask him. I don't go out much.'

A slightly uncomfortable silence then ensued, interrupted by the return of Maria with another silver tray, this time holding a bottle of gin, two glasses, two small bottles of tonic and a crystal bowl filled with ice. She set it down on the coffee table and retired, but Jane couldn't miss the expression of compassion on the housekeeper's face as she turned away. Jane wondered just how much of a habit Miss Leonard had developed. Certainly, working for an alcoholic wouldn't be easy and, for the first time, she began to question the wisdom of accepting what had seemed like a dream job. However, she was slightly reassured to see her employer add almost a whole bottle of tonic to a fairly modest quantity of spirit. After a few more moments of silence, she decided to ask the question that had been plaguing her ever since being offered the job.

'Could you satisfy my curiosity and tell me how come a British lady happens to be living here in Venice?'

She was relieved to see that this elicited a hint of a smile on her employer's face. 'Peter, my husband, was posted all over the world by the army and I followed him at first but when the children arrived we decided it was only fair to give them a settled family home. Although Peter was born and bred in Oxfordshire and we lived there for a while after getting married, he came from an old Venetian family on his mother's side and we decided to settle here in Venice when his father passed away almost thirty years ago now. I've always loved the country and, of course, for him, it was a sort of homecoming.'

'Well, I think your decision to come here was inspired. It's magnificent. Now, I wonder if you could give me an idea of my duties. Do you have a regular daily schedule? Do you have an office? Would I have an office? Do you write in the mornings or later on?'

'Do I write?' Miss Leonard took a mouthful of her drink before replying. 'The answer, Captain Reed, is that I don't write.'

'You don't write?' Jane looked up in amazement. 'But you've been publishing book after book. I imagined you at the computer all day long.'

Miss Leonard didn't raise her eyes from her glass. 'I used to be like that, but that's all changed now. About the only things I've written in the past two years have been replies to letters of condolence after my husband passed away.' For a second she glanced up and Jane read deep sorrow on her employer's face before the weary eyes dropped again. 'As for a regular daily schedule, that's what you're here for. I want you to be my eyes and my ears. You take the phone calls; you answer the emails and letters. I can't be bothered any more.' Her voice was flat, her demeanour, deflated.

Jane was beginning to see what Mr Russell had meant about this job involving treading carefully. Working for somebody suffering from serious depression was likely to be tricky. Still, she told herself, she was a fine one to talk. When it came to depression, she was no novice. Maybe this would be the opportunity for both of them to emerge from beneath their respective clouds of gloom. She took a deep breath and hoped for the best. There was no getting away from the fact that this job would be a chance in a million to work alongside a world-famous author and to experience life in these unique surroundings. Her counsellor and her mother had both urged her to make a radical change, and life in a seventeenth-century palazzo alongside the Grand Canal was certainly that.

Chapter 3

A fine old grandfather clock was striking seven when Maria reappeared and led Jane up to her accommodation, and it was well worth the climb up three more flights of stairs to get there. It turned out to be a self-contained apartment on the top floor of the palazzo and the views from the windows were stunning. Jane stood and gazed in awe at the red-tiled roofs, the spires, cupolas and towers of the city, as well as the network of canals of all sizes that sliced through the closely packed buildings. The sun was dropping towards the horizon and reflected on the waters of the lagoon, giving them and the city a pink glow, filling the whole scene with a magical feel. She was so enthralled that she barely heard Maria's voice behind her.

'Dino, you shouldn't be up here.'

Jane turned to find that the Labrador had followed them up the stairs and was sniffing her suitcase with interest. She smiled down at him.

'That's all right, Maria. I love dogs. It'll be nice to have some company. And many thanks to Alvise for bringing my suitcase up all those stairs. Tell him I'm sorry it's so heavy but I had to pack for a long stay.'

Maria showed her around the kitchen, the living room, the two bedrooms, both with scrupulously clean bathrooms, and a little room equipped with a desk and a telephone that would make a perfect office. Jane reflected that this was a whole lot more luxurious than any flat she had lived in before and in a unique, outstanding setting. Her new boss might be going to create problems for her of a different kind, but providing sumptuous accommodation wasn't one of them. She thanked Maria profusely and asked for her advice as to where to go to eat. 'I've heard that Venice can be very expensive. Are there any reasonably priced restaurants around here?'

'There's a pizzeria a couple of blocks away which isn't too expensive, but I'm afraid almost all the restaurants here in the centre aren't cheap.' Maria opened the fridge door. 'That's why I've filled the fridge for you. At least you should have enough to eat for a few days until you find your feet. If you like I can show you a couple of places where the food is good – even if it does cost a bit more than over on the mainland – so you won't get ripped off too badly if you do decide to go out to eat. Why don't you come shopping with me tomorrow morning and I can show you where I buy food for Her Ladyship?'

'That would be great but won't Her Ladyship want to see me?'

Maria shook her head. 'Not before mid-morning. She's never been a morning person and since Sir Peter died she's been getting up later and later.'

Jane wondered whether this might be connected with her employer's obvious depression and it struck a familiar chord in her. In the early months after Mark's death, she, too, had spent an inordinate amount of time in bed – and in her pyjamas around the house. She decided not to bring up the subject with Maria until they knew each other better. They arranged to meet up in the kitchen downstairs at nine next morning and Maria went off to prepare dinner for Miss Leonard. To Jane's surprise, the dog showed no sign of wanting to follow and settled himself down on a rather smart old rug in front of the huge empty fireplace while Jane pulled out her phone and called her mum to tell her she had arrived.

Later that evening she made herself a sandwich with some of the marvellous selection of sliced ham, cheese and salami from the fridge. She accompanied her meal with a glass of cold white wine from one of a row of unlabelled bottles that lined the fridge door. When she opened the wine it fizzed before settling down and she wondered if it might be Prosecco – although it was in an ordinary wine bottle – which she knew to be local to the Veneto area. Whatever it was, it was excellent.

At the end of the meal she stood at the open window and surveyed the lights of Venice below. The Grand Canal was still busy with boats chugging up and down while the orange glow of the lights of the mainland off to her right showed how densely populated this part of northern Italy had become. Up here on the top floor it was almost silent apart from the snores of the dog who was still snoozing happily on the rug. The whine of a mosquito by her ear finally decided her to step back and close the mesh screen across the window. Hearing her move, the dog woke up, sprang to his feet and shook himself.

'Had a good sleep, Dino?' Jane couldn't help thinking of Fred Flintstone's pet dinosaur as she used the dog's name and it brought a smile to her face. Just like her new employer, smiles had been lacking on her own face for some time now, and it felt good. She went over to the dog and ruffled his ears. 'You can't stay here all night, you know. Maybe I should take you for a walk.'

The dog immediately displayed his bilingual comprehension skills as the magic word started him bouncing up and down excitedly, uttering happy little whines of anticipation. Jane glanced at her watch, grabbed her purse and her phone and headed downstairs with him. It was half past nine and she wondered if this would mean that the streets would be less crowded.

They weren't.

Armed with a lead, a pocketful of poo bags and Maria's directions to a couple of large squares – the closest thing to open space for dog walkers here in this part of Venice – she set off into the night and found herself surrounded by a mass of humanity. There were people of all shapes, sizes and nationalities. Dino had no compunction about greeting many of the humans he saw – especially those wearing short shorts – with his cold, wet nose, and Jane had to keep a close eye on him to avoid angry reactions from non-dog lovers. Even so, she still had time to begin to take in the sheer variety of the buildings around her and the beauty of this incomparable city.

After a few minutes among the crowds, they finally emerged into the large open space of Campo Sant-Anzolo and she found herself doing her best to prevent Dino from pulling her arm out of its socket as he attempted to chase the flocks of pigeons. Although night had fallen, the birds were still on the lookout for food under the streetlights, even though their country cousins would no doubt all be asleep by now. At the far end of the piazza a group of colourful Peruvians were playing their panpipes and the music echoed around the square. She was wandering about, soaking up the atmosphere, when her phone started ringing.

She checked the caller ID and was surprised to see that it was Fergus. She wasn't sure whether to be happy to hear from him or not.

'Hi, Fergus. Long time no speak. How are you?'

'Hi, Jane. How are *you* is more to the point?' Fergus had been one of her fellow officers in the regiment and was one of the few people who knew the full horror of what had happened that day in Fallujah. Hearing his voice brought a whole host of memories rushing back – most of them unwelcome.

'I'm doing well, thanks.' She did her best to sound upbeat. 'In fact I've just started a new job in Venice of all places.'

'That sounds great. You always had a thing about Italy, didn't you?'

They chatted for a few minutes and he told her he had just been promoted to major. After she had given him her congratulations he got round to the reason for the call.

'Ginny and I are getting married on the twenty-fifth of August and we wondered if you'd like to come. Sorry it's a bit short notice, but I'm being posted in the autumn and we thought we'd better legalise things first.' He had obviously already considered how she might react at the thought of what would no doubt turn out to be a regimental reunion, with all the memories that could stir up, as he was quick to add. 'Anyway, just take your time. Why don't you save the date and think about it? No pressure. Let me have your address and we'll send you an invitation but, like I say, no pressure.'

'Thanks, Fergus, that's very kind. I don't know, though…' Her voice tailed off and he jumped in.

'Like I say, just think about it. We'd both love you to come but we would fully understand if you didn't feel up for it.'

'Thanks, Fergus, thanks a lot.' Automatically, she dictated her new address to him and told him she would definitely think about it. After he had rung off, she stood there for a few moments, staring blindly across the flagstones to the array of pink and white buildings all around the square and felt pretty sure that sending her an invitation was going to be a waste of a postage stamp. Any lengthier reflection was interrupted by the sight of the dog crouching down at her feet in an unmistakable pose. Hastily she stuffed the phone back in her pocket and reached for the poo bags.

—

Next morning she woke up with a feeling of considerable relief. Despite her new surroundings and even after receiving the call from Fergus, she had slept like a log, untroubled by any recurrence of her bad dreams. She went across to the bedroom window and opened the mesh screen that had done a good job of keeping away unwanted insects. She leant out and surveyed the view. It was another cloudless day and she felt sure the temperature would be high once more. Although the flat was on the top floor right up underneath the roof and she hadn't turned on the aircon, she hadn't been too hot in bed. Certainly, in comparison to Iraq, this was bearable heat. She spared a thought for her new canine friend underneath his thick fur coat. It must be hot being a Labrador in Venice in the summer.

After taking a shower she went through to the kitchen to make herself a coffee and heard scratching coming from outside the door. She opened it to find that Dino had come upstairs to greet her. She gave him a big smile and a bread stick. It was rather nice to have company.

At nine o'clock she and the dog descended the stairs and met Maria, who introduced her to her husband.

'Good morning, Signora Reed. This is Alvise.'

As Jane shook hands with the friendly-looking man, she couldn't miss the gnarly feel of his hands and the weather-beaten look to his face. Clearly he hadn't spent his whole life as a live-in servant.

'Good morning, Alvise, and please would both of you call me Jane. Thank you for carting my suitcase up all those stairs yesterday. Sorry I had to bring so much stuff.'

She had felt obliged to bring winter things in addition to lightweight summer clothes as well as the two smart dresses she owned in case she really did have to represent Miss Leonard at formal events. She hadn't taken much interest in her appearance for several years now and she felt sure she would have to think about doing a bit of shopping one of these days. No sooner had the thought occurred to her than she realised that this was the first time she had considered clothes shopping for ages and took it as a positive sign. If she had still been having sessions with Oscar, the counsellor the regiment had provided for her, she felt sure he would have approved.

'Don't worry about that, Sig— Jane.' Alvise had a stronger accent than his wife but Jane managed to follow what he was saying pretty well. 'I spent most of my life working as a stevedore at the docks so a little bag like yours was nothing.'

Leaving Dino with Alvise, Jane and Maria set off on their shopping trip. Even this early in the morning the narrow street was fast filling up with tourists and she was relieved when Maria led her off into a narrow lane away from the crowds. Jane did her best to memorise the route as they snaked through alleys sometimes little wider than her shoulders. After crossing a narrow humpbacked bridge over a far from fragrant-smelling canal, they reached a little square hemmed in by tall buildings which provided welcome shade from the morning sun. Here they found a neon sign above a shop front proudly describing itself as a supermarket despite the width of the shop barely reaching a few metres. Inside, however, it opened up into a complex labyrinth of rooms, many with ornate arched ceilings, all packed with supplies.

From there they carried on via the back lanes as Maria showed her the best shops to buy fish, meat, fruit and vegetables; most of them tucked away well off the tourist trail. On the occasions when the alleys were wide enough for them to walk two abreast, Maria explained the solution the Cooper family – in common with many of the inhabitants of Venice – had come up with so as to avoid the tsunami of tourists who descended on the city every summer.

It was very simple: they moved out.

'At the end of the month we'll head for the hills.' In answer to Jane's quizzical expression, she elaborated. 'As well as the palazzo, the family also has a country estate. Signora Flora, the general's mother, lives up there now.'

'Really?' Jane did a bit of quick calculation. If the general had been the same age as Lady Cooper or even a bit older, his mother was probably well into her nineties by now. 'Does she live there alone?'

'She has a companion.' Maria used the expression *dama di compagnia*, which sounded like something out of *A Room with a View*.

'And this lady looks after the general's mother?'

Maria's face broke into a little smile. 'I'm not quite sure who looks after who. Signora Flora's still a very feisty lady, even though she's just turned ninety-five and her companion is only a year or two younger. But they

29

manage – with a bit of help from Umberto who looks after the estate.'

'I see. And where's the country estate?'

'It's up in the Colli Euganei.' Seeing the look on Jane's face, she supplied some more detail. 'It's a hilly area just over an hour or so from here, on the other side of Padua. The temperature's a lot more manageable up there and there aren't so many people milling around.'

'Will that include me?'

'I'm sure it will. Alvise and I will close up the palazzo and we'll all go.'

'And you're happy to leave Venice?'

'I am. I'm not from the city. I'm a country girl originally and I'm dying for a bit of fresh air. Alvise is a Venetian through and through so it's tougher for him to leave all his friends, but even he enjoys getting away in summer. I'm sure you will, too.'

'And no doubt Dino will as well.'

'He lives up there anyway. That's where David, Her Ladyship's son, lives.'

'With his grandmother?'

'He lives in a separate house up there.' She caught Jane's eye and smiled. 'It's a very big estate.'

'I see. And what does he do? His mother said he used to be in the British Army, like his father.'

For a fraction of a second Jane thought she glimpsed a look of compassion on her face and she wondered what could have caused it. However, the expression disappeared again without trace as Maria answered.

'He's a writer now. He's ever so brainy.'

'Like mother, like son. It must run in the family.'

'Yes, indeed, but he writes history books – you know, serious non-fiction, not like his mother's books.'

Since they were well away from any curious ears, Jane decided to do a little bit of digging as far as their employer was concerned. 'Miss Leonard... Her Ladyship told me last night that she hasn't written a thing for ages. Is that because of the death of her husband?'

Maria nodded sadly. 'I'm afraid so. She and Sir Peter were together for forty years and she was devoted to him. I've been working for them ever since they moved into the palazzo thirty years ago. His death hit her hard, I'm afraid. It's been two years now and she's still not showing any signs of coming out of it.' She caught Jane's eye for a moment. 'Alvise and I are very worried for her, but what can we do?'

'Can't her son help? Or does she have other children?'

'There's not much help coming from him, I'm afraid. He's very much a recluse these days. He spends almost all his time up at the estate and doesn't come here often. Don't get me wrong – he and his mother get on well but he's decided to hide himself away.' Yet again that look of deep sympathy. 'Her Ladyship has two daughters; Beatrice and Diana. Beatrice is the eldest child. She's recently divorced and lives in Rome with her little girl, while Diana, the youngest, has been studying in New York and she only comes back every now and then. So Lady Cooper's left on her own – apart from Signora Flora and Alvise and me of course.'

'Poor lady. Well, I'll try to do my bit to help cheer her up.' Although, she told herself ruefully, it would help if she could learn how to cheer herself up first.

Chapter 4

It was almost midday before Miss Leonard emerged from her room.

After returning from the shopping expedition, Jane had pulled out her laptop and spent some time looking for books by David Cooper, but without success, even though she tried both UK and Italian retailers. Of course it was possible he hadn't had any books published yet, but the way Maria had spoken, she was surprised. Then she had a moment of inspiration and tried David Leonard and struck gold. Evidently he had adopted his mother's maiden name for his own pen name and she wondered why. There was a serious-looking book about the First World War, and a brief glance at the contents made it obvious that he had an almost encyclopaedic knowledge of his subject.

She did a bit more digging into the Cooper family background on Google and discovered mention of Beatrice's wedding ten years earlier. A photo showed a beaming bride and her husband standing outside a wonderful old church. Sadly, from what Maria had said, the marriage had turned sour and ended badly. Before she could get around to Diana, her research was interrupted as the phone on her desk started to ring. It was her employer. Clearly there was some sort of intercom facility incorporated in the phone system.

'Good morning, Captain Reed. If you could spare me a few minutes, I'll be in the lounge.' She sounded quite cordial and Jane was relieved.

'I'm on my way.'

When Jane opened her door, she almost tripped over a large back shape, almost invisible on the dark red rug, stretched out at the top of the stairs.

'Dino, you'll be the death of me.'

He just wagged his tail and stood up to lick her hand as she made a fuss of him. All the way down the stairs she could hear the clicking of his nails on the floor behind her. When she reached the door to the living room she hesitated before deciding she should knock. A voice from within answered her.

'No need to knock. Come in, come in.'

The Labrador nosed the door open and led the way. Inside, Jane found her employer standing at the window with a cup of coffee in her hand.

'Good morning, Captain Reed. Would you like a coffee? There's a fresh pot on the table. *Ciao, Dino, come stai?*' She patted the dog's head and Jane was pleased to see her expression soften.

'Good morning, Miss Leonard.' Jane went across and poured herself a little cup of strong black coffee from a well-used old Moka pot. 'Did you sleep well?'

'Not really, but I'm used to it now. I gather from Maria that she's been showing you the lesser-known sights of Venice.' There was a warmer note in her voice and Jane took heart.

'Definitely off the tourist trail – and that was welcome. I hadn't realised just how claustrophobic it could be here in Venice.'

'You think it's crowded now? Just you wait till next month. It's almost impossible to move in July and August. Did Maria tell you we'll be decamping for the hills in three or four weeks' time? We normally stay there until September; it's the only solution.'

'Yes, she did. In the Something-or-other Hills, I believe she said. I didn't quite catch it.'

'Colli Euganei or, as immortalised in the poem by Percy Bysshe Shelley, the Euganean Hills. My husband's family have a house up there and my mother-in-law still lives there. It's a beautiful area and it's also where David, my son, lives, although he's away this month.'

'Is that for work? I gather from Maria that he's also a writer.'

Lady Cooper nodded her head slowly and for a second or two Jane spotted that same compassionate expression she had seen on Maria's face. 'He's in northern France at the moment ferreting around the battlefields of the First World War – research for a book he's working on.' She drained the last of her coffee and set the cup down. 'Now then, let's have a talk about what I'd like you to do for me. Shall we sit down?'

They talked for well over an hour, during which Miss Leonard handed over a variety of documents including her diary – remarkable for the number of blank pages in it – and explained what commitments she had and what she would like Jane to do about them. Jane learnt the name of her literary agent in London as well as the people to contact at her publishers. These snippets of information came with a caveat.

'Eleanor, my agent, loves nothing better than to come over here and try to twist my arm. She's decided to make it her mission to get me writing again and she'll jump at

34

any opportunity to come and badger me. I'm counting on you, Captain Reed, to put her off. I'm not in the mood for being badgered.'

Jane added a few notes to the list she was compiling, but her employer hadn't finished yet.

'And the same applies to anybody from my publishers. They're constantly on at me to send them something. Now, in that bag over there's a heap of letters from readers. I'd like you to make a start at answering them – not all of them, just the non-crazy ones.'

'You get letters from crazy people?'

'Fans come in all shapes and sizes. You'd be surprised how many of them identify intimately with my characters. Some of them can be really deluded. At all costs don't get into lengthy correspondence with anybody too weird and, whatever you do, don't breathe a word of where I live, my address or my contact details.'

'How did the letters get to you if nobody knows your address?'

'Via the publishers or my agent or both.'

'What about your name? I imagine your married name is in the public domain?'

'Yes, people know I'm married but, like I told you yesterday, I think it's better if you always refer to me by my penname.'

By the time the meeting concluded, it had been agreed that Jane would work out of the office in her flat and she and Miss Leonard would meet up every day at noon so that Jane could discuss developments and receive orders. Finally, Miss Leonard sat back and breathed deeply.

'Excellent. Having you here is going to take a tremendous burden off my shoulders, Captain Reed.'

'On that subject, Miss Leonard, would you like to call me Jane? To be honest, I no longer use my military rank. That's the old me, not the new me.'

To her surprise, this drew a wry smile from her employer. 'You sound just like David. He's said those selfsame words to me on numerous occasions. I suppose civilian life is so very different from the army, isn't it?'

Jane glanced around this quiet, peaceful, luxurious room and out of the windows at the ever-changing spectacle that was the Grand Canal and nodded. 'Totally different, Miss Leonard.'

'Different in a good way?'

At that moment a gondolier in his striped jumper appeared just below the window and sculled past. There was a muffled call from the jetty as somebody, probably Alvise, shouted a greeting which the gondolier returned with a wave. It was beautiful, peaceful, and it couldn't have been more different from her experiences in the military. She returned her eyes to her employer.

'Definitely in a good way.' She even felt herself smiling. Progress.

—

Jane went for a little walk in the afternoon and when she got back to the palazzo, she found Alvise waiting for her with further instructions from Miss Leonard.

'If you're free now, I've been told to take you over to the mainland so you can equip yourself with everything you need for your office. There's a big office supplies store in Mestre where you should be able to find everything. Here's her credit card. The code is 1234.' He grinned. 'She's not very bothered about security matters. She told me to tell you to buy yourself a new computer and anything else you think you need.' He lowered his voice a little. 'And don't worry about the expense. One thing there's no shortage of in this house is money.'

To Jane's surprise, they were joined on their shopping trip by a very happy Labrador. As she followed him into the immaculately varnished wooden launch moored at the palazzo's private jetty, Alvise explained.

'While you go shopping, I'll take Dino for a quick run in the fields. He's used to having all the exercise he wants at the estate in the hills so he finds life in the *centro storico* a bit constricting. I take him out whenever I can.'

'When you say "estate"… Is it a big property?'

'It's huge. I forget how many hectares of land.' Seeing the expression on her face, he smiled. 'What did I just tell you about this family and money? It's been in the family for generations. They were a very important merchant family here in Venice with roots going back to the Middle Ages.'

'And that's where Signora Flora, Her Ladyship's mother-in-law, lives. Maria told me.'

'Yes, indeed, and she's a fine lady. I've known her for ages and she has a heart of gold.' He caught Jane's eye and grinned. 'Although she can hide it pretty well when she wants to.'

'Maria said she was a feisty old lady.'

'Definitely, and woe betide you if she hears you calling her "old".'

He cast off and they motored sedately – he told her there was a very strict speed limit all over the lagoon – back up the Grand Canal and he pointed out a number of places of interest as they passed. By the time they reached the station Jane was almost overwhelmed by the succession of iconic buildings they had seen, from art galleries and museums to imposing palazzi and, of course, the magnificent arches and pillars of Venice Casino – according to Alvise, the oldest casino in the world – its main entrance opening onto a landing stage protected from the elements by a very classy red cloth canopy. Jane could imagine a succession of launches like theirs, laden with formally dressed ladies and gentlemen, jockeying for position on busy nights, and she wondered if the inside of the building was as impressive as the exterior.

They left the launch just past the station at a private landing stage behind which was a solid old red brick garage. Inside there was a big Mercedes 4x4 and a little Fiat 500. Dino leapt eagerly into the rear of the Mercedes and they set off up the causeway to the mainland. The grey-green waters of the lagoon stretched out on both sides. Ahead of them to the left was an industrial sprawl of factories and petrol refineries, while to the right was just water, the reed-edged shoreline, and a few distant islands. The view in that direction probably hadn't changed much since the days of Marco Polo, although the roar of an aircraft coming in to land at the airport that bore his name indicated that things had moved on somewhat since then.

Jane spent almost half an hour and a considerable amount of her employer's money at the office supplies store and emerged laden down. She called Alvise and he arrived five minutes later to collect her. After loading everything into the car they set off back along the causeway again and he made a suggestion.

'Maria tells me this is your first time in Venice. If you like we could take the long way back and I'll give you a bit of a tour. I can show you where I used to work.'

Jane had no doubts on that score and accepted gratefully. After returning the car to its garage they loaded the shopping into the launch and he set off. He steered the boat expertly through the traffic as the canal narrowed until they emerged into a wide-open waterway, hundreds of metres across. Here he turned right and slowed as they reached a series of massive quays, alive with boats of all shapes and sizes, from large naval vessels to the ubiquitous barges that were Venice's delivery vehicles.

'This is the port. I worked here for fifty years, from when I was a youngster until two years ago. It still feels very familiar.'

They chugged slowly in among the other boats and from time to time he was greeted by people who knew him, and Jane could sense the camaraderie he must still feel. It reminded her of her time in the regiment. They, too, had been a close-knit community, and deep and lasting friendships had been formed. Thoughts of the regiment reminded her of Fergus's phone call last night and the wedding invitation. While her initial reaction had been to say no, she allowed herself to consider it. It would be good to meet up with her former brothers and sisters in arms in spite of the memories it would inevitably stir up. Maybe she should say yes after all.

Of course, Mark wouldn't be there, but there was nothing anybody could do about that now.

She resolved to see how she felt when the invitation landed on her desk and surprised herself by actually entertaining the possibility of accepting. Oscar, the counsellor, would no doubt have identified this as another positive sign, although she knew that considering and accepting were two very different things.

From there Alvise took her down the broad waterway in the direction of the open sea. The water here in the open channel was no longer so smooth and there was a very welcome breeze. The dog roused himself from his sleep inside the cabin and came out to enjoy the cooler air, and Alvise wagged an admonitory finger at him.

'You do not, repeat not, jump in the water, Dino. Got it?' He looked over at Jane. 'Like all Labradors he's got a thing for water but Her Ladyship wouldn't be too happy if we brought a smelly wet dog home to her. Will you keep an eye on him please?'

Jane kept one eye on the dog and one eye on the scenery as they approached the end of the island of Giudecca on their right. Alvise pointed out the impressive cupola and tower of the church of San Giorgio Maggiore on the next little island. Before they reached it, he spun the wheel and headed across to the other side of the waterway. He glanced across at her and pointed straight ahead at a scene she had seen many times in books and on the television but never before in the flesh. It was an unforgettable assortment of light cream-coloured stone buildings whose intricate maze of exotic Byzantine arches gave them an almost lacework appearance, while the pink and white bell tower and the massive dome of St Mark's basilica beyond were unmistakable.

'There's the Doge's Palace. Alongside it is St Mark's Square, the Basilica and the Campanile. If you like I could drop you here and you can walk back by yourself. It's not too hard. Just follow the signs for Rialto.'

Crowds flocked the area so Jane thanked him but said she would come back some time a bit quieter and just took a couple of photos to send to her mum. Alvise gave her an understanding nod of the head and turned the boat to the left, heading back into the Grand Canal again, but this time approaching the palazzo from the other end.

By the time they got back, Jane had seen so many stunning old buildings that her head was spinning. As a place to live and work, Venice certainly took some beating and she could feel her spirits rise.

Chapter 5

The next days flew by as Jane gradually settled into her new job, her new flat and this amazing city. She set up the new laptop and printer and made a start on the huge pile of fan mail, some of it going back several years. Most of the envelopes hadn't even been opened and she deliberately kept some of the better letters to one side to show her employer – although the usual reaction when she did so was little more than a casual glance. She also emailed the literary agent and publisher in London to introduce herself as the new PA and received almost instantaneous replies, both saying very much the same thing: when was Miss Leonard going to start writing again? When Jane referred the question to her employer, she was unsurprised to be given fairly terse instructions to tell them to get off her back. Jane replied in less corrosive terms, saying that they would be the first to know once the pall of depression that had settled on her employer began to lift – assuming it ever would.

She took over her boss's email account and sifted business from personal messages. In so doing, she came across a huge file of emails from readers, almost all of which had never received an answer. One thing was for sure: it didn't look as though she was going to be bored in this job. Rather surprisingly, she discovered that Miss Leonard had no social media presence and she queried whether this was something she should get onto. The reply was a determined shake of the head and a five-minute rant on the evils of the internet. She soon discovered that Miss Leonard had a horror of technology in general and computer screens in particular. She refused to carry a phone and, according to Maria, she apparently still wrote her books on the same old Remington typewriter she had used for decades – or at least she would do if she could ever get her mojo back. She obviously liked paper and the printed word. What her publishers thought of receiving a manuscript in the form of a hefty pile of typed sheets didn't bear thinking about, but this was Veronica Leonard, after all, and no doubt they had adapted their working practices to accommodate her.

Jane also made a point of going for a walk accompanied by the dog every morning before Miss Leonard stirred and before the crowds built up. She and Dino explored the backstreets and alleyways of Venice and she gradually began to get her bearings. Soon she got into the habit of stopping at a cafe in a little piazza just behind the Rialto bridge before returning to the palazzo. She would sit outside in the shade, sipping an espresso and scanning the headlines in the newspaper while the dog wandered around the other tables sporting his 'She doesn't feed me' expression that almost always resulted in a piece of croissant or doughnut coming his way.

She gradually began to recognise a few of the regulars and was soon on chatting terms with the owner. He, like Alvise, was a Venetian through and through, although he and his family lived on the mainland because of the prohibitive rents here in the old city. He was a mine of information on everything from upcoming events to scandalous goings-on in the local council. On more than one occasion Jane was even able to surprise Maria when she got home by relating some snippet of juicy local gossip before the housekeeper had heard of it. Yes, Jane told herself, she was definitely beginning to settle in and, as she did so, she could feel the memories of her military past slowly starting to fade.

It was while checking emails one morning during her second week that she came upon one asking whether Miss Leonard would be at a charity auction to take place at Venice Casino the following weekend. When she read this out to her employer, Jane received a shake of the head in return.

'I have no interest in socialising these days, but this is a major charity event and the family needs to be represented so I'd like you to go for me. This'll be the first function where you'll be representing me.'

Jane felt a shiver of apprehension even though this meant that she was going to see the interior of the beautiful old casino building sooner than she had expected. 'If that's what you want.'

'Yes, you go. I can't be bothered with all that.' Miss Leonard glanced across at her. 'You'll have to dress up a bit. How are you off for evening gowns?'

'I'm afraid I've only brought a couple of what you might call cocktail dresses with me, but no long dress. I've got a red velvet one back home in my parents' house, but I'd die of heatstroke if I wore it in this weather even if I could get Mum to send it over in time. I think I'd better go and buy something.'

'I see…' Miss Leonard didn't say anything for a few moments. She just sat there, subjecting Jane to one of her searching stares. Finally she hauled herself to her feet. 'We'd better make sure you're suitably dressed for the occasion but there's no need to go shopping. Come along with me and let's see what I've got. The crème de la crème of Venetian society will be there and, as the family's official representative, you need to look the part.'

As Jane followed her out of the living room and onto the stairs she couldn't help reflecting that Miss Leonard was probably twice as broad around the backside – and no doubt everywhere else – as she was, so if she was going to be lent one her employer's gowns, she was going to need a big box of pins and a sewing machine to prevent it falling off. But, as it turned out, Miss Leonard had quite a surprise in store.

Upstairs on the second floor there were various rooms, and one of them housed a sartorial treasure trove. Miss Leonard opened the door and flicked on the light, and Jane stopped dead, finding herself presented with the spectacle of row upon row of dresses almost filling up the little room. She took a couple of hesitant steps forward.

'Wow! I've never seen so many dresses outside of a clothes shop. Do you wear them all?'

Miss Leonard laughed. It was the first time Jane had heard her laugh properly and it was good to hear. 'You must be joking. I have a dozen or so gowns in my room for my personal use – not that I go out any more these days – but these here are a little hobby of mine. I've been collecting for decades, ever since I got my first royalty cheque back in the seventies.'

'And you don't wear them?'

'My daughters have used a few of them for big events in the past. Diana's about your size, but now she's in New York studying fashion. Her big sister's outgrown most of them and although I've worn some of them on special occasions, I'm afraid there's no way I could get into any of them now. The majority of them used to belong to

Hollywood stars of the Golden Age and most of those girls were stick thin – even slimmer than you and Diana are. Now then, let me see…' She took another long look at Jane before making her decision. 'Young Ingrid Bergman, I think.' Her hands flicked across the hangers until she found the one she wanted and pulled it out. 'Here, see what you think.'

Jane took it with awe. Had this dress really belonged to the star of *Casablanca*, *Notorious* and so many other classic movies? She could hardly believe it. It was a delicate off-white colour, quite sheer and unmistakably pure silk. It was as light as a feather and it shimmered in the light of the chandelier. Tentatively she held it up against her body.

'There's a mirror over there.' Miss Leonard pointed across to the other side of the room. 'Take a look. You'll need to try it on, but from here I'd say it should fit. Do you like it?'

'Do I like it? It's unbelievable.' Jane walked over to the full-length mirror and took a better look. 'Yes, I think you're right. It feels like it's about my size, maybe a bit long but I suppose I should wear heels.' She turned and glanced across at Miss Leonard, feeling almost overcome. 'I've never ever in my life even handled, let alone worn, anything like this. The thing is… surely it's far too precious. What if I spill wine all over it? I'd never forgive myself – and you'd probably never forgive me.'

Miss Leonard gave a dismissive wave of the hand. 'It wouldn't matter. Champagne washes out quite easily.' She produced a smile. 'And in a dress like this the only drink you could possibly be given is champagne. This was never designed to be worn while drinking pints of Guinness down at the pub. Why don't you go off and see how it fits?'

Jane almost ran up the stairs. Pulling off her blouse and skirt, she stood in front of the mirror and slipped the dress over her head. Miss Leonard certainly had a good eye. It fitted her like a glove. All right, she would need to buy some different underwear and some heels but there was no getting away from the fact that it could have been made for her.

'Can I come in, Jane?'

She heard Miss Leonard's voice from outside on the landing and hurried across to open the door. Her employer's reaction was enthusiastic.

'Absolutely perfect. Give me a twirl, would you? That's wonderful. You look lovely. Once we've got your hair done and maybe a pair of pendant earrings, you'll knock them all dead. How does it feel?'

'It's absolutely stunning.' She caught Miss Leonard's eye. 'I've never really been one for dressing up much. I've always felt more comfortable in jeans and a T-shirt – or in uniform – but this is something else! Are you sure you want me to wear it?'

'Of course. Besides, like I say, you'll be representing me, and I'd like you to look good. And don't forget that as my representative that brings certain responsibilities. You need to look the part, but you also need to act the part.'

'I promise I'll do my very best for you. It's just that… you know you said you felt like an impostor when people call Lady Cooper? Well, how do you think I'm going to feel, decked out in something as exquisite as this? Looking in the mirror, it's like looking at somebody else.'

'I told you before and I'm telling you again. You are a very good-looking girl and, in Ingrid Bergman's dress, you're going to be outstandingly beautiful.' She held up her hands in mock defence. 'Now don't get all sniffy about it. I'm just telling you the truth.'

Jane produced a smile in return. 'I promise I could never be sniffy about something as gorgeous as this. I just hope I don't let you down.'

'Well, we'll soon find out if you do. The bush telegraph here is very efficient and very unforgiving. If you get drunk and start doing a striptease in the middle of the auction, Maria will have heard the news before you get back home.'

'I promise that won't happen.' Jane felt her cheeks blushing at the thought. 'So, tell me, what exactly happens at a charity auction?'

Chapter 6

The charity auction started at eight o'clock and, as she had imagined, Jane was delivered to the casino's covered landing stage by launch – piloted by Alvise decked out in the sort of uniform an admiral of the fleet might have worn. He offered her a steadying hand as she stepped off the boat and she took it gratefully. The new heels she had bought were higher than any she had owned before and it felt a bit like walking on stilts. Miss Leonard had insisted on – and paid for – sending her to a very posh hair stylist who had curled her hair into an updo with the addition of what looked like chopsticks and Jane was afraid to make any sudden moves for fear they might fall out and she might find herself with hair all over her face. If this wasn't bad enough, she had the added complication of knowing that the dress she was wearing was worth countless thousands and the diamond earrings provided by Miss Leonard were probably worth as much as the big Mercedes 4x4.

She was greeted deferentially at the doors by an immaculate usher in a tuxedo. He gave her invitation a cursory check before waving her through into an open hallway at water level, not dissimilar to the one in Miss Leonard's palazzo. A broad stone stairway led up to the *piano nobile* and Jane was relieved she managed to climb the stairs without tripping over the hem of her gown or toppling off her heels. Emerging into the bright lights at the top, she was surprised to find that she had been expected. A figure appeared alongside her and tapped her forearm. She looked around to find herself in the company of an elegant lady *d'un certain âge* wearing a diamond tiara, earrings and necklace which, if authentic, were probably worth as much as the casino.

'Good evening, signora. Are you here to represent Lady Veronica by any chance?' She extended a silk-gloved hand in greeting.

Jane took the hand and shook it. 'Yes, my name's Jane Reed. I didn't think anybody was going to know me. How did you recognise me?'

'Veronica told me to look out for a beautiful fair-haired woman in the most stylish gown in the house – I couldn't fail. My name is Lavinia di Pontegrande and this is my husband, Alessandro.' She indicated an imposing elderly gentleman in an evening suit at her side. He had an unruly mop of silver hair that made him look vaguely like Albert Einstein. Jane held out her hand towards him and he took it formally, leaning forward to kiss it.

'Delighted to meet you, signora. My compliments on your Italian. Alas, command of your language is something that has always eluded me.' His speech was as formal as his actions.

'Veronica tells me this is your first foray into Venetian society and charity events.' His wife had clearly been given instructions to take Jane under her wing.

'That's right. It's all new to me. I've never been inside a casino before and it's my first time at an auction of any kind.'

She took a good look around. The wooden floor was polished mahogany laid in a herringbone pattern; the walls were adorned with massive oil paintings of Venetian scenes, and monumental chandeliers hung from the ceilings. Uniformed waiters and waitresses circulated with drinks and canapés and there was an unmistakable atmosphere of opulence both in these fine surroundings and among the guests. Jane wasn't too sure she felt comfortable in such a gathering but she had a job to do so she straightened her back and decided to take all the help she could get.

'Can you give me an idea of what to expect, please? I'd hate to make a fool of myself and let Her Ladyship down.'

'I'm sure you'll do just fine, but of course I'll be happy to help. Now, has Veronica told you to bid for any items?'

Jane nodded. 'Yes, just one.'

She had her employer's gold card in her sparkly little clutch bag – also on loan – and had received instructions to bid for lot number 37. This was a gown which had once belonged to Italian film icon Sophia Loren, and Miss Leonard had told her to bid anything up to ten thousand euros for it. Jane had been gob-smacked at the astronomical figure but her employer hadn't batted an eyelid, telling her the auction was in aid of a very good cause and she really wanted it as an important addition to her collection.

She saw Signora di Pontegrande smile. 'The Loren dress, I wouldn't mind betting. Am I right?' Jane nodded. 'Well, you come along with me and I'll give you a helping hand if you need it, but you'll be fine.'

'Some champagne, signora?' A waiter materialised at her side and, seeing that the other two were already clutching glasses, Jane automatically reached out for one, murmuring a silent prayer that she wouldn't spill it on her precious dress. She resolved to take her time drinking it. One thing was for sure: tonight was definitely not the night for getting plastered.

She chatted to the elderly couple, telling them about her recent Masters degree but not about her military service. They then guided her around the room and introduced to a host of elegant people whose names Jane knew she would never remember. Finally a gong sounded and the guests all gradually made their way into a separate room with a charming frescoed ceiling and wood-panelled walls. In here rows of seats had been arranged facing a low stage. Once almost all the seats were filled, the master of ceremonies appeared and introduced the president of the child poverty charity that would benefit from tonight's auction. As this gentleman thanked them all in advance for their generosity, Jane couldn't help reflecting that if all the ladies here simply handed over their jewels, several million kids could be lifted out of poverty in one go. Still, she told herself, at least these people appeared to be using some of their money for a good cause.

After polite applause the master of ceremonies took over and the auction began. On entering the room, the guests had been issued with little wooden paddles, each bearing a number, and all the members of the audience needed to do was to hold up a paddle to bid. The system worked remarkably smoothly and a number of items sold for several thousands of euros. Interestingly, a signed set of first editions of Miss Leonard's early books appeared as lot number 29 and raised almost a thousand euros. Shortly afterwards it was the turn of the Sophia Loren gown and Jane clutched her paddle firmly, hoping she wouldn't make a mess of things. The bidding started at a thousand and moved quickly up to five thousand euros before slowing. At this point Signora di Pontegrande whispered to her that it was probably time to start raising her paddle to bid. Jane did as instructed and waited to be noticed.

'Five thousand five hundred.' The auctioneer pointed at her with his gavel and heads turned in her direction.

'Six thousand.' The auctioneer was pointing off to the left and the attention of the crowd changed.

Jane raised her paddle again and again and soon found herself in a bidding war with just one other bidder. She couldn't see his face, but he had dark hair and he was sitting a few rows in front of her, off to one side. Finally the bidding reached ten thousand euros and it was against her. The auctioneer looked out hopefully around the audience for any other bidders but there were none and Jane knew she had to make a quick decision. She knew Miss Leonard really wanted this dress so she took a deep breath and decided to disobey her instructions and make one more bid, telling herself she could always pay the extra five hundred euros if her boss objected. She raised her paddle and waited.

'Ten thousand five hundred euros.' The auctioneer pointed in her direction and all eyes turned to her once more as silence descended on the room. She saw the auctioneer cast an interrogative glance across at the other bidder and distinctly saw him give a little shake of the head. After giving fair warning to any other bidders, the gavel came down and Jane knew she had successfully carried out her mission.

While the auction continued around her she sat back and relaxed. Carrying out orders and accomplishing missions had been her life in the regiment, and over these past two tough years she had missed the feeling of accomplishment that this could bring. Life since the army had been a physical struggle to regain her health and fitness after her injuries, and a mental struggle to come to terms with the loss of the man she had loved. Looking back she could see the huge black cloud that had been hanging over her. Now, at least, she could think of her time in the regiment without welling up. Could it be that this cloud was finally beginning to shrink?

At the end of the auction she bade farewell to her companions, thanking Signora Lavinia for her help and advice, and went over to the desk at the back to complete the formalities. She was just completing the transaction when she heard a male voice from close behind her.

'*Buona sera.*'

Picking up the gold card and the receipt she turned to find that the owner of the voice was a tall, good-looking man with dark hair and a neatly trimmed beard. She had a sudden feeling of familiarity which was confirmed by what he said next.

'Congratulations on beating me to the Loren gown.' He had to be the other bidder. 'Are you planning on wearing it yourself?' He was smiling.

'I'm afraid not. I was bidding for my employer.' She found herself smiling back at him and this was puzzling. Smiling and making small talk had been absent from her life for some time now. She even managed a bit of cheek. 'Sorry you didn't get it. Were *you* planning on wearing it yourself?'

His smile broadened. 'I fear I don't have the figure for it.' He held out his hand towards her. 'Paolo Padovan, I'm pleased to meet you. I'm the curator of the Mantua Costume Museum. We have a fine collection of clothes throughout the ages and I wanted to add a bit of twentieth-century glamour to it. Never mind, I'm sure something else will come up soon. Can I offer you a drink?'

She had been studying him closely. In fact he was *very* good-looking, with his dark brown eyes, immaculately groomed hair, and equally well-tailored dinner jacket. He was probably five or even ten years older than she was but very appealing and she felt a little spark of attraction. This, too, came as something of a surprise to her. Checking out random men had also been off her agenda for ages and her mind inevitably turned to Mark. Still, she decided, it wouldn't hurt to accept this man's offer. It was the polite thing to do under the circumstances.

'Thank you, that's very kind. Now that the auction's finished and I've managed to do what I was sent here to do, I think I could allow myself a second glass of something.'

They walked out and through one of the gaming halls to the bar. All around were intense-looking people playing blackjack and roulette. There were all ages and all nationalities and a surprising number of the players were elderly ladies. Unfamiliar with casinos, she had been expecting men in tuxedos and glamorous women like in the James Bond films.

When they reached the bar Paolo turned towards her. 'What'll it be? Champagne? In a dress like that, champagne is almost obligatory.'

She felt another smile appear on her face. 'Funnily enough, that's exactly what my employer said to me but she was probably just thinking of possible stains. You see, it's her dress. And yes, champagne or Prosecco would be lovely, thank you.'

He ordered two glasses of champagne and then turned back to her, his eyes running across her gown – and body – before he grunted approvingly. 'Your employer has immaculate taste and the dress could have been made for you.'

Jane decided that he deserved to hear the full story. 'Since you're involved with this sort of thing, it might interest you to know that the dress was actually made for Ingrid Bergman.'

She saw his eyes light up. 'Is that so? It's absolutely stunning. Would you mind if I touch it?'

Somewhat apprehensively, she nodded and he reached out to take the cloth of the sleeve between his thumb and forefinger. He stood there for several seconds, his eyes trained on the dress, before passing judgement.

'Exquisite. There's something about the feel of vintage silk. It's hard to explain but it's a material that, unlike almost any other fabric, manages to conserve its integrity and somehow acquire character with age.' He released his hold on her sleeve and caught her eye for a moment. 'It's a beautiful dress on a beautiful woman.' Then he turned away to collect the glasses from the barman, leaving Jane to digest his words. Although it was always nice to receive compliments, she hoped this didn't mean he was making a pass at her because she knew full well she wasn't ready for anything like that. At least, not yet.

They sat down at a nearby table and chatted. He told her more about the Mantua Costume Museum while she told him about her aspirations of becoming a writer. She didn't mention the army, nor the name of her employer, and neither of them made reference to any partners. She enjoyed being with him more than she could possibly have expected and it appeared that he was enjoying her company just as much. Of course, she reminded herself, this could just be because she was wearing a dress belonging to one of the most famous actresses of all time and the fact that he had built a career among such things, but she had her doubts. Finally, as ten o'clock approached, she swallowed the last of her wine and stood up.

'I'm afraid I have to leave. I'm being picked up by launch at ten and I don't want to keep the driver waiting. Or should that be the "captain"?'

He stood up as well. 'I'm going home by more pedestrian means, but let me walk you to the boat.'

'There's no need for that, really.'

'I'd like to. Humour me, please.'

Emerging from the building, they walked down the staircase to the water's edge and Jane was relieved to see Alvise already moored at the end of the jetty. Although Paolo was very polite and very nice, she had been dreading finding herself alone in the dark with a man for the first time in two long years. She turned towards him and held out her hand formally.

'Thank you for your company and for the drink. Sorry, once again, for depriving you of the Sophia Loren dress. No hard feelings, I hope?'

He took her hand and held onto it for a second or two longer than necessary before releasing it. 'No hard feelings. I've enjoyed this evening and I was wondering if maybe we could meet up again. I don't suppose you might feel like letting me have your phone number by any chance?'

Jane hesitated for a few moments before agreeing. She knew she wasn't ready for a relationship with any man, but when all was said and done, it was just a phone number. She didn't need to agree to see him again even if he did call her. They exchanged numbers and he gave her a broader smile.

'Thanks for that. I was afraid you might disappear into the night like Cinderella and I'd just be left with a glass slipper.'

She smiled back. 'I shudder to think how uncomfortable glass slippers could be. I'm wearing new high heels and I feel as if my calves are about to explode. Thanks again and good night, Paolo.'

'*Arrivederci*, Jane.'

He offered her his hand to help her step into the launch and then stood on the jetty and watched while Alvise reversed away and turned for home. Before they disappeared into the night, she gave him a little wave and he waved back. *Arrivederci*, till we meet again, was what he had said – if that was what she wanted.

She sat back and relaxed as the launch took her down this most romantic of waterways, passing wonderful historic buildings on both sides, and she reflected on the unexpected turn her life had now taken. Only a month ago she had been marking time in her parents' house, wandering around in old jeans, still deep in a slough of despair, with little hope and little joy. Now here she was in this dreamy setting, dressed as a diva with a two-hundred-euro hairstyle, travelling down the Grand Canal from one magnificent palazzo to another, and with a handsome man standing on a jetty receding into the distance behind her. Captain J. V. Reed, Royal Engineers, had never in her wildest dreams envisioned such a spectacularly different career path as this. Could it really be that this was what her life was going to be like from now on?

Chapter 7

'So you see, I'm very sorry but I disobeyed your orders and paid five hundred euros more for it, but if I did wrong please take that out of my pay. I just got the impression you really wanted to have it.'

Miss Leonard looked up from the Sophie Loren dress which had been delivered earlier that morning and smiled – a broad smile that didn't look in the least bit forced. 'No apology needed and thank you for the kind offer, but it's perfectly all right. I'm delighted you decided to go the extra mile. This will make a wonderful addition to my collection.' Her smile broadened even more. 'Now, do tell me about the handsome man I hear you were with last night.'

'The handsome man?' Jane did her best to affect an air of insouciance. 'I presume you mean the director of the Mantua Costume Museum. His name's Paolo Padovan. He was the other bidder who pushed the price of the dress up.' She returned her employer's smile. 'The bush telegraph really does work well here, just like you said.'

'Padovan – that's a good local name. I used to know a Paolo Padovan years ago. As for the bush telegraph, I got a call from the duchess a little while ago, telling me all about it. It appears you made quite an impression last night.'

'A *good* impression, I hope. But, did you say, "duchess"? You mean Lavinia di Pontegrande is a duchess? I had no idea. Good lord, should I have been addressing them as milord and milady?'

'Of course not. There's no such thing as the aristocracy here in Italy any more. Those titles are all just hang backs to a bygone age. That's partly why I never use mine either – although I'm powerless to make Maria and Alvise call me anything but "your ladyship". Anyway, Lavinia and Alessandro were most impressed by you – and I'm not just talking about your looks, so no need for you to get sniffy again.'

Jane shot her employer a smile. 'I promise I'll never ever be sniffy in front of you. Well, I'm glad they thought I did all right. I felt like a fish out of water in the midst of all that opulence.'

To her surprise, Miss Leonard actually clasped her hand for a few seconds before releasing it again. 'If it makes you feel any better, I spent years feeling like that, but you get used to it after a while. Don't worry. Most of them are good people underneath the bling.'

'Well, I have to say that the signora… the duchess and her husband were charming and very supportive.'

'So, tell me about this man.' Miss Leonard sounded genuinely interested and Jane registered this as a good sign that she might be cheering up – at least a bit.

'Paolo Padovan? He's a nice guy and I had a drink with him before Alvise came to collect me.'

'And are you going to see him again?'

'I'm not sure. We exchanged phone numbers but I don't think I'll be saying yes if he asks me out.'

'Why's that, if you don't mind me being nosey? Is there someone else? I told Gordon to say there would be room for two in the flat upstairs if needed when he placed the advert.'

'Yes, Mr Russell did ask me, thank you, but there's nobody else… now.'

Noting her tone, Miss Leonard's voice became surprisingly warm. 'But no longer. Want to talk about it?'

Instinctively Jane shook her head, but then relented. 'Not really, if you don't mind. At least, not yet. There was a man who was very dear to me, but he died.'

'I'm so sorry to hear that. Well, if you ever want to talk about it, I know a thing or two about grief.'

Jane was genuinely moved at this sensitive and caring side to her employer. Maybe talking might do both of them some good but not now, not yet. 'Thank you, Miss Leonard. That's very kind. Maybe one of these days…'

'Of course. You take your time. And would you start calling me Veronica? I think we know each other well enough now. Miss Leonard makes me sound so stodgy.'

'I would like that. Thank you.'

'Anyway, going back to the man from Mantua, would you mind meeting up with him again – with me as chaperone? You see, I'd already heard about the Costume Museum from my daughter, Diana, and I've been meaning to visit it. It only opened a couple of years ago but I'm afraid I haven't been in the mood for sightseeing or museum visits of late. But now, seeing as you know the curator, it seems like too good an opportunity to miss. Besides, I'm sure you might enjoy a trip to Mantua. Do you know the city?'

Jane shook her head. 'No, this area's all new to me.'

'It's a charming little city situated on a curve of the river so that it almost feels as though it's an island. All very quaint and medieval with cobbled streets and a magnificent Palazzo Ducale. The dukes of Mantua were big players in Italian history. It's a couple of hours away by car and we could drive over one day, visit the museum and I can check out the costumes. I promise I won't leave you alone with your man unless you want me to. How does that strike you?'

The idea definitely appealed. It sounded like a lovely place to visit and Jane was confident that the fact she would have her boss with her should ensure that Paolo wouldn't get the wrong impression. 'That sounds great.'

'Shall we get Alvise to drive us or how would you feel about doing it? I'm afraid I gave up driving some time ago. Everybody goes so fast these days.'

'No need to bother Alvise, I can drive us by all means. Just say when.'

'How about early next week, Monday or Tuesday?'

'That's absolutely fine by me. I'll check the opening times.'

Later that day, Jane decided to call Paolo. She had given it a lot of thought before getting in touch with him but Veronica had clearly indicated she was interested in meeting him. Jane had enjoyed his company and she knew it would be pleasant to see him again and, luckily, Veronica would provide a perfect excuse for not getting too friendly – unless she decided she wanted to.

He answered almost immediately. 'Jane? Ciao, it's good to hear from you. I was hoping you'd call.'

'Hi, Paolo. I told my employer I'd met you and she's keen to visit the Costume Museum next week. I'll come with her and I thought maybe if you're around I could return the favour and buy *you* a drink.'

'It'll be great to see you again but let me offer you lunch or dinner.' He definitely sounded eager, but she stuck to her softly-softly approach.

'That's very kind, but I can't really. I'll be with my employer and working, you see, but I'm sure I could take half an hour off to buy you that drink.'

He had another couple of goes at persuading her but she stuck to her guns and he finally relented. He told her the museum was closed on Monday but said he would be only too pleased to give them a private tour that day if that suited them. Jane felt sure Veronica would be pleased to receive special treatment so she thanked him and they agreed to meet there on Monday afternoon at three.

That evening she really felt the need to get some exercise. She had always kept herself very fit and the physios had been keen to get her back onto a regular running routine once her wounds had healed. It was now a week since her last run and she knew she needed to restart. The problem was that here in Venice there were precious few places suitable for a run without bumping into people at every turn. She mentioned the problem to Alvise and he came up with an excellent solution.

'I have to go over to Murano to pick up some replacement pieces of glass for one of the chandeliers in the living room. When the decorators were in recently, they managed to give it a clout with a ladder and broke four of the little crystal pendants. As you can imagine, Her Ladyship wasn't best pleased. It's all handmade and it's been there for hundreds of years, so the replacement pieces had to be specially made. Why don't you come with me? I'll show you where you can go for a run without bumping into too many tourists. Down by Murano sports ground there's space.' He had another idea. 'Come to think of it, you could take Dino with you if you like, unless you're afraid he might trip you up. You can let him off the lead and the only worry is that he might choose to go for a swim.' He grinned. 'But even if he does jump in, we should be able to dry him off before we get back home.'

'I'd love to take him for a proper run. He's still quite young, isn't he? I bet he'd love it.'

'He's barely two years old now. Like I told you he normally roams all over the estate up in the hills so he'll probably run you into the ground.'

Jane went up to change and then they set off. This time after barely a couple of hundred metres or so Alvise turned off the Grand Canal into a considerably narrower canal between the houses, regularly passing underneath humpbacked bridges that seemed almost to graze the top of the little cabin. Each time Jane instinctively ducked, just in case. Gondolas and other boats – some of them long, low delivery vessels and even a municipal rubbish barge – came past in the other direction and Alvise had to nip in and out between the moored boats to avoid the larger ones. He had an expert touch on the tiller and was clearly enjoying himself. Dino, too, was having a marvellous time charging from side to side of the launch, occasionally barking at other dogs, or simply for the hell of it. When Jane considered that this was simply the Venetian equivalent of being given a lift from one part of the city to another, it was a surreal experience. She still hadn't fully come to terms with living in a city built on water.

After a few minutes they emerged from among the houses into the open lagoon and Alvise pointed across the smooth surface of the water to a low island some distance away.

'That's where we're going: Murano. Know the name?'

'Murano's famous for glass, isn't it? I'm sure my parents have got a glass jug at home from Murano. Of course, I suppose that's why you get the chandelier parts made there. Is that right?'

Alvise nodded. 'It's famous worldwide. You should go over some time and take a look around. They do tours of the factories where you can see glass blowers and all that. There are some amazing craftsmen there.'

It took them fifteen minute or so to motor across to the island, which he told her was actually a collection of half a dozen separate little islands linked together by bridges. Instead of heading for the centre, he took her round to the north of the island where there were fewer buildings and what looked like a sports complex. He dropped her and the dog at the entrance to a broad canal that he told her would lead him to the glass factory, and they arranged to meet back here again in forty-five minutes. After he had chugged away again, she looked down at Dino who was clearly raring to go. She pointed her finger sternly at him as Alvise had taught her.

'No swimming. Got that?'

He just wagged his tail harder and she unclipped the lead. He set off at a gallop along a broad strip of grass beside the canal and she followed. There weren't many people walking about and as a result she and the dog had a fine run and she was able to relax and just concentrate on her cadence. A daily run had been a regular feature of her army life and this simple activity stirred memories, but now she was almost able to think back on her former life with nostalgia rather than remorse. Being out in the fresh air gave her time to reflect on her first two weeks in Venice and she had to admit that it was working out far better than she might have hoped. Her boss was not the dragon she had feared and her accommodation was spectacular; she was beginning to make a few friends, was feeling more cheerful, not to mention she had found herself a lovely canine companion and a good-looking man who appeared interested in her. Now all she had to do was to figure out if she was interested in him.

Chapter 8

Monday's trip to Mantua was fascinating. Veronica insisted they take the big Mercedes rather than the little Fiat but Jane didn't mind in the slightest. She had got used to driving big vehicles in the army, although they had been nothing as luxurious as this modern automatic car with feather soft suspension and comfortable leather-clad interior. On the way there Veronica was soon chatting freely and appeared genuinely excited at the prospect of what would apparently be one of her very first outings since her husband's death. When Jane had told Maria what they were planning, the response had been delight that Veronica was venturing out of the house at last. The elderly housekeeper had caught hold of Jane by the shoulders and kissed her on the cheeks, telling her she was a miracle worker.

In response to Jane's queries as they drove along the autostrada, Veronica told her more about her life from her early years as a school teacher – surprisingly maths, not English – to becoming a world-renowned author. In return, Jane told her about her own dreams of becoming a published author. Veronica then asked the sixty-four-thousand-dollar question.

'So what are you planning on writing, or have you already started?'

Jane didn't reply immediately; by then they had reached the outskirts of Padua where the traffic had intensified noticeably and the cars in front of her all started slowing down and braking. Alvise had warned her that this stretch of the main Venice to Milan motorway was notorious for heavy traffic and he was being proved right. However, after a minute or two it gradually started to speed up again and she relaxed once more.

'That's the problem, I just can't decide. I love romance novels – particularly those with a happy ending – and I've devoured almost all of your books. The thing is, though, I also rather like the idea of something with a bit more action.'

'Why not combine the two? Have you actually sat down and made a start on anything?'

'While I was doing my Masters I wrote a couple of short novellas as assignments – one a romance and the other an attempt at a thriller.'

'And which did your tutors prefer?'

'Annoyingly, one preferred the thriller and one the romance, so I'm sort of back to square one.'

'Would you like me to read them and tell you what I think?'

Jane nodded heartily. 'That would be amazing, thank you, but don't expect too much. These are very much first steps and I'm still just finding my way. I'd be ever so grateful if you could look at them, but only if you can spare the time.'

'Spare the time?' Jane heard her snort. 'I'm bored stiff these days. I used to spend five, six hours a day at the typewriter. Now I find myself with all that spare time and I don't know what else to do.' There was a catch in her voice now. 'That's why I lie in bed so much. At least if I'm in bed I don't feel quite so listless.'

'But you said you don't sleep much. Does that mean you just lie there and stare at the ceiling?'

'For hours on end.'

Jane decided to take a chance and pop the question that had been uppermost in her mind ever since learning of her new employer's identity. 'So what's stopping you writing again?' There was silence for several minutes and she was beginning to fear that she had overstepped the mark when she heard Veronica reply, thankfully in even tones.

'Don't think I haven't tried. Time after time I've sat myself down at the typewriter, put in a clean sheet of paper, and tried to make a start. Regular as clockwork I find myself still sitting there two or three hours later still staring at that blank page. I'm afraid that bird has flown.'

'You're saying your muse has left you?'

'I'm saying exactly that. I used to have ideas for plot-lines piling up in my head and scribbled on odd bits of paper all over my desk but ever since Peter, my husband, passed away, I seem to have run out of any kind of inspiration. Grief can do that to a person.' A more tender note entered her voice. 'But you maybe know all about that.'

Jane just nodded. 'It can be tough.'

An hour or so later she saw the signs for Mantua and turned off the autostrada. Although there had been the foothills of the Alps off to their right as they drove from Venice past Padua, Vicenza and Verona, the countryside down here was as flat as a pancake and the temperature and humidity were, if anything, even higher here than in Venice. Reluctantly leaving the air-conditioned car, they walked past the imposing bulk of the Palazzo Ducale into the *centro storico*. The very air they breathed was hot. Beside her she heard Veronica sigh.

'It's only the middle of June and it's boiling already – and it's only going to get hotter and hotter. I can't wait for us to head for the hills.'

'At the end of the month, you said?'

'Yes, I was planning on going in two weeks' time but if it carries on getting hotter and stickier, we might do well to go sooner. Besides, Italian school holidays are starting any day now so the crowds in Venice are going to get worse and worse. When we get back home, I'll have a word with Maria and see how she feels about shutting up the house and going as soon next week.'

'And will you stay with your mother-in-law?'

'In the same building but she has her own part and we have ours.'

Jane wondered if the old lady's alleged feistiness made for an awkward relationship with her daughter-in-law but decided not to ask anything so personal. She would find out in due course. 'Is it a long journey?'

'Not too long – shorter than today, an hour and a half or so. Because of the dog and all our stuff, we'd better go in two cars. Would you mind driving one and Alvise the other?'

'Not at all.' Jane realised that leaving Venice for two whole months would mean that the chances for Paolo to attempt to see her again before the autumn would diminish accordingly and spare her a possibly embarrassing conversation. Nevertheless, she had to admit that these first couple of weeks here in Italy had been very positive so far. She felt more relaxed than even just a month ago and there had been no repetition of her nightmares. Hopefully the change of setting from the coast to the hills wouldn't alter the trajectory of her return to some sort of happiness. 'I'm looking forward to some cool air as well.'

They met up with Paolo in the main square as planned, and Jane could instantly tell he was pleased to see her again. He was wearing a blue polo shirt and chinos and there was a welcoming smile on his face. She was about to make the introductions when it emerged that he and Veronica already knew each other.

'Lady Cooper, it's lovely to see you again. You remember me, don't you?' Jane could see recognition dawn on Veronica's face. 'I'm Paolo... Paolo Padovan. I used to come up to the villa.'

'Of course, Paolo. I was telling Jane your name sounded familiar and I wondered if it might be you. I'm sorry, it's the beard, or I would have recognised you immediately. It's been quite a few years now, hasn't it?'

'It has indeed.' His expression became more serious. 'I was sorry to hear of your husband's death. My condolences.'

'Thank you, Paolo, but life has to go on.'

Jane was relieved to hear Veronica talking about her husband without sounding totally grief-stricken. Maybe she, too, was beginning to come out from under the grey cloud of sorrow which had gripped her.

'And now you're the curator of this museum. You've done very well for yourself, Paolo. Congratulations.'

He shook hands formally with her as Jane wondered how they came to know each other but, as neither of them offered an explanation, she left it at that.

He took them into the Costume Museum by a side door and gave them the tour. The collection was housed in a handsome red brick palazzo set in a road just off Mantua's main square, and the contents proved to be fascinating. Even Jane, who freely acknowledged she had little knowledge of fashion, found it interesting as he took them through garments from as early as the Middle Ages to the modern era. There were clothes belonging to men, women and children, rich and poor, stretching back over the centuries.

The juxtaposition of a wonderful lacy eighteenth-century formal dress, complete with bustle wider than most doorways, alongside a Flower Power miniskirt that barely grazed the tops of the thighs was striking. There were male mannequins in doublets, breeches and codpieces alongside slick-haired rockers in long coats and crepe-soled shoes from the Rock 'n' Roll era. And there were plenty more. He told them that the exhibits were regularly rotated so as to conserve them from the effects of over exposure to the light and the passage of people, and that they had hundreds of other costumes safely stored away in the climate-controlled basement.

Altogether they were in there for almost two hours and Jane could see how animated her employer had become. It certainly looked as though the outing was doing her good and Jane was happy for her. And if this was a success, she resolved to try to organise other ways of getting Veronica out and about. By the time they finally left the museum with Paolo and walked back to the cobbled expanse of Piazza Sordello for the drink she had promised him, Veronica was chatting volubly and even invited him to come and inspect her own collection after they got back from the hills. According to Maria, this sort of social interaction was something that had been missing from her employer's life for ages now and Jane took it as a good sign. Things were looking up for Veronica – and for Jane herself as she settled into life in Italy.

Paolo opted for a glass of Prosecco, but as she was going to be driving, Jane just had freshly squeezed orange juice with sparkling water and loads of ice, and she was pleased to hear Veronica order the same. Fears that her boss might have developed a sinister drinking problem had been decreasing day by day and this was just further proof that such was not the case after all. She tried to persuade Paolo to have champagne, just like he had given her, but he refused, saying he preferred to drink local wine from the Veneto region.

Over their drinks they chatted and Veronica asked him if he saw much of his parents.

'Whenever I can. I live here in Mantua now but it's only an hour in the car back to Monselice so I see them most weeks.' He glanced across at Jane. 'Monselice is where I grew up. It's on the edge of the Colli Euganei, not far from Villa Morea.'

'And it's a pretty little town.' Veronica nodded approvingly. 'Jane, you'll have to go and visit when we're at the villa.'

'I'd be very happy to show you around if I can get away.' Paolo looked as though he meant it. 'Unfortunately the summer months are my busiest time of the year here at the museum so I don't get over there as often as my mother would like, but I try to make it once or twice a month.'

Jane filed away the possibility that she might see him again this summer after all, but decided to cross that bridge when she came to it.

They chatted for almost an hour before Veronica cast Paolo an apologetic glance and told him she thought it was time to go. She then went off to the Ladies, leaving Jane alone with Paolo.

Jane looked across the table at him. 'Thank you for the tour.'

'Thank you for coming all the way from Venice to see the museum.'

'I'm glad I came. I'm sorry to have to rush off.'

'It's a pity, but maybe we can meet up in Monselice or up in the Colli Euganei.'

Not wanting to commit to a response, Jane changed to what she thought would be a safer subject. 'It's quite a coincidence that you already knew Lady Cooper, isn't it?'

A funny expression spread across his face. It was hard to pin it down but Jane felt sure she could see regret. 'I lived only ten kilometres or so away from their estate so I used to have a holiday job working in the grounds during my university vacations. I got to know them and the estate pretty well.'

After checking that Veronica wasn't on her way back to the table Jane leant forward and lowered her voice. 'What was Veronica's husband like?'

'He was a nice man, a bit old-fashioned, but very pleasant. You could tell that he and Lady Cooper were very fond of each other and his death must have been an awful blow to her. I'd heard on the grapevine how distraught she was, and I'm glad to see her looking and sounding a bit more like her old self today.'

'What about the rest of the family? Did you meet the old lady?'

'Signora Flora? Of course. She was a very hands-on sort of lady – probably still is.'

'And did you get to know Veronica's children?'

'Yes, I did. Really well…' He looked up and hastily changed the subject as Veronica appeared. 'I hope to see you again soon.'

Chapter 9

They drove up to the hills the following week. A few days before they left, an envelope with a British stamp arrived for Jane and she found a stiff white card inside inviting her to Fergus and Virginia's wedding on the twenty-fifth of August. She stared at it blankly for several minutes before stuffing it into her bag for now. It said RSVP at the bottom so she knew she would have to make up her mind before long, but it wasn't an easy decision and she needed time to think. She had told Fergus it was unlikely but maybe, just maybe, it might be the right opportunity for her to try to confront her demons and re-establish contact with so many friends and former colleagues. If she accepted the invitation, this would be an important milestone for her, and she wanted to be absolutely sure she made the right decision.

Veronica was already up by nine o'clock and Alvise ferried her, along with Jane and the dog, to the garage with a heap of bags and boxes, including Jane's new laptop and printer. He then went back to help Maria finish closing up the palazzo for the summer while Jane piled all the baggage onto the back seats of the Mercedes and settled the dog in the boot space. When everything was all securely stowed away, they set off, heading west, and as they travelled, Veronica explained what lay ahead.

'The family estate's almost four hundred metres up. The air temperature's noticeably fresher than it is down here and there are so few people. It's totally refreshing.'

'That sounds wonderful. What's it like?'

'It was built in the late seventeen hundreds in the Palladian style. You probably know that Andrea Palladio was a famous Renaissance architect and his villas have been copied for centuries. The villa's a lot smaller than most, but still very striking.'

'So is it smaller than the palazzo in Venice?'

'In terms of floor space in the villa itself, probably about the same. I'll be staying there with Maria and Alvise. We occupy part of the ground floor and all of the first and second floors. My mother-in-law has her own apartment on the ground floor. A couple of hundred metres away there's the original medieval house where my son David has been living. Over to the other side is what we call the summer house and that'll be all yours.' She smiled at Jane. 'Don't worry, we're not putting you in a shed in the garden. The summer house has two big bedrooms and we use it for guests – not that there have been any for years. You'll be completely independent so you'll be free to come and go as you please.'

'And the estate itself? Is it farmed or what?'

'Partially; we have red and white grape vineyards and a small olive grove – just for our own consumption really. The rest is grassland and there's a little lake. I'm sure you'll find it's rather nice and very relaxing after the bustle of Venice.' She was sounding quite animated today and Jane was pleased for her.

After initially heading west towards Vicenza, they turned south, bypassing Padua. The terrain here was still dead flat but ahead of them through the heat haze Jane began to make out an island of dark green rising up from the plains. As they drew closer and closer, Jane realised that there was to be no gradual transition. One minute they were on the flat, the next they were climbing. The hills suddenly rose up from the plains and, in a matter of seconds, they had gone from a long straight, level road to a series of sinuous bends that climbed steadily and the scenery changed radically. Here, they found themselves in the midst of wooded valleys, vineyards, olive groves and remarkably green fields, with woodland covering the tops of the hills which Veronica told her were long extinct volcanoes.

The road narrowed considerably as it snaked through a little village before starting to climb steeply. After rounding a sharp bend Veronica pointed to the right.

'We're here. I'll open the gates.'

Jane turned off and drew up in front of a pair of sturdy metal gates set between hefty stone pillars. Veronica produced a remote control from the glove compartment and the gates hummed open. They drove through and onto a long drive that curled steeply upwards. The sound of the gravel crunching beneath the car tyres stirred movement from behind her as Dino – who had been sleeping soundly up to this point – recognised where he was. Just to underline this, he produced a prolonged half whine, half howl, that ended with what could have been a laugh – or he may just have been sneezing. Whatever it was, it was clear that he was happy to be home.

Their home for the next few months was set on the hillside, just below the top of a rise, and the views were spectacular, but not as spectacular as the villa itself. It was dramatic. Clad with white marble, the first impression was of a Greek or Roman temple, complete with massive columns supporting the gently sloping roof. Half a dozen curved stone steps, three or four metres across, led up to the double height front doors. It was ornate, it was imposing, and it certainly wasn't for the unassuming. When this had been built it had been a statement of the power and wealth of the owners. Alvise had been right: there was no shortage of money in this family.

Jane drew up in front of the building and switched off the engine. She climbed out of the car and went around to let the dog out and, as she did so, she took a closer look at the place. The formal flower beds on either side of the stairway were filled with red and pink blooms and immaculately cared for. The gardener responsible for looking after the house had done an excellent job. While definitely not cold by any means, as Veronica had said it was noticeably fresher up here than in Venice, and Jane breathed in deeply, relishing the clean, much less humid, air. Yes, it might look like a National Trust property, but she had a really good feeling about this place.

'Jane, come and let me introduce you to my mother-in-law.'

Veronica had only just started walking across to the front door when it opened and a figure appeared.

She was an old lady – of that there could be no doubt – but she looked unlike any other nonagenarian Jane had ever seen. She was tiny, but emanated an aura of confidence that was unmistakable. Her snow-white hair was curled up on her head in an elegant swirl, and pendant earrings sparkled in the sunlight. She was wearing jeans – real blue denim jeans – and a remarkably modern-looking pink top. On her feet were leopard-print shoes and there was a big smile on her aged face.

'Veronica, carissima, how wonderful to see you again.'

78

Jane stood back as the two ladies embraced warmly and she could sense real affection there. Moments later they were joined by the dog who greeted his master's grandmother remarkably gently. After making a fuss of him, she raised her head and gave Jane a searching look.

'And you must be...' She impressed Jane by speaking in impeccable English.

Veronica leapt in to make the introductions. 'This is Jane. She's my new personal assistant and she's worth her weight in gold.'

Jane blushed as she responded to the old lady's gestures to approach and found herself on the receiving end of a handshake that would have done a sergeant major proud; this lady certainly wasn't frail.

'I'm delighted to meet you, Jane. Tell me, how are you at bicycle repairs?'

Momentarily blindsided by this unexpected question, Jane hesitated but then rallied. 'I'm not too great with gears but I'm okay at stuff like punctures and brakes.'

'Excellent. You see, I've got a puncture. David normally sorts out that sort of thing for me but he's away at the moment. Once you're all settled in, I wonder if you could take a look at it for me.'

'Of course, I'd be glad to.' A ninety-five-year-old on a bike? Jane caught Veronica's eye for a moment and distinctly saw a twinkle in it.

She started to unload the bags and boxes while Veronica and her mother-in-law went back into the house. Jane wondered idly where the *dama di compagnia* was – preparing lunch quite possibly. Dino, looking very bouncy, made a beeline for what was presumably his home, some way off to the left. This was a lovely old red brick building, partly hidden and shaded by cypress trees. Over in the other direction was a quaint wooden construction that looked like a cross between a pagoda and a cricket pavilion. Presumably this was the summer house so, after carrying Veronica's things up the steps to the front door, Jane took her things over to the pagoda, starting with a box containing the food from her fridge and then the laptop, printer, and other tools of her PA trade, and then finally her heavy suitcase. She hadn't been sure what clothes she was going to need in the country so had thought it wiser to bring almost all her things with her from Venice.

'Here are your keys, Jane.' Veronica emerged from the front door and handed over a small bunch. 'If you want to go out in a car any time, just take your pick. I won't be doing any driving but do check with Alvise first in case he has plans. There's a remote control in each car which opens and closes the gates. If you want to go out on foot, there's a pedestrian gate by the main entrance and the key to that's on the ring. Now, what do you want to do about lunch today? My mother-in-law says she's saving herself till dinner – to which we are both invited by the way – so for now we could order something in from the bar in the village if you like.'

'I should maybe take a look at your mother-in-law's bike first, shouldn't I?'

'Don't worry about that. She'll be having a siesta and she probably won't surface for a couple of hours. Wait until this evening when it's a bit cooler.'

'As far as lunch is concerned, to be honest I had an enormous pizza last night so I'm not really that hungry. I've brought the contents of my fridge with me so I've got lots of stuff that needs to be eaten. Would you like to come and have a lunch of salad and bits and pieces with me? That way you can show me where everything is in the summer house.'

'That sounds excellent, thank you. I'll be delighted to take you up on your kind offer. Alvise and Maria will be here in an hour or two if you need anything, but I should be able to show you how most of it works.' She turned and called out to the dog who was just visible in the distance, sniffing about in the trees around his house. 'Dino, come here. David's not back yet.'

Jane's accommodation might not have had the historic allure of the palazzo in Venice or the striking appearance of the Palladian villa but it was exceedingly charming and comfortable all the same. There was an enormous open plan living room with a well-equipped kitchen to one side downstairs, and two big bedrooms upstairs, both with ensuite bathrooms. The floors were pine and there were bare beams throughout and wood panelling on the walls. The last time Jane had been somewhere like this had been the skiing holiday she and Mark had had in Austria barely a few months before his death. She felt quite nostalgic for a moment but was heartened not to feel her eyes begin to water.

'The summer house was built in the twenties.' Veronica went around opening curtains and windows. 'The people who were living at the villa then did a lot of entertaining and I gather this little place was constantly full of guests. Like I said, we haven't had guests here for years; it's good to see it being used.'

'It's simply lovely. I can almost see the ladies in their long dresses and the men in their blazers and flannels.'

'I'm not sure about blazers, but hunting clothes would have been common. Hunting was popular then and it wasn't until thirty years ago that this whole area became a national park and they put a stop to it. I imagine back between the wars you could hardly hear yourself think on a Sunday morning with all the intrepid hunters out there shooting sparrows and protected species.' Veronica shot her a rueful glance. 'One of my least favourite facets of Italian country life, but at least that's all over now as far as this area's concerned.'

'What about your father-in-law? Did he hunt?'

Veronica shook her head. 'He had a horror of guns. He was in the RAF during the war and he must have seen more than enough violence. No, the only hunter here was Flora – and she was a crack shot. She even won competitions.'

'Now, why doesn't that come as a surprise to me? Your mother-in-law's very different from any other grand-mother I've ever known.'

'*Great*-grandmother. Don't forget little Linda, my own granddaughter. But yes, she's quite a lady. Mind you, in spite of their wealth, she's had a tough life. Living under the Nazi occupation can't have been easy.'

She and Veronica carried on eating their lunch and chatting – increasingly freely these days – until there was a bleep from the iPad and Jane saw that her boss had just received an email.

'It's from your daughter, Diana. Are you happy to read it on the screen or do you want to wait until I've set up the printer?'

'Just read it out to me if you don't mind.' Veronica took a sip of wine. 'I can't stand those damn computers.'

Jane clicked on the message and read it out loud as instructed. It wasn't very long.

Ciao, Mamma. I'm flying back on Saturday morning. Should be arriving British Airways at Marco Polo at five p.m. Could Alvise come and pick me up? Are you already up at the villa or still in Venice? Really looking forward to seeing you again. Hope all is well. I'm fine. Love to Nonna. xxx

'She never was one for long letters – mind you, she's still miles better than her brother.' Veronica was smiling, presumably at the thought of being reunited with her youngest before long. 'Can you ask Alvise to pick her up?'

'Of course, and if it's a problem for him I'm happy to do it.'

'That's kind. I'll give her a call later on. I'm so looking forward to seeing her again. I haven't seen her since Christmas so we'll have a lot of catching up to do.'

'What about your other daughter? Will she be coming for the summer?'

'Beatrice brings my little granddaughter, Linda, for a few weeks every summer. Hopefully she'll stick around for a while. She and her husband split up last year and the divorce has just come through. I'm sure she could do with a break.'

'I'm sorry to hear that. Is she going to stay on in Rome? Does she work?'

'She works for a TV channel and she's always busy. I sometimes worry that Linda doesn't see enough of her mum. I have no idea whether she'll end up staying in Rome. She says she's trying to get transferred a bit closer to here but who knows?'

'And David should be back by then so it'll be a nice family get-together for you all.'

Veronica's smile slipped. 'Not all… The family will never be fully together again.'

Jane immediately did her best to add a bit of encouragement. 'Of course, but still, it'll be good for you to see all your kids. What age are they?'

'Beatrice is the eldest. She's…' Veronica did a quick calculation. '…thirty-six now, while David's thirty-three and Diana's almost exactly eight years younger than him.'

Jane decided it would be a good idea to try to keep Veronica talking. As her own therapist had never stopped telling her, talking was good. 'And are they all bilingual, like you and your mother-in-law?'

'Yes, I'm pleased to say. We always spoke English in the house and they went to school here in Venice so they automatically learnt both languages. All three went to university in the UK as well so they're as bilingual as you could hope for. They certainly speak Italian a whole lot better than I ever will.'

'What about little Linda? Does she speak English? How old is she?'

'She's seven. She just had her birthday last month. She doesn't speak a lot of English, but she's getting better. Her father, Dario, only spoke Italian and he insisted on sending her to an Italian school in Rome, so although Beatrice tried talking to her in English it's been mostly Italian in their house up till last year and the divorce. Still, she understands pretty well and her mum's been speaking more English to her recently so who knows? You know what kids are like for picking things up.'

'She sounds like a bright little girl.'

'Oh, she's bright all right. I'm sure you two will get on like a house on fire.' She was sounding noticeably enthused at the prospect of seeing her granddaughter again.

'And you said that Diana's studying fashion. She gets that from you, presumably.'

Veronica nodded. 'I suppose so. She's determined to become the next Coco Chanel... or more probably the next Vivienne Westwood or somebody equally eccentric. You wait until you see her clothes. When she came over at Christmas she was half naked underneath what looked like a native American blanket.'

Jane giggled at the thought. 'Can't have been too comfortable on a transatlantic flight.'

'Comfort doesn't register with her. It's all about making an impression; shock and awe. You'll see.'

Jane couldn't miss the life that had come into Veronica's eyes since they'd started talking about family. It made sense that, even as Veronica withdrew from society and locked herself away, she'd still want to be with her nearest and dearest. Jane was looking forward to seeing the family reunited and, hopefully, seeing Veronica's mood continue to lift.

'And David, does he share Diana's taste in extravagant clothing?'

'Anything but. He spends most of his time looking like a tramp.' Veronica's tone was sombre once again, and Jane realised she might have inadvertently spoiled the mood. 'I wish he would look after himself a bit more but he just doesn't care.'

'Do he and his sisters get on?'

'Very well. He dotes on his little sister in particular.'

'Any idea when he's coming back?'

Veronica held up her hands helplessly. 'That's anybody's guess. Some time in early July, I believe. He'll just turn up one day and that'll be that. Like I said, he's not exactly the world's greatest communicator.'

Chapter 10

Late that afternoon, after unpacking and setting up the computer and printer, Jane slipped into her running gear and went out to survey the terrain before turning her hand to bicycle maintenance. Opening her front door, she almost tripped over a sleeping Dino stretched out on her doormat, enjoying the shade as the sun began to set on the rear of the house. He opened one eye, looked up and his tail began to wag lazily.

'Hello, dog. Are you going to show me around? Coming for a walk?'

The magic word did the trick and she was soon jogging down through open fields towards a little copse of trees, the dog scampering happily ahead of her. From here she had an excellent view down over the red tiled roofs of the little village they had passed on the way up. There was a very old-looking church tower, and beyond it, the other side of the valley rose steeply to the pyramid-shaped summit of a big hill, on top of which there was an unsightly cluster of TV masts. She resolved to explore the area in depth as the weeks went by. It certainly looked as though there would be no shortage of picturesque walks or running trails.

When they reached the trees at the bottom of the property, the dog disappeared down a path into thick bushes and she followed. Seconds later there was an almighty splash and she emerged from the bushes to find a very happy-looking Labrador doggy-paddling about in a lake the size of a pair of tennis courts. All around were weeping willows whose branches cast shadows across the remarkably blue water.

'Oh, God, Dino. You're going to get me into trouble. Come on out, will you?'

He made no attempt to comply, even when she scouted around for a stick and threw it in for him to retrieve. He did indeed swim over and catch it in his mouth, but he didn't show any signs of wanting to bring it back to her, so she resigned herself to spending the rest of her run in the company of a smelly wet dog. She stood and looked on, noticing for the first time that there was a raft moored in the middle of the lake with a ladder attached to the side. Presumably this meant that the pool wasn't just for dogs. The sun was low on the horizon by now and the shadows were lengthening, but she decided to come back one day when it was hot and try it for herself – after checking with Alvise first to be sure it was all right to swim here.

After a while she thought it was time to carry on with her run – with or without the dog – so she addressed him in her sternest voice. 'Dino, come on. I'm off. You heard – come here, boy!'

To her surprise it worked and the next thing she knew she was running for shelter as the bouncy – and very soggy – dog decided to come up to her and shake himself enthusiastically. Just managing to avoid a shower of probably not very fragrant water, she set off again and Dino was soon running ahead of her, leading her on a tour through the grasslands surrounding the villa. There was a clearly discernible path that snaked across the open fields before looping back again, so presumably it was a regular circuit for the occupants of the property – presumably David and his four-legged friend. It took about twenty minutes to run all the way round, so she did two circuits before heading back up to the villa. By this time the Labrador, while still not exactly dry, was a lot less wet than before, but she felt she should warn Veronica and her mother-in-law just in case he decided to trot into the villa and start rolling about on the carpets. By this time the little Fiat was parked outside and she found Alvise sitting on a bench by the back door, enjoying the last rays of the setting sun. Attached to the villa beyond them was an amazing domed conservatory, packed with a seemingly impenetrable wall of greenery, that looked more like Kew Gardens than Italy.

'Good evening, Jane. Had a good run?'

'Yes, thanks. I've just come to warn you that the dog's been for a swim and he's still wet.'

'We're used to that here. We keep a towel specially for that purpose.' He turned and called through the open door and Maria appeared almost immediately with a big towel in her hands. Jane reached for it.

'I'll do that. It's my fault for taking him down by the lake. I didn't realise it was there but I'll know for the future.'

Maria protested but Jane grabbed the towel and set about drying the dog who quite clearly loved this part of the operation and was soon rolling about on the grass making happy little grunting noises as she dried his tummy. Finally, as she dried the dog's paws one by one, she glanced up at Alvise.

'So does Dino just run free?'

'Around here, yes. I don't think he'd run off – unless he was chasing a squirrel or a rabbit. He's got a thing about squirrels in particular for some reason, but the whole estate's fenced off anyway so he can't go far. He hasn't learned how to unlock the gates yet so there's no problem.' He grinned. 'He's a clever dog, but not that clever.'

Jane had just straightened up again when Maria appeared at the kitchen door with a tray in her hands. 'Here, Jane, I've made fresh lemonade. You look like you could use a glass of something cold. I could do with a little sit down myself.'

Jane took it gratefully and took a seat alongside Alvise on the bench while Maria pulled up a chair and sat opposite them. The sun was already grazing the tops of the hills behind the house and the air had turned a little bit cooler now. After the suffocating heat of Venice, it made a very pleasant change, as did the wide-open spaces all around with hardly a single human in sight. They chatted for ten minutes or so and Alvise asked her what she thought of the villa. Jane answered honestly.

'It's amazing although, to tell the truth, I wouldn't want to live in a house like this. It's just too…' She hesitated. She had been about to say *vistosa*, which translated as 'flashy' but this was her employer's family's residence she was talking about after all, so she adopted a less judgemental adjective. 'It's just a bit too grand for my taste. Give me the little summer house any day.'

He nodded slowly. 'I know what you mean, but the general loved it and Signora Flora says the only way she'll ever leave will be feet first.' He glanced around to be sure they weren't in danger of being overheard. 'The way she's going, that probably won't be for a good long while.'

Jane grinned. 'She's quite a lady. I wonder what her secret is.'

'She puts it down to the hills. She says this is the healthiest place in the whole of Italy.'

'It's certainly green enough so the air must be a whole lot cleaner than down on the plain.'

'And, of course, she's out and about all the time. Exercise is so good for all of us.'

'And she really rides a bike?' Jane had a sudden image of ninety-year-old Flora freewheeling down the hills and smiled to herself.

'She certainly does. Because of the hills it was getting a bit hard for her so David managed to get her to change to an electric bike last year and she rides it down to the village two or three times a week to see her friends or do the shopping and, of course, for mass on Sundays.'

'That reminds me, I promised to mend her puncture.'

'Already done. I saw the tyre was down when I got here so I've fixed it.'

'That's great, thanks. Tell me, is that a greenhouse attached to the back of the villa?'

'That's her pride and joy. She occupies all the ground floor of the east wing and she spends most of her time out in what she calls the orangery. You wait until you see what she's got in there. Talk about green fingers; she's got plants from around the world.'

Jane had the chance to inspect Signora Flora's plants that same evening when she walked across to the villa at seven o'clock sharp. The inside was, if anything, even more overwhelming than the outside. The high ceilings were frescoed with nymphs, shepherds and pastoral scenes; the floors were polished marble and the furnishings looked as if they had been looted from Napoleon's personal collection. It was way over the top as far as Jane was concerned, but there was no denying that it all fitted together perfectly.

Veronica accompanied her through a fine old door on the far side of the marble-clad entrance hallway into the old lady's apartments. Dino led the way along a cool corridor lined with portraits of no doubt long dead ancestors, through a charming living room and out into the orangery. Out here, perfectly shaded from the setting sun by the bulk of the house, it was unexpectedly cool and they found Flora and her *dama di compagnia*.

The first thing to strike Jane was the fact that the carer looked, if anything, even older than Flora. She was introduced to Jane as Luciana and she rested heavily on a stick as she reached out to shake hands. Her handshake was more what you would expect from a lady of mature years; however, she made up for her frailty with a sparkling sense of humour and soon had Jane and the others giggling as she recounted how a young deer had managed to get into the orangery a few days earlier, managing to make the resulting chase to get rid of it sound like an episode of Indiana Jones.

The orangery itself was spectacular with, as Alvise had indicated, a mass of exotic plants ranging from huge cactus plants to a very healthy-looking vine, already hung with little bunches of tiny green grapes which would no doubt ripen in a month or two. But for Jane, the nicest thing was the wonderful song of a little robin that filled the whole room from his vantage spot on top of a banana palm. Luciana pointed to the ventilation openings high up in the glass walls which provided access to the robin and his wife who had set up home here some years ago. It was charming – almost like being in the jungle but without the cloying heat of the tropics.

It came as no surprise to Jane to find that the evening meal had been prepared by Flora herself – ninety-five years old or not. When she went off to the kitchen to make the final preparations, Jane got up and followed her, keen to help. Luciana, who had mobility problems, remained in her seat. The kitchen was a huge old-fashioned room dominated by a monumental fireplace occupying most of the end wall with a massive and evidently ancient cast iron range set inside it. The floor was made of old terracotta tiles and the centre of the room was taken up by a huge table, about the same length as the Mercedes. On it was a broad dish with another dish upturned on top of it to ward off any insects. Signora Flora removed the cover to reveal slices of toasted bread topped with chopped tomatoes and basil leaves, all soaked in thick extra virgin olive oil.

'This is very kind of you to help, Jane. If you'd like to take the *bruschette* out to the orangery, I'll get the rest of the stuff from the fridge.'

By the time Jane returned, the kitchen table was laden with other plates containing cold chicken, ham and salami, what looked like polenta slices spread with pâté and goat's cheese, and a huge bowl of mixed salad. There was potato salad, slices of tomato with mozzarella and basil, and bottles of ice-cold white wine and mineral water. Jane looked on in awe – Flora really was an amazingly active old lady. It took three trips with a loaded tray to ferry everything outside and lay it all out on a long side table in the orangery, from which people helped themselves. Jane acted as wine waiter, making sure everyone had a drink in their hands, before sitting down to sip the excellent wine herself. The bottles were unlabelled so she queried their provenance. The answer also came as no surprise.

'This is our own homemade wine. I'm so pleased you like it.' Flora smiled. 'Umberto – he's our groundsman – is a real expert and last year was a very good year for the vines up here.' She took a sip herself and addressed Jane directly. 'So, Jane, what brings you to Italy? Veronica tells me your mother's from Milan. Is this a return to your roots?'

'I suppose you could say that. I was born and brought up in the UK, but I do feel a real connection to Italy.' As she spoke, she realised just how true that was. She had been feeling more and more at home.

'That's what I did, you know.' In response to the expression on Jane's face, Flora elaborated. 'I got married and moved to England when I was in my early twenties and I lived happily over there until my husband passed away thirty years ago. After his death, I knew I wanted to come back to the family home in Italy and I'm so pleased I did, particularly as Veronica and Peter also decided to move to Venice at the same time. It's good to know that the villa here and the palazzo in Venice are being lived in by members of our family once more.'

'This is a wonderful place, as is the palazzo in Venice.'

'Veronica tells me you were in the army. You probably know that my grandson, David followed in the Cooper family tradition and joined the army. Do you come from a military background?'

'Not at all. Originally I joined up so the army would pay to put me through university. That way I didn't end up with a massive student loan.' Jane was pleased to find she was able to talk about her military career without it arousing any unwanted upsurge of emotion. Even just a few weeks ago this wouldn't have been possible.

'That sounds very sensible. But you enjoyed your time in the army?'

Jane had to stop and think for a moment. Her memory had been so clouded by the way her army career had come to an end that she had forgotten the good times – and there had been a lot of them. Realising as she spoke that this was just about the first time she had talked about this sort of thing for several years, she felt pleased to be able to reply in even tones.

'Overall, yes. I made many very good friends and I got to see a lot of different places.'

Veronica then intervened to change the subject and Jane was relieved. Even so, the fact that she had started talking about her former life felt like a massive step in the right direction.

Chapter 11

On Saturday, Jane volunteered to drive down to Venice airport to pick up Diana. This was partly to save Alvise the trouble, but also so she could go to a big shopping mall she had located in the outskirts of Mestre to do some shopping. She had only brought one old pair of shorts from England and she got the feeling she would be wearing shorts most of the summer up here in the hills, so she knew she needed more. The shops had a good range of clothing and she bought two more pairs, deliberately choosing those that were long enough to cover the jagged white scar on her thigh. As well as shorts, she bought a lightweight rain jacket, a little backpack, new walking boots and thick socks to go in them. For old time's sake she bought herself a compass, a Swiss army knife and a detailed map of the Euganean Hills. If she was going to do some serious exploring, she knew she would feel happier with the right equipment.

Suitably kitted out, she drove on to the airport, left the car in the short-term parking area, and was waiting in the Arrivals section by five p.m. Veronica had shown her a photo of her daughter so Jane was expecting a twenty-five-year-old girl with long brown hair and probably wearing outlandish clothes. Just to be on the safe side she had also made a sign with Diana's name on it and, as it turned out, it was just as well she did.

She had been standing there for some time, studying the new arrivals emerging through the automatic doors, when she felt a tap on her arm and heard a voice at her ear.

'Hi, I'm Diana. You must be Jane.'

Jane swung round to find herself confronted by a young woman with short blonde hair in a pixie cut, wearing jeans and a red T-shirt advertising Woodstock Music and Art Fair, August 1969. Apart from the T-shirt being twice as old she was, she looked remarkably normal; not in the least bit wacky.

'Hi, Diana. I'm sorry I didn't recognise you. Your mum showed me a photo but you've changed a bit.' She held out her hand but was slightly taken aback as Diana leant over and gave her a hug and kisses on the cheeks.

'Hi, Jane. It's really good of you to come and pick me up. Sorry about changing my hair. I do it every now and then. It was getting too long so I got it chopped off.' She grinned and Jane took an instant liking to this chirpy girl. 'You're lucky – last month it was green.'

'Green hair?'

'So as to go with my spring collection. The colours are predominantly oranges and greens so I thought I'd better look the part. I modelled most of it myself.'

'Was this as part of your course?'

'Yes, and I got a commendation. I've brought photos to show everybody.'

Jane led her over to the short-term car park and together they lifted the remarkably large suitcase – with an advisory *Heavy* label stuck on it by the airline – into the cavernous boot. She had toyed with the idea of driving down today in the little Fiat but Veronica had warned her that her daughter didn't travel light. Jane pressed the button to bring down the tailgate, reflecting it was just as well she had heeded that advice. Trying to get this beast into the back of a 500 would have been a real challenge.

On the way back to the villa Diana chatted almost non-stop and Jane learned all about her life in New York and her course at what sounded like a very exclusive fashion and design school there. Although Jane's military service had taken her to a lot of different countries, she had never visited the US, and New York sounded like a fun city. Diana was both friendly and approachable – not in the least bit stuck up. In return Jane told her how she was hoping to become a writer and how pleased she was to be working for such a famous author. For now at least, she didn't mention her time in the army, but she went on to provide a positive update on Diana's mother.

'I can honestly say I've noticed an improvement in your mum since I arrived less than a month ago. She seems more animated and Maria was gobsmacked when she heard that we were taking a trip to the Costume Museum in Mantua the other week. Apparently it was one of the first times your mum's been out of the house since your father passed away. Since Mantua I've even managed to get her to come for a few walks with me around Venice as well.'

'That's amazing. I'm so glad. It's hard for me being thousands of miles away and knowing that there's little or nothing I can do. What did you think of the Costume Museum? I've read about it but I've never been.'

Jane gave her a brief description of the museum and the collection of costumes but decided not to mention that the curator might have taken a fancy to her. Inside her head she repeated her regular mantra that she wasn't interested in any man for the foreseeable future.

She delivered Diana to the villa and helped her carry the suitcase up the steps where Alvise appeared and hoisted it easily onto his shoulder. Jane then headed back to the summer house so as to give mother and daughter some time alone together. Half an hour later she was just beginning to think about making herself something to eat when there was a tap at the door. She opened it to find Diana with an invitation. At her side was the dog who came trotting across to greet her.

'Mum asks if you'd like to come to dinner. Maria's roasted a whole goose and there's enough food to feed an army.'

'Well, only if you're sure. You and your mum must have all sorts of stuff to talk about.'

'Please come. By the way, you're right, I can see it as well. Mum's definitely looking and sounding brighter than when I last saw her.' She reached out a hand and squeezed Jane's arm. 'Maria told me it's all down to you. Thank you so much.'

'If I've helped, that's great but, as far as I can see, she's pretty much done it all herself.'

Together they walked over to the villa where she found Veronica in the massive living room looking happy. Tall French windows were open wide and faint mooing in the distance was the only sound to be heard. It was pastoral, it was peaceful and it couldn't have been any more different from the dust and destruction of Iraq.

'Help yourselves to some Prosecco and come and join me outside. I told Maria we'll eat in a few minutes' time but it's just such a delightful evening, it's too good to miss.'

Jane took this as another very good sign. Clearly the arrival of her daughter had been a welcome boost to her employer's morale. Diana filled two glasses with Prosecco, handed one to Jane, and they all went out onto the impressive terrace where comfortable wicker armchairs had been arranged.

'Take a seat and breathe deeply. Much as I love Venice, you can't beat a bit of clean country air.' Veronica sat down alongside Diana, while Jane took a seat nearby and admired the view down the valley, over the village, to the plains beyond almost hidden by the heat haze.

'Cheers.' Veronica held up her glass. 'Diana, darling, it's so lovely to have you back home, and Jane, thank you for fitting in here so beautifully.'

'Is Mum working you hard, Jane? She used to bully me to do my homework.' Diana softened the impact of her words by leaning over and kissing her mother on the cheek.

'I can honestly say I'm enjoying every minute of it.' Jane realised that she really did mean what she said. 'Your mum's the best boss I've ever had.'

'So I'm not as tough as some of your superiors in the army?' Veronica gave Jane a little smile while Diana looked up in surprise.

'You were in the army? Like David?'

Jane nodded. 'Yes, for six years. I was in the Sappers… the Royal Engineers. What regiment was he in?'

'The Rifles.'

'Ah… PBI.'

'PBI?' Both mother and daughter looked puzzled.

'Poor Bloody Infantry. Traditionally they always get the worst jobs.'

'And what was your job, Jane?'

'Bomb disposal and mine clearance.' She suddenly felt her throat dry and she took a sip of wine. As the bubbles hissed over her tongue, she saw the other two exchange glances. It was Diana who commented first, looking aghast.

'And yet, you reckon the infantry get the worst jobs? I can't imagine anything worse than yours.' The expression on Diana's face wasn't new to Jane. Most people looked at her as if she were crazy when they found out what she did – or rather, what she used to do.

'If you're well trained and you know what you're doing, it's just another job.' Jane was very pleased to find she was able to talk about this in measured tones.

'And if you're very, very lucky.' Diana was looking at her goggle-eyed.

'Yes, luck helps… for as long as it holds out.'

'But yours held out, didn't it?'

Jane was surprised to see Veronica's hand snake out and catch hold of her daughter's arm. 'Of course it did. Now, I think it might be time to go and eat. Maria's beckoning.' Without more ado, she stood up and, still holding Diana's arm, turned and headed back inside. Jane walked in behind them taking a few deep, calming breaths. Two things were clear. The first was that Veronica either knew more than she was letting on or she had intuitively guessed that something bad had happened. The second was that she herself had managed to talk – albeit only minimally – about her military service without welling up. Oscar the counsellor would have been pleased.

Dinner that night was spectacular, not just because it was taken in the cavernous dining room with the three of them, accompanied by Flora and Luciana, sitting at one end of a highly polished table that could have housed another couple of dozen people. As a starter Maria presented them with a wonderful selection of olives, sundried tomatoes, smoked and cured hams, salami and local cheese. Jane was greatly relieved to discover that, in view of the size of the goose, Maria had decided not to make a pasta course, and they went from antipasti straight to the main. The roast goose was exquisite and Maria served it with little roast potatoes, tasty fresh asparagus, and fennel roasted in the oven and smothered with grated cheese. This was all accompanied by an unlabelled bottle of excellent red wine that Flora said was also made from their own grapes. By the time Jane had finished the homemade panna cotta, she was absolutely full. She just about managed to find the strength to ask for a little espresso but that was that.

After her long journey Diana was looking weary and, without waiting for coffee, she kissed her mother and grandmother, waved to Jane and to Luciana, and headed straight off to bed. The two elderly ladies followed suit shortly after. After they had left, Jane glanced across the table to Veronica. 'It's been a delightful evening and thank you for sparing me any more questions about what happened in Fallujah.' The realisation dawned on her that this was another first. Veronica was the first person apart from close family, military personnel and medical practitioners to whom she had mentioned that name.

Veronica smiled back at her. 'Like I said, any time you want to talk about it, I'm here.'

'Thank you. That means a lot.' Jane hesitated for a moment and then added. 'And the same goes for you. If you ever want a shoulder to lean on, to cry on or laugh on, I'm here for you.'

Chapter 12

The beginning of July arrived and Jane carried on working her way through Veronica's fan mail, emails and messages. She also went out every day with Dino, enjoying being in the fresh air and returning to full fitness with the dog as company. Apart from running through the open grassland around the villa, she also followed the dog at a more sedate pace up through the vineyards where she met and chatted to Umberto, a weather-beaten man in his sixties who looked after the estate. She thought of asking him if he remembered Paolo Padovan who had helped out in his summer holidays but though it better not to ask too many questions until she got to know Umberto better. She didn't want to give the impression of being a busybody.

One afternoon she was sitting at her kitchen table with the front and back door open to allow a cool draught to combat the heat of the day when she heard a voice.

'Who are you?' It was a child's voice, speaking Italian.

Jane looked up to see a little dark-haired girl standing in the doorway with a teddy bear in one hand. She smiled back at her and replied in Italian.

'Ciao, I'm Jane. What's your name?'

'I'm Linda. Do you live here?'

Jane realised that Veronica's granddaughter must have arrived for her annual holiday in the country. 'I do at the moment, but I'll be going back to Venice with your grandmother at the end of the summer. Why don't you come in?'

'Is she your nonna too?' The little girl wandered in and climbed onto a chair alongside Jane, setting the teddy down carefully on the table in front of her, facing them. She was so small her head barely poked up above the tabletop.

'No, she's my boss. I work for her.' Jane went and collected a couple of cushions from the sofa. 'Jump off a moment and you can sit on these. That way you and I'll be at the same height.' The little girl obeyed and was soon sitting happily, if precariously, perched at eye level. Jane sat back down again and gave her a smile. 'That's a nice teddy. What's he called?'

Linda gave her a look as much as to say, *what a silly question*. 'He's called Teddy.' She then transferred her attention to the computer screen. 'What are you doing?'

Jane had limited experience with kids and had forgotten how inquisitive they could be. 'I'm writing an email.'

If she had been expecting Linda to ask what an email was, she was to be disappointed. This seven-year-old was already computer savvy. 'I got an email from my friend Violetta the other day. She's a year older than me.'

Jane decided to start asking a few questions of her own. 'And what did it say?'

'It didn't say anything. It was a photo of her birthday cake. It was pink.'

Jane gradually brought the conversation around to more relevant issues.

'Are you here with your mummy? Is she going to stay with you?'

'Yes, we're going to have a *super holiday*.' The last two words were delivered in perfect English and Jane realised her mother must have been using the language more now that her husband was out of the equation. She grinned and switched to English.

'Do you speak English? It sounds like you speak it very well.'

'I can speak English and Italian.' This, too, came out in fluent English and not without considerable pride – and rightly so. 'So can you. We're clever.'

'Mind you, Dino the dog understands both languages, too. I sometimes speak to him in English and sometimes in Italian and I'm sure he knows exactly what I'm saying – particularly if it's about food.'

At that moment there was a movement at the door and the Labrador himself put in an appearance, panting loudly, with his pink tongue hanging out. Jane saw that the water bowl she kept for him was almost empty so she got up and refilled it. When she returned to the table and they were both watching the dog slurping up big messy mouthfuls of water, she had an idea and glanced back at Linda. 'When he finishes drinking, try asking him if he'd like a biscuit, but do it in English. You'll see how well he understands.'

She got up and went over to her special packet of dog biscuits, listening with a little smile as Linda addressed the dog in slow, clear tones so he would understand. 'Dino, do you want a biscuit?'

He immediately trotted across to the little girl and sat down primly at her side just as Jane had been teaching him.

Jane nodded approvingly. 'Very good, Linda. Now tell him to give you his paw and to say "please".'

'What's a paw?' Clearly this was unfamiliar vocabulary for the little girl so Jane explained and then, after the dog had obediently obeyed the command, she handed Linda a biscuit to give to him. Both dog and girl looked satisfied as he took it most delicately and settled down at their feet to crunch it up.

His arrival was followed not long after by Veronica and her elder daughter.

'Jane, can we come in?'

'Of course. What can I offer you? It's a bit hot for tea but I've made some fresh lemonade if you're interested. Maria's trusted me with her secret recipe. Would you like some?'

'I'd like some lemonade.' Linda had understood and was proudly showing her mum and grandma how good her English comprehension skills were.

Beatrice was quick to remind her of her manners: 'No, Linda, "I'd like some, *please*."'

Veronica answered for all of them. 'That's kind. I'm sure we'd all love some… please. You've met Diana, so now let me introduce you to my other daughter. This is Beatrice.'

'Ciao, Jane. Mum's been telling me how you've changed her life.' Just like her sister, Beatrice spoke impeccable English. She was a good-looking woman in her mid-thirties, and she had a friendly, if slightly weary, smile. As Jane shook hands with her, she couldn't miss the worry lines around the eyes. What was that old saying about death, divorce and house moves being the worst?

'Hi, Beatrice. Your daughter's just been showing me how well she speaks English. She's a bright girl.'

'I'm a bright girl.' Clearly Linda was not one to hide her light under a bushel, but it then emerged that she was at least prepared to share the credit. 'And Dino speaks English too. I've just been talking to him and he understood what I said.'

Jane pointed towards the open door. 'Shall we sit outside? It's a gorgeous afternoon.' The others trooped out and sat down in the shade at the rear of the pavilion, while Jane grabbed four glasses and the jug of lemonade from the fridge and put them on a tray. For good measure she added a bowl of ice cubes and a plate of biscuits – not the canine variety, although Dino eyed them covetously.

They sat and chatted about everything from the weather to life in Rome, Linda's school and Jane's literary aspirations. Her military career was not mentioned and she was pleased about that. She found herself drawn to Beatrice, just as she had been to Diana, but this was different. She knew that Beatrice had been through a tough spell and must have suffered emotionally. In consequence she felt an immediate bond with her and was pleased to hear that she would be staying three full weeks and her daughter a few weeks longer. Veronica was looking and sounding perkier than ever and Jane was pleased for her too.

In the course of the conversation she learnt about Beatrice's job with an Italian TV company, which sounded fascinating although it was clear that life as a single parent wasn't making things easy for her or for her daughter. By the sound of it, this holiday would be the first real together time the two of them had had for ages. After a bit, Beatrice turned the subject to her siblings.

'Di sounds as if she's enjoying life in New York. Did you see the photos of her spring collection?' She glanced across at Jane with a smile. 'Believe it or not, there were some dresses I wouldn't mind wearing myself – unlike last year's collection that looked as though it was inspired by pole dancers.'

Diana had shown Jane the photos and she agreed with Beatrice's assessment.

'I thought some of them were very stylish.' She grinned at her employer. 'Although I only wear Ingrid Bergman gowns myself…'

'Jane had to represent me at a charity auction, so I gave her the cream Bergman dress to wear. Remember, Beatrice, that was the one you wore on your twenty-first.'

Beatrice smiled across at Jane. 'Lucky you. It's gorgeous isn't it. The trouble with dresses like that is there aren't that many occasions when you can wear them. In my job most of the time all the viewers see of me is from the waist up. I could be wearing pyjama bottoms underneath if I felt like it.'

Veronica had also been favourably impressed by Diana's collection. 'Diana tells me what she wants to do is to set up her own design studio.'

'Where?' Beatrice looked up with interest. 'Over here or over there?'

'She doesn't know. She was muttering about Paris, but seeing as she doesn't speak the language, I would think she'd be better off here or in the States.'

'Surely Milan is one of the big centres for fashion, isn't it?' Jane didn't know a lot about designer clothes. 'That would be conveniently close to here so you'd see more of her.'

'She's got to finish the final year of her course first but yes, Milan would be good. Or even Venice…'

'And what about David?' It sounded as though Beatrice hadn't seen her brother for a while. 'How's he doing these days?' That same note of compassion was evident in her tone. 'Did I hear that he's gone off again?'

'Yes, for a whole month. I'm hoping he'll be back soon but, you know him, he hasn't said a word.' Veronica gave a heartfelt sigh. 'Hopefully the change of air will have done him good.'

Beatrice exchanged glances with her mother. 'Still miserable?'

Jane was ever more curious to know what was troubling Veronica's son but she refrained from commenting. This was family business, after all, and she was just a bystander.

Veronica nodded her head slowly. 'I'm afraid so. Sooner or later he's got to snap out of it.' She looked helplessly across at her daughter. 'I just wish there was something I could do.'

'I suppose he's got to work through it by himself. Still, when he comes back, Di and I can have a go at him. Maybe we can at least get him talking. When did you say he's expected back?'

'Your guess is as good as mine.'

Chapter 13

Over the next few days, Jane was regularly visited by Linda and her teddy, usually accompanied by the Labrador. Beatrice was also a frequent visitor and Jane got on increasingly well with her. She told Jane about the final months of her marriage and how stressful she had found everything. The reasons for the break-up were complex but the nub of it appeared to be the bitter jealousy of her husband – not of other men but of Beatrice's rising popularity as a TV personality. He had been unable to stomach the fact that his wife was better-known and more popular than he was, and his ever-increasing resentment had led to the divorce.

Jane provided a sympathetic ear and came close to recounting her own recent history but stopped short. Seeing her burst into tears would have done little to cheer Beatrice up so she just listened and sympathised for now. There would come a time when she would be able to talk about Fallujah and Mark and everything else, but not yet.

The other person she saw quite regularly was Flora on her bike. On Sunday morning as she was out for a jog, she was confronted by the sight of her employer's mother-in-law dressed in her Sunday best, hurtling down the gravel drive with gay abandon. When she spotted Jane she even lifted one hand from the handlebars to give her a cheery wave. Watching her disappear into the distance, Jane had to admit that Flora was a one-off.

She also spent quite a bit of time with Diana, finding that the two of them also got on very well together. They visited the nearby village, which boasted only three shops, but one of these was a fabulous *gelateria* serving home-made ice cream in no fewer than twenty-four flavours. The Euganean Hills might not be the earthly paradise but they came close.

One lunchtime she and Diana drove down to Padua and met up with a group of Diana's friends in the town centre. The city came as a very pleasant surprise to Jane, who knew next to nothing about it – apart from a vague memory of it being mentioned in a Shakespeare play. The *centro storico* of this ancient university city was made up of tortuous, narrow cobbled streets with historic buildings popping up all along the way. In particular the basilica was a stunning building in the Byzantine style that wouldn't have looked out of place alongside the Bosporus. She spent a fascinating hour with Diana walking around, doing her best to take in the main sights – from the spectacular Piazza delle Erbe, the medieval Palazzo Ragione and the Piazza della Frutta with its bars and restaurants. It was here that they stopped for lunch at tables set outside under sun-bleached parasols.

Diana's friends were a group of a dozen or so that she had known since childhood. Some lived locally but many, like Diana, lived in Venice or beyond, but had spent their holidays in the hills every summer since they were little, as their families tried to get away from the suffocating heat of the plains. They were all in their early or mid-twenties, and Jane, with everything she had already been through in her life, felt as if she was twice their age, even though the difference was probably only four or five years. She ate her way through an excellent thin crust *pizza montanara* heaped with smoked speck and wild mushrooms, and listened to the others' conversations with interest, but detachment.

She couldn't miss the fact that two of the men appeared particularly keen on Diana and had positioned themselves on either side of her, and it looked as though they were vying with each other for her attention. Diana, on the other hand, didn't appear particularly interested in either of them and Jane wondered how it would work out. When they all decided to go dancing that night at a disco on the outskirts of town, Jane hastily invented an excuse and declined the invitation to join them.

Later that afternoon, Diana came over to Jane's house in an attempt to persuade her to change her mind and come out dancing that evening, but Jane steadfastly refused. They sat down for a cup of tea together and Jane took the opportunity to quiz her about the two men who had been courting her at lunch, and the answer was unexpected.

'They're nice boys but nothing's going to happen there. The thing is, I know they aren't interested in me for me. They're interested in me for the family's money.' She shot a serious look across the table at Jane. 'Having pots of money's great in so many ways. I can go off to the States and sign up for a course that most people just wouldn't be able to afford. It means I've been able to rent a great little apartment in downtown New York and I can go for holidays to the Caribbean or the Rockies if I want – not that I do – but there's one big drawback. When people find out who I am and my family background, I suddenly become flavour of the month with a whole heap of guys, but how can I tell if they're really interested in me or if they just see a couple of glowing dollar signs when they look at me? And to make things worse, my girlfriends get jealous of all the attention I get, and that leads to arguments.' She managed a wry smile. 'Poor little rich girl, eh?'

This was a facet of wealth that Jane had never considered. Maybe there was such a thing as having too much of a good thing. She gave Diana an encouraging smile. 'You're still young. It'll all work out. You'll see.'

'I really hope so. What about you? Have you got a man hidden away somewhere?' Diana must have noticed the expression that flooded Jane's face because she immediately reached across the table and squeezed her arm. 'I'm sorry, that's no business of mine.'

Jane swallowed hard and was mildly surprised to find that she was able to answer in a fairly steady voice. 'No apology necessary. There was a man, but he's not around anymore. To be honest, I'm concentrating on work now, and working for your mum's great.'

The following day she decided it was warm enough to try going down to the lake for a swim. Alvise had told her it was quite safe but that the water was, as he put it, 'a little chilly'. When she got down there, she immediately discovered that he had been guilty of almost Anglo-Saxon understatement. After stripping to her costume, she put her toes in the water and the immediate impact almost took her breath away. Nevertheless, slowly and cautiously she waded in among the weeds until the water was up to the scar at the top of her thigh, and then lowered herself gingerly until she was floating. However, after the initial shock she soon began to enjoy herself.

In fact it wasn't too terribly cold and it was unquestionably refreshing after the heat of the day. She swam out and around the floating platform, deciding not to climb the ladder out of the water as this would only result in having to steel herself to slip back into the cold water again. She wondered idly where Dino was this evening. Normally he was to be found snoozing on her doormat but today he must have had a prior commitment.

When she came out of the water it was too fiddly to change out of her wet costume, so she decided to stay as she was for the short walk back to her house. She was just rolling up her shorts, top and towel and enjoying the warmth of the last rays of the setting sun when the dog suddenly appeared. There was the thunder of charging paws and his familiar black shape came bursting through the bushes and he flung himself into the water with gusto. He surfaced with a big canine smile on his face, noticed her for the first time and immediately doggy-paddled energetically back to the bank and climbed out, clearly intent on saying hello.

Well aware by now of the icy and malodorous shower that would accompany him, she backed away along the path into the bushes and took refuge behind a particu-larly thick clump of gorse as he shook himself violently, sending Labrador-perfumed pond water all over the place but fortunately not too much her way. When he had finished, she was just emerging from her shelter when she suddenly heard footsteps and almost bumped into a tall figure who appeared on the path. She took one look at him and stepped back apprehensively.

He looked like a cross between a caveman, a tramp and a yeti. His tangled hair hung down past his shoulders and he had a bushy beard that almost completely masked his face and could probably have housed a family of baby birds. He was wearing sunglasses, a crumpled khaki T-shirt and shorts, and from the look of his strong arms he would know how to handle himself if it came to a fight. She was just looking warily for alternative escape routes when Dino came bounding up and jumped at the man, scrabbling at his waist with his paws in cheery greeting.

'Dino, you pest, get off. You're soaking wet.'

It was only when Jane registered that the yeti was speaking fluent native English that the penny dropped. This had to be David, Veronica's son. She managed to produce a friendly smile and held out her hand towards him, acutely conscious that all she was wearing was a wet swimming costume.

'Hello, you must be David. I'm Jane… Jane Reed, your mother's new PA.'

'Oh, yes, hi.' He sounded polite rather than warm and friendly.

He shook her hand and then an awkward silence ensued. It didn't last long because at that moment the dog decided he was still feeling a bit damp so he dropped back onto all fours and proceeded to shake himself violently once more, soaking both of them. His master gave an exasperated groan.

'Dino, you monster. Go back in the water, will you? Look what you've done to the nice lady.'

Jane hadn't often been referred to as a nice lady before and it brought a smile to her lips. 'No harm done but I think I'd better head off home and change. Good to meet you, David. Bye.'

'Oh yes, good.' She had already turned away when he remembered his manners. 'Goodbye.'

–

That evening she had a visitor. She had just finished a plate of salad with delicious local salami and goat's cheese when there was a tap at the door. She opened it to find Veronica standing there, holding a sheaf of papers which Jane instantly recognised as her two novellas. A sudden wave of apprehension ran through her but she, too, remembered her manners.

'Hi, Veronica, do come in. Feel like a coffee? I've just finished eating and I'm about to make some.'

'That would be nice.' Veronica stepped inside and closed the door behind her. 'I finished reading the second of your two novellas this afternoon and I thought I could give you a bit of feedback if you like. Is now a good time?'

'Now's great, thanks. Thank you so much for reading them so quickly.' Jane was dying to ask what the great author though of her work but she forced herself to be patient and busied herself at the coffee machine. She glanced over her shoulder and made a bit of small talk as Veronica took a seat at the kitchen table. 'I met David earlier on.'

'I thought you might have. I hadn't heard a thing from him for weeks and then he just appeared this afternoon. What did you think of him?'

Jane felt she could hardly tell her boss that her son looked like a caveman so she prevaricated. 'We barely exchanged more than a couple of words. The dog had just soaked me and I was rushing off to change.'

'I bet he didn't look like any army officer you knew back in the day.' There was a melancholy half-smile on Veronica's face so Jane decided to be honest.

'It was hard to see anything of him under all that hair. Has he got something against hairdressers and razor blades?'

'God only knows when the last time he went to a hairdresser was. Certainly not for ages. Since before his father's death, definitely. I did warn you that he takes absolutely no interest in his appearance. I suppose it's partly a reaction after years of short back and sides in the army.'

'When did he come out of the army?'

'Three years ago. Probably when he was about your age now.'

Jane set the cups of coffee on the table and sat down as well. 'Why did he leave?'

A shadow passed across her boss's face. 'You'd better ask *him*. In fact, it might not be a bad thing if he tells you why he left and you tell him why you did. It might be good for both of you. Now, let me tell you what I got out of reading your work.' It was clear that she was deliberately changing the subject.

Jane filed away the fact that it would appear that David had also left the army under unusual circumstances and her curiosity was piqued even more, but for now, she listened partly in anticipation, partly in trepidation, as Veronica passed judgement.

'I liked both of the novellas in different ways. The thriller was well written – they both were – but I felt it lacked intensity somehow. I thought your main protagonist was a bit too impassive. I wanted more emotion from him.' She looked up and smiled. 'But your romance, on the other hand, had me gripped from the start. The former Olympic swimmer with the tragic past really hit the spot with me and I was genuinely disappointed when it finished after only thirty thousand words or so.'

'So you're saying I should concentrate on writing romance?'

'On what I've seen of your work so far, definitely. You managed to produce believable and sympathetic male and female characters and the twist at the end came as a real surprise. Well done. So, yes, my advice, for what it's worth, is to concentrate on writing romance. You mentioned an interest in historical romance so why not try that, if you can think of an era that appeals to you? Also, if I were you I'd go for something a bit grittier. You've showed from your thriller that you can write about the seamier side of life. Why don't you see if you can combine both works into a romantic thriller?'

Jane felt a wave of relief. 'That's great to hear, Veronica. Thank you so much. I really value your opinion. Getting feedback from a writer of your calibre is a chance in a million for me. I was terrified you were going to tell me I was wasting my time. I'm so, so grateful.'

'Any time.' Veronica took a sip of coffee. 'I just wish the roles were reversed. I would love to be able to start writing again.'

'Still no sign of your muse returning?'

Veronica shook her head sadly. 'Still nothing.'

'Well, give it time. I'm sure the inspiration will come.'

'I do so hope you're right, but I'm not holding my breath.'

Chapter 14

A few days later, Jane was sitting at her laptop when her now regular little visitor put in another appearance.

'Ciao, Jane. Can I have some lemonade?' There was a momentary pause before she added as an afterthought, 'Please.'

Jane looked up and saw Linda at the door, her teddy in her hand as always.

'Ciao, Linda. Come on in. Of course you can. I think I'll have some myself.' She went over to the fridge and heard the familiar clicking of Labrador nails on the floor behind her, followed by a friendly nudge from his cold wet nose. She turned to see him panting. 'And hi to you, too, Dino. Feeling hot?' Although they were up here in the hills, the temperature had been rising all week and Jane had even been considering another swim in the icy waters of the lake later this afternoon. She glanced across at the little girl who had piled the cushions onto her chair and was once more sitting level with the table. 'I'll get him a biscuit if you ask him to say please.'

By the time she had poured two glasses of lemonade – to which she was rapidly becoming addicted – the dog was sitting at Linda's side with one big hairy paw on her lap. Jane handed the biscuit to the little girl who gave it to the Labrador. He settled onto the floor to eat it while Jane sat down alongside the little girl and they chatted. Just like with the girl's mother, Jane found herself increasingly drawn to this little mite.

'I love your lemonade.' Linda offered her glass to the inscrutable teddy but received no response so she turned back to Jane and explained. 'Teddy doesn't like lemons.'

'Well then, there's all the more for us, isn't there?'

'My mummy says you work for my nonna. What do you do?'

'I help her with her work.'

'My mummy works. She's on TV.'

'I know. How clever of her.'

'So's my daddy, but I don't see him very much now.' She looked very serious. 'They're *divorziati*.' Although they were speaking English, she used the Italian word.

'That's a pity, but maybe it was for the best if your mummy and daddy weren't happy.' Jane was feeling her way here. Talking to a seven-year-old about divorce was well outside her comfort zone.

'They used to argue all the time.' Linda picked up her teddy and hugged him. 'Teddy and I both heard them. It was horrid.'

'But now your mummy and daddy are happy. So that should make you feel happy, too.'

'I suppose so. Are you *divorziata*?'

'Not exactly, but I'm on my own. Your mummy's lucky. She's got you.'

'Why are you alone?'

Jane could hardly tell her the full details of what had happened so she improvised. 'I had a boyfriend but he went away.'

'Is he coming back?'

'I'm afraid not.'

'Why not?'

Jane was struggling now and it came as a mighty relief to hear Beatrice's voice at the door.

'I've been wondering where you were, Linda. You were sent over to ask Jane to come for tea, not to plonk yourself down here and stay.' She waved to Jane. 'Hi, Jane, Mum says there's tea in the garden if you're interested.'

Together they went over to the villa and Jane was glad to have been rescued from a potentially tricky Q&A session with the little girl. They found Veronica and her mother-in-law sitting in front of a low table set with cups of tea and one of Maria's cakes.

'Ciao, Jane. Tea? Cake?'

'Cake! Yes, please, Nonna.'

From the expression on the Labrador's face, he felt the same way about the offer of cake.

Jane accepted willingly and helped herself to a cup from the tray and a small slice of chocolate cake. A cold wet nose prodded her thigh and she looked down to see the dog standing beside her, tail wagging, his eyes trained on the cake.

'Sorry, but I'm afraid you aren't allowed chocolate cake.' She took her cup and sat down opposite her employer while Beatrice and Linda settled down between Veronica and Flora. After a vain attempt to scrounge more food, the dog stretched out on his back at Jane's feet, tail wagging lazily. Flora looked down at him and smiled.

'Looks like you've got a friend for life there.'

'He's a lovely dog and he's great company. As it's so hot today I think I might see if he wants to come for a swim with me later on. It's just a pity the water's so cold in the lake – not that it seems to bother Dino in the slightest.'

Flora nodded. 'That's one disadvantage of the villa being here. If it had been built only a bit further down valley, we might have had our own hot spring. The Romans discovered the hot water bubbling up from beneath their feet and built thermal baths just a short way from here in Montegrotto Terme. This whole area has over a hundred spas and yet we end up with the one cold pool for miles around. Not that I swim any more these days. The doctor says I have to take it easy.' There was a mischievous twinkle in her eye. 'Doctors? What do they know?'

'What about going to one of the spas? Aren't they supposed to be relaxing?'

Flora shook her head. 'Not for me. When you get to my age the last thing you want is to start parading around in a swimming costume. It's all very well for young girls like you but I prefer to stay covered up.'

Veronica, on the other hand, picked up on the suggestion. 'I know, why don't the rest of us go to a spa one of these days? My treat. It's supposed to be good for aches and pains and the older I get, the more of those I seem to accumulate.'

Jane smiled – yet another sign of her employer beginning to break out of her self-imposed isolation.

Her daughter obviously felt the same way. 'That sounds like a great day out, Mum. Sure you won't come with us, Nonna?' Seeing Flora shudder at the thought, she returned her attention to her mother. 'And you never know, Mamma, you might find inspiration for a new book there.'

Jane joined in. 'That would be amazing. You just need that one spark to get you going again.'

'Well, if the truth be told, I've never included a spa visit in any of my books. Who knows? Wouldn't it be wonderful if something clicked and it meant I could sit down at my typewriter again? It's amazing how just one single place or object can very quickly become the stimulus for a whole book.' Veronica settled back in her chair and Jane could see a faraway look on her face. She exchanged glances with Beatrice who gave her a little wink. This was sounding good. 'The plot of my Paris book all came from a tattered cloakroom ticket I found in the pocket of an old dress I bought at auction – and that book sold over two million copies worldwide.' Veronica glanced across at them. 'What I wouldn't give for another of those cloakroom tickets to come along now.'

They were still chatting when Diana appeared. Along with her were two of her girlfriends that Jane had met the other day in Padua. These two were Silvia and Grazia, and Jane knew that they were both teachers in Vicenza. Beatrice clearly knew them as well and they all embraced.

'Ciao, everybody. We've come for a swim.' Diana was speaking Italian but by now Jane had got used to the way the members of this family managed to switch seamlessly into whichever language suited them at the time. Diana headed back inside and emerged a minute later with cans of Coke from the fridge, which she distributed to Silvia and Grazia before swallowing half of hers in one go. 'God, it's hot today. It's almost like being back down in Venice.' She glanced at Linda. 'Feel like a swim?'

'Oh yes, please. Mamma, can we go swimming, please?' Linda was hopping up and down at the thought.

'That sounds like a very good idea, but we need to get you changed first and we need your armbands. You know the water down there's deep as well as cold, don't you? Jane and Dino will probably come swimming as well. She was just saying the same thing. What about you, Mum?'

Diana added her own weight to the suggestion. 'Yes, do come, Mamma.'

Veronica held up her hand before her daughters could say any more. 'I'm with your grandmother on this one. It's no good you bullying me, I have no intention of splashing about in that freezing pond. But I will come and watch you swim.'

A few minutes later, Jane went back home, changed into her costume, pulled her shorts and T-shirt back on over the top and made her way down to the lake. From the sound of splashing, she felt sure Dino had got there first and as she emerged from the bushes, she saw that not only was he already in the water, but so was his master. With his wet hair plastered down across his scalp David looked a bit less like a woolly mammoth than before, but from behind it could still have been an old English sheepdog in there alongside Dino. Screams and giggles indicated that the three girls were in the process of inching their way into the chilly waters, and Jane spotted an expression of what could have been annoyance on his face as he looked towards them.

Taking advantage of the distraction created by the three girls, Jane slipped out of her clothes and waded into the lake, reminding herself to keep breathing as the cold water climbed up her body. Finally she pushed herself forward and, as she became acclimatised to the chill, she started swimming about in a lazy breaststroke. In the meantime the three girls were engaged in a splashing contest in the shallows and their squeals had attracted the attention of Dino who doggy-paddled enthusiastically across to join in the fun. Jane left them to it and swam over to the far side of the raft, where she suddenly found herself face to face with David. He came powering across the lake in a stylish front crawl and surfaced abruptly right in front of her, looking surprised.

She looked into his deep blue eyes and a shiver which had nothing to do with the temperature of the water ran through her. His eyes seemed to reach deep inside her and she felt her cheeks colour as she realised that the shiver had been one of attraction. Struggling to collect herself she took a deep breath.

'Hi, David. Great minds think alike. You looking for a bit of peace and quiet too?' She was relieved to hear her voice sounding almost normal.

In spite of all the hair she distinctly saw him smile. 'Dead right. What a racket!' They floated there in silence for a few moments before he came up with a comment. 'Hot today, isn't it?'

The tension inside her dissolved in an instant and Jane almost burst out laughing. He might look like a caveman but he certainly knew how to make polite English conversation: the weather, as ever, a safe topic. She smiled back. 'You aren't joking. I shudder to think how hot and sticky it must be down in Venice.' A thought occurred to her. 'By the way, how deep is this lake? If I were brave enough to climb onto the raft and dive back in again, would there be enough water?'

He nodded. 'Ample. Alvise reckons it's five or six metres deep in the middle. I was about to do just that, so I'll show you.'

He swam over to the stainless-steel ladder and climbed up onto the raft. Watching his athletic form emerge from the pool there was no doubting the feeling this inspired in her. The muscles of his back formed a perfect V-shape and her eyes followed the rivulets of water as they ran down his body, plastering his swimming shorts tightly against him. She was still dealing with the wave of attraction – or at least lust – that swept over her when he turned and executed a very tidy dive into the water. He surfaced a few metres away and immediately gave her a wave of the hand.

'See? Loads of depth. Now I'm off. Bye.' And he dropped his face back into the water and set off for the shore again.

Jane swam over to the raft and climbed out onto the wooden surface, enjoying the warmth of the sun-scorched timbers. She spotted Flora over on the shore, looking on, and received a little wave from her. Before diving back in she sat down with her feet in the water, still watching David's back as he waded out of the lake and disappeared up the track towards home, followed a few seconds later by his dog. She sat there, trying to get her head around the fact that this was the first time in more than two years that she had felt physically attraction to a man. She was still struggling with the ramifications of this discovery when her thoughts were disturbed by Diana's voice.

'I see we've frightened David off.' Diana hauled herself up the ladder and was soon joined by the other two girls. They sat there, basking in the sunshine, and Jane rapidly discovered that she wasn't the only one to find Diana's hirsute brother attractive. Grazia's voice sounded decidedly dreamy.

'He's such a hunk, your brother. Does he really live all alone?'

Diana nodded. 'Apart from the dog.'

'Wish I was that dog.' There was real longing in Grazia's voice now. 'He could pet me and tickle my tummy any time he wanted.'

'Don't waste your time. The man's a hermit nowadays. He never goes out, he never talks to anybody; he just lives for his books and his work.' Jane could hear the regret in Diana's tone. 'More's the pity.'

Jane would dearly have liked to ask for a bit more information about why this desirable man was so closed off from society and unapproachable, but she decided it wasn't her place to ask such a personal question of her employer's daughter, so she stood up and braced herself.

'Well, I can't put it off any longer. I'm going back into the freezing cold water before I get too warm and don't want to leave the raft at all.'

With this she dived back in and by the time she had got her breath back after the shock of the impact she was already halfway towards the shore. She was just wading out of the water when she heard Flora's voice.

'Poor David...' Flora was still staring up the path towards David's house and she sounded unusually subdued.

'Poor David?' Jane reached for her towel and stretched it around her shoulders. Here in the shade of the trees she was almost cold. 'Why do you say that?'

'He's had his problems. He's not the boy he used to be.'

Considering he was thirty-three, he was hardly a boy, but to a nonagenarian it probably felt that way. 'What sort of problems?'

Flora turned towards her and for the first time Jane noticed that she had the same blue eyes as her grandson – just a bit faded by the passage of time. 'The sort of problems only you are likely to understand.'

'Only me? I don't understand.' Although she had an inkling it might have something to do with his time in the army...

The old lady reached out and patted her arm. 'You will. Believe me, you will.'

Chapter 15

The following Sunday Jane decided it was time to put on her new walking boots and climb up to the TV masts. By now she had discovered that this was called Monte Venda and it rose to over six hundred metres. Her map showed a number of paths and tracks leading up its flanks but she decided to check the best way by asking the resident expert. Although she felt sure this should really be Umberto, the groundsman, she decided to ask David. After all, she told herself, he did live up here all year round, didn't he? The fact that this would give her an excuse to talk to him again was not lost on her but she managed to avoid obsessing about why she so badly wanted to see him, or any man, again.

She had only glimpsed him a couple of times since meeting him in the lake – usually when he was out running laps around the perimeter – but hadn't spoken to him again. Secretly she was a bit sorry that since his return she saw less of the friendly Labrador, but Dino was his dog so she could hardly complain and, besides, she now often had regular company in the shape of a seven-year-old girl and her teddy. However, she still hadn't been able to shake Flora's words down by the lake out of her head. What was the trouble with 'poor David' and why did she find herself thinking about him so often?

That morning, she spotted him and his dog out for a run and decided this was the perfect opportunity. She did a quick change into her running things and timed her exit from the house to coincide with when his next circuit would take him past her part of the house. Her plan worked perfectly and she came out to find Dino right outside her door with his master only twenty or thirty yards behind. She stopped to make a fuss of the dog before falling into step alongside his master and broaching the subject.

'Hi, David. I was hoping I'd see you. I'm thinking of climbing Monte Venda later today and I thought you could maybe tell me the best tracks to take to get up there. There seems to be a choice.'

He didn't break step but he did acknowledge her presence and her request for help. 'Good morning, Jane. Of course I can help.' He sounded cordial enough, but just a bit distant.

At that moment the path narrowed between the trees and he slowed to allow her to go first, so she was unable to respond for a minute or so. When they once more emerged into the open, she tried again.

'I've bought a pretty detailed map of the area but a bit of local knowledge would be a big help.'

'No problem; whenever you like.' Still little trace of warmth but at least he had said yes.

'What about a cup of coffee at my place after your run?'

He didn't reply immediately and she had the feeling he was searching for a suitable excuse to say no. Presumably he must have drawn a blank as he nodded. 'Of course.' He glanced at his watch. 'Would ten thirty be okay?'

At ten thirty, after a quick shower, Jane had just spread out her map on the kitchen table when she heard a familiar scratching sound at the door. She went across and opened it to see the Labrador standing there, tail wagging, with David behind him. The dog stretched up on his hind legs to be petted and she beckoned his master in.

'Hi, again, David. Do come in. This is very kind of you. This is the map I bought. Is it detailed enough?'

He bent forward and studied it closely before nodding. 'It looks pretty good but I've also brought a more detailed one of mine. It's very old but it shows most of the little paths as well as the bigger tracks.' He set a map down on the table and glanced across at her. He had taken his sunglasses off and she found herself once more looking into his deep blue eyes at close range. As she did so, she felt that same feeling of attraction – or more – run through her and she was still trying to work out what this might mean when she remembered the coffee.

'That sounds perfect. What can I offer you? Espresso, cappuccino, or there's tea if you prefer. I've got some real English tea if that appeals.'

'A mug of tea sounds good, thanks.' He made no move to sit down and just stood there, idly scratching his dog's ears, as she boiled the kettle. Acutely conscious of him behind her, and the fact that her new shorts were still pretty tight across her bottom, she tried to make the tea as quickly as possible, exchanging a few stilted banalities, but that was all. Finally she was able to give him his tea.

'Here, I hope you like it. I brought it from home.'

'Thanks. And where's home?' She was pleased to hear him at least making a stab at conversation – and not the weather this time.

'I've been living with my parents since I left the army. They're in west London.'

He showed no sign of having heard her mention the army. 'Ah, right, wonderful city London.' This must have drained his reservoir of small talk as a more businesslike note entered his voice. 'Now, let me show you the best way of getting up to the top of Venda.'

He launched into a detailed description of the main places of interest around here and she sensed he was a lot more relaxed talking about such matters than about anything more personal. Whether he had always been so reclusive or whether this was as a result of something that had happened to him was anybody's guess, but it was clear he didn't feel comfortable.

She sipped her tea, stroked the dog's head and listened intently.

'There's actually a proper footpath all the way to the summit and you'll meet everything from tourists to mushroom hunters to wheelchairs and mountain bikes. Personally, I like a more direct route which avoids the crowds.' He paused for reflection. 'Well, not just crowds, but people in general. I tend to prefer keeping myself to myself.'

Jane had already got that message loud and clear so she didn't pick him up on it. 'I'm like you. I'd much rather go off-piste.'

He showed her his favourite route and she marked it on her map. He finished with the words. 'You'll find yourself in dense woodland for some of the climb. It's very pretty but just be careful. It's very easy to get disorientated in the forest.'

Jane pulled out her new compass and waved it in front of him. 'I'll be fine, thanks. It's not the first time I've been walking in the woods.'

He might even have smiled at her but, apart from a slight crinkling alongside those almost hypnotic eyes, it was impossible to tell. 'Just saying…'

She smiled back. 'I'll be careful. I'm hoping I'll see something that'll give me some good ideas for a book I'm planning.'

'You're a writer as well? I didn't know.' He looked interested.

'I'm a *wannabe* writer if the truth be told. That's part of the reason I was so pleased to be offered the chance of working alongside your mother. I've got a lot to learn and she is one of the very best, after all.'

'If only she could manage to find the spark that gets her writing again. I feel so sorry for her.'

Jane nodded. 'Me, too, but I'm doing all I can. Hopefully as she comes out of her shell a bit more, the muse will return.'

Just before he left he made a suggestion that seemed out of character – at first. 'Are you happy to be on your own today or would you like some company?'

She hadn't been expecting this and, bearded wildman or not, she knew she would be very happy if he came with her. 'I'd love a bit of company and I know Diana's going out for lunch today.'

'Then why don't you take Truffaldino with you? I have to work this afternoon and he'd love a long walk.'

The feeling that washed over her was disappointment, closely followed by pleasure at the idea of having a companion – albeit with four legs rather than two – for her walk in the woods.

'That would be great, thanks. He and I get on very well together.'

'Just keep an eye on him if he spots a squirrel. He's got a thing about squirrels.'

'Alvise already told me. Don't worry, I'll make sure he doesn't climb any trees.' A thought occurred to her. 'Tell me, why did you call him Truffaldino? It's a bit of a mouthful.'

This time he definitely did smile. She could read it in his eyes. '*Mouthful* is the appropriate word. We had to study Goldoni's play *The Servant of Two Masters* when I was at school and Truffaldino, the main comic character, was always hungry. Somehow that seemed to suit this one perfectly. When he was a puppy, he was a real comedian – he still is – and you must have discovered by now just how greedy he is.'

'Labs must have gluttony in their DNA. But at least this Truffaldino only has one master.'

'I'm not so sure about that. He spends half his time scratching at your door or sleeping on your doormat.'

After he had left and she was moving about, making herself some sandwiches for lunch, her head was full of thoughts of David. She realised she had to accept that she found him unexpectedly attractive in spite of his tramp-like appearance. What did this signify? She had come over to Italy with her head and her heart still filled with memories of Mark, but now she had met this clearly troubled man and he risked arousing feelings in her she had thought lost forever. Was this what she wanted? Even just considering this made her feel somehow disloyal to Mark's memory. Could she really ever see herself allowing another man into her heart?

–

At noon she put her packed lunch and two bottles of water into her little backpack and went over to David's house. She knocked on the door and there was a single loud woof from inside. The door opened and she couldn't miss the frisson of pleasure that shot through her at the sight of David, but she tried hard not to show it.

'Hi, David, I've come to borrow your dog if that's still okay.'

'He's all yours. Take care in the woods.'

'Thanks. Enjoy your afternoon and don't work too hard.'

She set off on foot with the dog, and together they headed down a winding path into the valley before beginning the climb up the steep slope on the far side. David had shown her a route that avoided almost all roads so she didn't need to put Dino on a lead. There was only one place where they had to cross a quiet lane, but otherwise she saw virtually nobody apart from a few men working in the fields. All around were vineyards, the vines covered in fresh green foliage and the young grapes – barely the size of green peas – already forming into bunches beneath them. No doubt this whole area would suddenly become a hive of activity in the autumn as the *vendemmia*, the grape harvest, took place.

She thoroughly enjoyed herself navigating with the aid of her map and compass as she scrambled up towards the top of the hill. Although far from complicated, it reminded her of operations she had undertaken in the army and she felt genuinely nostalgic for what had been an exciting period of her life. Although this brought back the memory of Mark, she didn't descend into melancholy and she found herself smiling contentedly as she soaked up the natural beauty of her surroundings.

Once she had climbed past the last of the vine-yards, she found that David's route took her into thick deciduous forest, mainly composed of chestnut trees, with the ground littered with the spiny cases of the nuts left over from the previous autumn. She kept a weather eye out for squirrels but neither she nor Dino spotted any, although she did see a big bird of prey with bright yellow legs, and then a moment later a curious black and white striped bird with a chestnut brown head sporting an extravagant crest and a long curved beak. With the aid of her phone, she discovered that this was called a hoopoe and she tried to take a photo, but it flew off before she could get more than a blurred snap.

Oblivious to the birds, Dino trotted ahead of her most of the time and was evidently enjoying his long walk as much as she was. At one point she crossed what was obviously the track David had spoken of but saw nobody. Presumably most people were finding today too hot for strenuous activity. Finally they climbed the last few hundred metres to the top. By this time she was perspiring freely and was ready for a rest and a drink. By the look of the panting Labrador, so was he.

Perching on an outcrop of stone just alongside the TV masts, she took a good look around. From up here she had a three-hundred-and-sixty-degree view and, even through the heat haze, she was able to make out the urban sprawl of Padua to the east and even what was probably the Venice lagoon in the far distance. To the north, again in the far distance, was the dark bulk of the Alps, arching around from west to east. To the south of her were the other pyramid-shaped hills that made up the Colli Euganei, rising up like an island in the midst of the plains far below. The sky was clear, the sun scorching but the air up here was definitely fresher than further down, and she breathed deeply, enjoying the spectacle, and could almost feel her batteries – both physical and emotional – being recharged. Compared to the last ten years of her life, this was an oasis of calm and it was doing her good.

After a while, she shrugged off her backpack and reached inside. Predictably, the Labrador raised his nose and adopted his familiar 'I'm starving' look. She grinned at him. 'It's all right, Dino, I haven't forgotten you.'

She took out a plastic bowl and filled it from one of the water bottles she had brought. He slurped up half the contents in one go and she followed his example – although less messily. She then pulled out a large dog biscuit and held it out towards him. He took it from her delicately and then settled down with the biscuit gripped between his front paws to crunch it up as she helped herself to a sandwich.

She had just finished her sandwiches and was nibbling at a banana when her phone started ringing. She pulled it out and checked the caller ID. So the curator of the Mantua Costume Museum had decided to get in touch…

'Ciao, Paolo, how are you? Where are you calling from?'

'Ciao, Jane. I'm still in Mantua but I'm coming over to Monselice tonight to see my parents and I wondered if I could maybe take you out for lunch tomorrow. It's Monday so it'll be my day off.'

For a moment Jane hesitated. She didn't want him to get the wrong idea and consider this as a date. At the same time, he had been very kind to her and her employer and it seemed churlish to refuse, so she agreed, telling herself that if it looked like he was getting ideas about the two of them, she could spell out to him that she just saw him as a friend. 'I'd like that, thanks, but I'll just have to check with Lady Cooper first. I wouldn't think she'll have any objections though. Where were you planning on going? I'm out for a walk in the hills at the moment and I've just had a picnic lunch. We could do something like that if you like.'

'Another time I certainly would like that, but I'm afraid the weather forecast is for rain overnight tonight and throughout most of tomorrow morning. Let's have a lazy day.'

She promised to call him that evening after she had spoken to Veronica. After he had rung off, she slipped her phone back into the pocket of her shorts and took stock. The interesting thing was that her head was filled with thoughts of a completely different man – one who looked like a woolly mammoth.

Chapter 16

The weather forecast was dead right. It rained all night and when Jane woke up next morning it was to wet grass and muddy paths and she decided not to take her usual daily run. It finally stopped drizzling but the air was a whole lot fresher by the time Paolo came to pick her up at noon, and she took a jumper and a waterproof with her just in case. She gave him a cheerful welcome but limited herself to shaking his hand rather than kissing him on the cheek.

'Ciao, Paolo. At least the rain's lowered the temperature.' What was that thing about the English taking refuge in talking about the weather?

'It's been over thirty degrees and really humid all week in Mantua. It's wonderful to be able to breathe again… and to see you.'

'It's good to see you too. What's your plan for today?'

'Lunch, but something a little bit different, if you're happy with it. It's a restaurant in the suburbs of Padua. It's well outside the *centro storico*, in a very ordinary-looking place with no frills, but the food's excellent. It started life as a project for former prisoners at the local prison – where there's a very good restaurant as well by the way – and I often eat there. I think you might like it. Feel like giving it a try?'

'Sounds exciting.'

The restaurant was a fairly unprepossessing large wooden structure set in the middle of a vegetable garden, surrounded by apartment blocks. It wasn't exactly scenic but it was clear that the produce was going to be home-grown and completely fresh. They sat outside on a terrace that steamed as the sun broke through the clouds and rapidly began to dry everything out. Although she had brought her jumper Jane didn't need it as the temperature climbed steadily from then on.

After ordering a *spiedino misto* of grilled meat, she settled back with a glass of very good Merlot from the Colli Euganei and enjoyed Paolo's company. They chatted about their respective jobs, his family and hers, and her ever-improving relationship with Veronica. She told him about her idea of writing a romantic thriller and he was supportive, telling her to go for it and asking if he could read what she had written so far. It was a most enjoyable meal and the chunks of grilled meat on a skewer were tender and tasty. Accompanying it were roast potatoes and a selection of vegetables cooked on the charcoal grill. There were slices of aubergines and courgettes, red and green peppers and, interestingly, half a red radicchio lettuce – all hot from the grill. Jane had never had cooked lettuce before but, doused with olive oil and with the charred outer leaves removed, it was delicious.

She found herself relaxing in his company, right up until he asked her what she had been doing since leaving university. After a few seconds' hesitation she decided to tell him.

'I was in the army.'

'The army?' He looked amazed. 'You were a soldier?'

She nodded. 'An officer in the British Army, for five years.'

'But… were you on active service? I mean, do women fight… did you fight?'

She was all too familiar with this reaction by now. Over the years she had been in the regiment, she had grown used to the disbelief on the faces of people – especially men – when she told them what she did for a living.

'I never shot anybody, if that's what you mean. I'm an engineer by training.'

For a moment he looked almost disappointed. 'I see. But now you've left the army.'

'That's right. I wanted a change and I've always been interested in writing so I dug into my savings and went to Cambridge to do a Masters in Creative Writing.'

'Cambridge University? Congratulations. And now you're hoping to become a world-famous author.'

She grinned at him. 'That's the plan. Now all I've got to do is write something.'

When they got back to her house, the rain had cleared completely and the sky was once again blue and cloudless. Since she had promised him her manuscript, she invited him in for coffee, hoping he wouldn't think anything more than coffee was on offer. Yes, she had enjoyed his company, but talk of her military service had only served to remind her yet again of everything that had happened, and she knew she still wasn't free from her past. Even so, it occurred to her as she led him into the house that she still hadn't had a single recurrence of her bad dreams since arriving in Italy. That really had to be terrific progress.

She made two cups of coffee and gave him the manuscript of her romance novella to take away. To avoid any misunderstandings, she deliberately made sure they stayed in the kitchen area, seated chastely on either side of the big table. They carried on chatting and it was gone four o'clock when he shook his head apologetically and rose to his feet.

'I'm afraid I'd better make a move. I have to be back down in Mantua tonight and I promised my parents I'd set up their new printer for them and show them how to use it before I go. I'll get your story back to you as soon as possible. I'm in Paris for a collectors' fair next weekend, but hopefully I should be able to come up and see you again in a couple of weeks if you're free.'

Jane stood up as well and led him out to his car. When they got there, she gave him a big smile and kissed him on both cheeks. It had been an enjoyable day. 'Thank you for a super lunch, Paolo, but remember, if we do it again, next time I'm paying.'

She stepped back and heard her boss's voice just a short distance away.

'Paolo, how lovely to see you again.'

They both turned in unison, and while Jane said hello to the affectionate dog who had followed Veronica out of the villa, Paolo went over to shake hands with her. 'Lady Cooper, it's good to see you too. Jane and I have been out for lunch.'

Jane was quick to confirm this. 'To an excellent restaurant in Padua.'

At that moment there was a movement behind Veronica and Jane saw Diana and her brother come out of from the main door. She was about to make the introductions when it emerged that they already knew each other. Although Diana was gushing and cheery towards Paolo, David did little more than shake hands and exchange a few quick words. Jane was actually quite pleased to see that it clearly wasn't just with her that he appeared uncomfortable, and she remembered what he had said about keeping himself to himself. In fact, only a minute later, while Veronica and Diana were still chatting to Paolo about the Costume Museum, David excused himself and headed back to his part of the house, leaving his four-legged friend rolling happily about at Jane's feet while she rubbed his tummy with the toe of her shoe.

Finally Paolo took his leave and drove off. Once his car had disappeared down the drive and Veronica had gone back into the house, Diana glanced across at Jane and grinned. 'Now that is one very good-looking man. I always thought so. You've done well, Jane.'

Jane felt she had better set the record straight. 'He's a very nice guy and a friend but that's all.'

For some reason that appeared to please Diana, and Jane soon found out why as she went on to explain. 'I don't know if he told you this, but he and Bee used to have a thing.'

'What, Paolo and Beatrice were...?'

'That's right. It all happened one summer.'

'He told me he used to help Umberto in the grounds. Was that when he and Beatrice met? That must be ten, fifteen years ago now.'

Diana nodded. 'I don't remember much about it – I was probably only ten or eleven at the time, but I know Bee was very fond of him. The problem was that she was studying in the UK and when the summer came to an end so did their little liaison – if you can call it that.'

'And nothing came of it?'

'No, she was very cut up about it but like they say, life goes on... What's his situation now? Is he married?'

'Not that I'm aware of, I don't think so, in fact I'm sure he isn't. He would've said something.'

'And you're sure you aren't interested in him?'

'I'm sure. He's a very nice guy but that's all there is to it.'

'Definite?'

'Positive. Are you going to tell Beatrice about him? I think you should. After all, she's a free agent now.'

'Well, if you really don't mind then, I will.' Diana grinned. 'It's a small world, isn't it?'

Chapter 17

That evening Jane made a big decision. After a lot of thought – and a couple of glasses of Prosecco – she sent Fergus an email thanking Virginia and him for the invitation to their wedding and saying yes. Although she had a moment of panic after pressing *Send*, she went to bed feeling satisfied with her decision. It wasn't going to be easy to meet up with so many of her former comrades but she knew she had to try. Life didn't stand still and she knew she had to make this attempt to begin moving on.

Over the next week or so the weather remained mixed and she spent much of her free time at the kitchen table – often with her neighbour's dog snoozing at her feet or with Linda and her teddy alongside her – handling Veronica's affairs and gradually starting to work out the plot of her book. Combining her two novellas was beginning to look too complicated so she decided to expand the plot of the romance and add in a bit of intrigue. Drawing on recent events, she rather liked the idea of a former boyfriend from fifteen years earlier putting in an appearance and sparking off a chain reaction that would lead to mystery, suspicion, heartache, but ultimately happiness.

When she wasn't working or writing, she managed to persuade her employer to accompany her for a couple of walks in the fresh air and they chatted, increasingly freely. Maria definitely approved and congratulated her on her success in getting Veronica out and about at last after her long months of purdah. Diana and Beatrice added their best efforts and even got their mother to start making a few trips into Padua with them. It looked as though Veronica's rehabilitation was improving in pace with Jane's own.

One morning she was surprised to receive a visit from Veronica at just after nine. They now knew each other sufficiently well for Jane to feel she could comment.

'Is it my imagination or are you getting up earlier these days?'

Veronica smiled. 'It's not your imagination and, believe it or not, I've already been up for over an hour. I'm sleeping a lot better. Whether it's the cooler nights or the drier air or something else, I feel a lot more relaxed. Now then, I have a favour to ask. How would you feel about popping down to Venice and back today?'

'Of course, no problem. Is there something special you want me to do?'

'Two things: first, I'd like you to call in at the house. Just take a quick look around to see that all's well, grab a couple of jumpers and some shoes for me and pick up any post that's arrived. It shouldn't take you more than a few minutes.' She went on to tell Jane where to find the jumpers and shoes in the dressing room off the main bedroom.

'And the second thing?'

'And the second thing is that I'd like you to keep an eye on David.'

'On David?'

'He's had terrible toothache for the past few days and he's finally managed to get an appointment for two o'clock this afternoon with our regular dentist in Venice. He's been having awful trouble trying to find a dentist around here. They all appear to be either on holiday or off sick. The thing is, he once had a nasty allergic reaction to an anaesthetic so if you could go with him and be prepared to drive home again if necessary, I'd feel a lot happier. Beatrice is tied up with little Linda, and Diana would have done it but she's got an upset stomach. Too much beer and pizza with her friends, if you ask me. Anyway, would you mind?'

'Of course not. I love Venice and it'll be nice to see it again. You'll need to tell me how to get into the house and turn off the alarm, but I can go any time you want.'

'Thank you, that's a relief. I'll go and see David and you can sort out all the details together.'

Ten minutes later there was a knock at the door. Jane opened it to find David standing there and he didn't look happy. At least, that was the impression she got from his eyes. The rest of his face, as usual, was shrouded in hair. Beside him was his much shorter-haired dog who looked anything but unhappy.

'Look, Jane, there's really no need for you to come all the way down to Venice with me. Mum's freaking out because of something that happened twenty-five years ago and it's never happened since.'

'She told me you had an allergic reaction.' By this time Dino was pressed up against her and was doing his best to climb up her thigh. She gently pushed him back down again and glanced back up at his master as she carried on scratching the dog's ears. 'Whatever you want, it's no trouble to me. Your mother said she'd like me to drop into the palazzo and pick up some clothes for her.' A thought occurred to her. She was going to need something to wear at Fergus's wedding. 'To be honest, I wouldn't mind doing a bit of shopping myself if there's time.'

'Ah, I didn't realise you both wanted clothes.' She could see him rethinking his objections. 'Well, in that case if you really don't mind, then come by all means, but come for Mum or yourself but not for me. I have no doubt I'll be fine.'

They set off in the Mercedes at half past ten and they didn't talk much, but that came as no surprise to her. She could almost feel the protective wall that surrounded him go back up again and she wondered yet again why this should be. From what Flora had said she somehow felt convinced it had something to do with how and when he had left the army, but what could that have been? She was dying to ask him but she decided to be patient. It was clear he still didn't feel comfortable with her so there was no point in pushing things. Besides, when all was said and done, she was an employee, rather than a friend, so it wasn't her place to ask personal questions. Hopefully he would begin to relax in her company as they got to know each other better, although if he wasn't going to say more than a few words, getting to know each other wasn't going to be easy.

Getting into Venice along the causeway took a while as there was a line of slow-moving traffic and Jane could see that the city was going to be packed with tourists as Alvise had predicted. At last, they managed to reach the garage and left the car there. The launch was still tied up on the pontoon at the rear of the garage, protected by a thick canvas cover. Jane helped David unhook the cover and roll it up before stowing it in the cabin. He started the engine and headed out into the canal with a practised hand. This at least gave her something to talk about.

'Have you been motoring up and down the Grand Canal since you were a boy? You seem really at home on the water.'

He glanced across at her and she thought she identified the beginnings of a smile in those bright blue eyes of his. 'Motoring, sailing, canoeing, paddling… I've even learnt how to scull a gondola – and that's not easy, I can tell you.'

'Somehow I wouldn't think there are many British Army officers who can double as gondoliers.'

The smile went out of his eyes like a candle flame in a sudden draft of air. 'Probably not.'

Once again it would appear that she had overstepped the mark so she hastened to change the subject away from the army. 'I suppose if we were to try and walk from here to the palazzo today, it would take ages.'

'July's always awful and next month will be even worse. You can hardly move in Venice in the summer. Thank goodness for boats.'

'Where's your dentist?'

'In San Marco; a five-minute walk from home in midwinter, but on a sunny summer day like today I bet it'll take me a quarter of an hour of pushing and shoving.'

They made good time on the canal and Jane couldn't help noticing that every bridge they passed was packed with tourists. Thank goodness for the boat indeed. They got to the palazzo and she hopped out to help moor up. Once the launch was secure, David led her into the house, stopping to show her how to turn off the alarm and then set it again. She wasn't surprised to find that the code was 1234.

Once they were inside he tried a light switch, but nothing happened. 'I thought so. Alvise always switches off the power – the alarm's on a separate circuit – when we leave the house for any length of time. Come and I'll switch it on and show you how to turn it off again.'

She followed him through to the kitchen and from there he opened the door to a dark windowless little pantry and beckoned to her. It was cramped in there and she found herself rubbing up against him as he pointed out the fuse board. She caught her breath. There could be no doubt about it: being so close to him might feel a bit awkward but it also felt good. As the realisation took root, so did a feeling of guilt at the thought of what this might mean as far as her feelings towards her former boyfriend were concerned.

Apparently unaware of her discomfort and certainly not displaying any sort of emotion himself, David showed her the switch to flick and, as he did so, light flooded the room and brought her back to her senses. He was only showing her how to turn the electricity on – it wasn't as if he was propositioning her, after all. Muttering 'Get a grip,' under her breath, she thanked him and they arranged to meet back at the car at four o'clock. This should give him ample time for his tooth to be fixed and should give her time to locate a suitable dress for the wedding, but they exchanged phone numbers just in case.

After he had gone off, she went up to Veronica's bedroom – the first time she had been in here – and located the jumpers and shoes. Opening the window, she pushed one shutter open so she could look out over the roofs of the city, as ever admiring this incomparable view that had changed so little since Renaissance times. By the window, facing out, was Veronica's desk with the battered old typewriter on it. Alongside this was an untouched ream of paper and the desolate scene made her feel deeply saddened. That a great author could lose the will to write as the result of a broken heart was truly touching. Somehow this highlighted just what love really was: a force so powerful it could stifle creativity and snuff out a successful career in an instant.

Inevitably she thought of her own career and how it had ended. Had she left the regiment because of what had happened to Mark, what had happened to herself, or for some other reason? The fact was that she had already been thinking about leaving when her initial term came to an end, partly because of stress, but mainly because she had been longing for a bit of permanence in her nomadic lifestyle. Of course the memory of what had happened that day in Fallujah would never leave her and would forever remain embedded within her, but there had been more to it than that. She had needed a change and she had certainly got that now.

Resting her elbows on the window sill she stared out over the ever-changing spectacle of the Grand Canal and found herself questioning – for the very first time – just how deep her feelings for Mark had been. Had his death deprived her of the one and only man there would ever be in her life? They had been together for a year before that fateful day in Iraq and she had liked him a lot and, if asked, she felt sure she would have said she loved him. But now, thinking back on it, could she honestly say she had truly loved him? Had he really been The One? Had she loved him as deeply as Veronica had loved her husband?

The answer was that she didn't know. And now, of course, she never would.

Rousing herself from her introspection she closed the shutter and window and was just about to leave the bedroom when her eyes landed on a series of photos in silver frames standing on the ornate marble mantelpiece.

Out of curiosity she walked over to take a closer look and switched on the light so she could see better. The middle one showed a much younger Veronica standing in front of the ornate pillared entrance arches of the basilica of San Marco. Beside her was the handsome figure of her husband with a little toddler between them, hanging onto their hands and clearly fascinated by a nearby pigeon. Presumably this was David. Holding her mother's other hand was five- or six-year-old Beatrice, already recognisable. In a silver frame to the left of this photo was a studio portrait of Beatrice and teenage Diana, both dolled up to the eyeballs in readiness for a formal soirée, and on the other side was a framed photograph of David that almost took Jane's breath away.

He was in the full-dress uniform of a captain in the Rifles and he looked good. Without the beard, without all the hair, she realised he was startlingly good-looking, and with a confident smile on his face she found him fascinating. He had high cheekbones and a resolute jaw similar to his father, and his looks coupled with his athletic physique came as a shock to the system for Jane and she actually felt that selfsame shiver of what could only be described as desire flash through her. To her own considerable surprise she pulled out her phone, glanced apprehensively over her shoulder to check that the real David hadn't come back, and took a quick photo of the photo. Just why she did this was not something she chose to debate for now so she stuffed her phone away guiltily, put Veronica's clothes into a bag, and headed out of the room.

She went up to her own apartment on the top floor to check that all was well there before coming back down to the *piano nobile*. Everything looked fine here, although the white dust sheets that Maria and Alvise had stretched over the furniture gave the place a rather ghostly feel, not helped by the fact that the louvred shutters were closed and the only light came in thin strips that gave the wooden floor the appearance of a toast rack. Finally she went to the side door, collected the envelopes and magazines that were lying on the doormat, and returned to the pantry where she turned off the mains switch, plunging the rooms into darkness. Then, after setting the alarm as David had shown her, she locked up again and went out into the clammy heat of a July afternoon and did battle with the crowds.

Fighting her way back to the car along the main thoroughfare – barely a few metres wide in places – squeezing through the mass of tourists, delivery men with barrows and street vendors, was hard work but not as difficult as selecting a dress for Fergus and Ginny's wedding. She had no intention of turning up in anything too revealing or too flashy and it took a lot of time before she ended up buying a floral print dress which looked fairly good on her, if not exactly dazzling. She told herself that at least this meant she wouldn't draw attention away from the bride.

When she reached the garage she found David already there, just finishing securing the cover on the launch. He looked up as she appeared and she gave him a little wave.

'Toothache sorted?'

'All good, thanks. And you?'

'Yes, the house is fine, I got the bits and pieces your mum wanted and I bought a dress for the wedding.'

She was gratified to see his eyebrows raise. 'The wedding?'

'A fellow officer from the Sappers is getting married next month and I needed something to wear. I haven't done much clothes shopping over the past few years.' She wondered if this might elicit some reaction from him and was pleasantly surprised to find that it did.

'Where's the wedding taking place; here in Italy?'

'No, back in the UK, in a village near Bath.'

'I imagine it'll be nice to see your old friends again.' This was just about the first spontaneous observation of an even vaguely personal nature he had made to her. Might this be progress?

'Yes and no – I'm not so sure. I'm a bit nervous about it, to be honest. It'll be the first time I'll be catching up with my former comrades in over two years.'

'You haven't stayed in touch with them?'

'I haven't really stayed in touch with anybody.' She caught his eye. 'I'm afraid my departure from the regiment wasn't exactly the way I would have planned it. I'll tell you about it some time.'

'Don't feel you need to tell me anything.' Although this could have sounded dismissive, it almost brought a lump to Jane's throat. It was as though he was saying he wasn't worthy of knowing her secret. She very nearly told him she would tell him her story if he would reveal his but, instead, she just followed him to the car in silence.

Chapter 18

Next morning she awoke to find the sun shining brightly from a clear blue sky and she decided the time had come for her to do a bit more exploration of the Colli Euganei. She was just finishing a late breakfast when there was a knock at the door. It was Veronica.

Jane hadn't seen her last night when she and David had returned from Venice and she had given him the clothes and the mail to deliver to her. 'Hi, Veronica. I'm just making coffee. Interested?'

'Thank you, I'd love one.' Veronica came in, taking evasive action as a dark shape squeezed past her legs and came bounding in to say hello to Jane, who bent down to stroke him.

'Ciao, Dino, you're looking bouncy today. Maybe you feel like coming for a good long W – A – L – K with me later on.'

'I'm sure he will.' Veronica sat down at the kitchen table and looked across at Jane. 'How did it go with David yesterday?'

'He got his tooth fixed. He said it's stopped hurting.' Jane busied herself at the coffee machine.

'Yes, he told me, but I was wondering how things went between you and him.'

Jane glanced around in surprise. 'It was fine. He was a bit taciturn at first but we did a fair bit of chatting.' This was stretching the truth but she felt she had to give his mother an encouraging account of how the day had gone.

'That's good to hear.' There was a pause and Jane realised that her employer was maybe feeling a bit reticent, but she soon saw her rally. 'He's got to get out more. He needs somebody to talk to. I've been speaking to Flora and she feels the same way. It's not natural for a man in his thirties to lock himself away and bury himself in his books like this.' Jane set down her coffee in front of her and Veronica looked up and produced a little smile. 'And before you say it, I'm aware of the irony that while the son can't get away from books, his mother can't start writing one.'

'Still no ideas?' Jane sat down opposite her and felt the dog sit down heavily on her foot as she did so. 'Dino, get off, you great lump. You've got a bony backside.' Shifting her foot slightly, she tried again in her most encouraging tone. 'Have you considered a change of genre? Maybe try turning your hand to a thriller or a detective story? You know what they say about a change being as good as…'

'I don't know, Jane, I honestly don't.' The frustration in Veronica's voice was plain to hear. 'What about you? Started your romance?'

Jane told her how far she had got with her planning of the book while in the back of her mind the suspicion began to dawn that maybe Veronica had had an ulterior motive in sending her to Venice in the company of her son. Was her boss counting on her to shake him out of his depression and his near hermitic state? Could it be that Jane now found herself in the position of having to provide encouragement and support not only to her employer but also to her employer's son? That was quite some job description and one that had been singularly lacking from the sheet the solicitor had read out to her. The other question was how Jane felt about adding this to her *To Do* list.

The answer didn't require much thought. It was a resounding yes. Nothing would give her greater pleasure than to cheer him up and maybe, just maybe, get him to a stage when he might be prepared to shave off the unsightly mass of hair that threatened to smother him, and reveal the very handsome man she had spotted in the photo. What might happen after that, of course, was anybody's guess. Determined not to waste time, she made a suggestion.

'I was going to pop across to see him in a minute to ask if I could borrow Dino for my walk. Maybe I could try to persuade him to come too.'

'That sounds like an excellent idea, but don't get your hopes up too much.' Veronica was still looking gloomy. 'That trip to the dentist yesterday was his first excursion out since he came back from France.'

Jane took a sip of her coffee. 'Has he always been so antisocial?'

'Very much the opposite. He was always very outgoing.'

'Lot of friends?'

'Loads – male and female. He's been back in Italy now for two years and, as far as I know, he hasn't been in contact with any of them.' This struck a familiar chord with Jane but she didn't comment other than to ask the same question she had already asked, to which she received the same answer.

'So what happened to make him suddenly want to go off the grid?'

'You'd better ask him.' An unmistakable pall of sadness flooded across Veronica's face. 'He doesn't want to talk about it, but I know it would help him if he could only begin to open up.' She looked across the table at Jane. 'Somehow I get the feeling you might be the one to get him to start.'

'That's what your mother-in-law said. Why me?'

'The army: you were both in it and you both left under unhappy circumstances.'

Jane just nodded. 'I certainly did and I owe you the full story, but it's tough. Maybe it's the same for him but it brings back so many bitter memories. I promise I *will* tell you what happened. I haven't really told anybody yet.'

To her surprise, Veronica smiled back at her. 'You see? This is why I think you and David should be able to talk. Shared experiences, shared suffering and, hopefully, shared healing.'

In spite of herself, Jane had to ask. 'Suffering? Was he wounded too?'

Veronica reached across the table and caught hold of Jane's hand. 'I'm afraid so, but what about you? You're all right now, aren't you?' She looked genuinely concerned.

'I'm fine, thanks.' Jane had to take another sip of coffee before continuing. 'So, what about David? Was he invalided out?'

'Not exactly.' Veronica squeezed her hand before releasing it. 'But it's best if he tells you himself.'

What on earth did 'not exactly' mean?

–

Half an hour later Jane was just about to go over to see David to ask if he wanted a walk or at least if she could take Dino with her – although the dog had set up camp in her kitchen and was sleeping peacefully under the table with his nose on her feet – when she had another visitor.

'Ciao, Jane.'

'Hi, Beatrice. No Linda today?'

'No, she's got the same tummy bug that Di had yesterday.'

'I'm sorry to hear that. How about you? Are you okay? I saw your mum earlier and she looked fine.'

'Touch wood, I'm fine, thanks. I thought I'd come and see if you fancy going for a walk somewhere today. Di's feeling better but she doesn't want to go out so she's volunteered to look after Linda. I feel I need to get out in the fresh air. I've been inside too much this week.'

'Funnily enough, I was just thinking the same thing. I was wondering if your brother would mind if we borrowed his dog, or even if he might come with us himself?'

Beatrice shook her head and Jane felt a distinct stab of disappointment. 'I'm sure we can take Dino but I've just asked David if he wants to come for a walk and he told me he's tied up all day. Some international online convention or some such. Apparently he has to give a talk and then do a Q&A session afterwards.' She looked up from stroking the Labrador. 'It might even be true this time, but Mum says he's always inventing excuses for not doing stuff.'

Jane did go and check with David but received the same response he had given his sister, along with his blessing for them to take Dino with them. Leaving him to his online lecture, Jane and Beatrice took the car and headed for the village of Arquà Petrarca down in the southernmost part of the hills. On the way there, Beatrice explained that the famous scholar and poet, Petrarch, the man credited with starting the Renaissance no less, had spent the last years of his life there. In fact, so famous was he that the village authorities had subsequently changed the name of the place from simple Arquà to Arquà Petrarca in his honour.

It didn't take long to get there. Most of the way they drove past a succession of vineyards extending up the sides of the valleys and through lovely historic villages with red-roofed stone houses and ancient churches. Arquà Petrarca was a small and very beautiful village surrounded by car parks full of cars belonging to people who had come to see the final resting place of one of Italy's most famous poets – or maybe to have lunch in one of the numerous restaurants. They strolled through the picturesque but busy streets for a while, Jane hanging onto Dino's lead in case he became too affectionate with the people and dogs he met, before they decided that it really was too crowded. They returned to the car and headed up a very narrow road towards the tree-covered summit of Monte Ventolone, which dominated the town. Leaving the car in a convenient lay-by, they set off through the woods with the dog running free.

The more they climbed, the better the view behind them grew, and within half an hour they had reached the top. They sat down on a fallen tree trunk and admired the scenery. From here they were looking south, over a couple of much lower hills and from there onto the broad expanse of the plains stretching off towards Rovigo, Ferrara and beyond. Arquà Petrarca itself was below them, surrounded by vineyards and olive groves.

After they had been sitting there for a few minutes, Beatrice asked Jane a question that didn't come as a complete surprise. 'Jane...' She sounded unusually hesitant. 'Mum and Di told me you had lunch with Paolo Padovan yesterday. I was wondering... Di said you and Paolo are just friends. Is that true? Did you mean it?'

'Yes. He's a nice guy but that's all there is to it. I met him at a charity auction while I was bidding for a dress on your mum's behalf. I like him, but that's it. Like I told her, I'm not in the market for a man at the moment, but Diana did mention that you and he used to be close.'

'It was a long time ago, but yes, I liked him a lot but life got in the way. She maybe told you it was while I was studying in the UK.'

'Yes, she did, and you know that he's now curator of the Costume Museum in Mantua?'

'Yes, he's done well. I'm happy for him.'

'Are you going to contact him? I can give you his number if you haven't already got it.'

Beatrice looked uncomfortable. 'Part of me would really like to but I wouldn't want to put him in an awkward position. That was fifteen years ago now. I'm sure he's changed. I know I've changed. I'm a divorcee with a child for a start. I can hardly phone him up and say "Hi, Paolo, feel like going out again?", can I?'

Jane gave it some thought. 'How's this for a solution? You call him to say that as your sister is studying fashion, you and she would like to visit the museum. Hopefully he'll offer to give you a private tour like he did for your mum and me, and you'll have a chance to pick up where you left off with him – or not, depending on how you feel. What do you think about that as a plan?'

Beatrice looked up with interest. 'And are you sure you wouldn't mind?'

'Of course I'm sure. I bet he'd be happy to help a fashion student and I bet he'd love to see you again. The only thing is that I know he's away in Paris this weekend. He told me there's a collectors' fair. I think it's just for a day or two but I'm not sure exactly when he'll be back.'

'Oh, right, thanks.' Beatrice was still sounding tentative. 'I just didn't want you to think I was trying to poach your man or anything.'

'Poach my man? There's nothing between us, so you don't need to worry about treading on my toes.' She grinned at Beatrice. 'Besides, you saw him first.' The fact of the matter was that she really didn't see Paolo in a romantic light. Plus, ever since seeing that photo of David in her employer's bedroom, she knew there was potentially another man already in her head, if not her heart. And, of course, there was the memory of Mark...

'That's a relief.' Beatrice sounded it. 'Well, I think I will give him a call. Nothing ventured...' She hesitated. 'So how come you aren't on the lookout for a man? You told Di there used to be a guy but he's no longer in the equation. Was it a bad break-up?'

Jane dropped her eyes to the dog who was rolling about on his back at their feet, making vain attempts to catch his tail in his mouth. It would be good to be like him, without a care in the world – apart from squirrels. Taking a deep breath, she told Beatrice more than she had told most people.

'The worst. I loved him dearly but he was killed. That was two years ago and I'm still coming to terms with it.'

Just like her mother had done, Beatrice immediately reached for Jane's hand and gave it a supportive squeeze. 'How awful. Were you together long?'

'Long enough: just over a year.'

'And you said you loved him. Were you engaged, married?'

'No, but we were very close.'

'And you would have married him?'

'Definitely. I was convinced he was the man for me. We had so much in common and I'm sure we would have got married. The funny thing is, though, that since coming over here, I'm no longer quite so sure it really was the Real Thing.' She looked up from her hands and even managed to muster a little smile. 'But I'll never know now, will I? Still, I *am* getting over it. I really am. I can feel things changing inside me, hopefully for the better.'

'You don't deserve to be on your own forever. Life goes on, Jane.'

'I know it does. I've even started telling myself the same thing. I suppose it'll just take time.'

Chapter 19

Veronica was as good as her word and arranged for them to visit to a spa. On Wednesday of the following week, she and her daughters, along with little Linda and Jane – but unsurprisingly not David – set off in the Mercedes for Montegrotto Terme. Jane volunteered to drive and it took barely a quarter of an hour to get there. She hadn't been quite sure what to expect. Maybe a waterfall, a lake or a sulphurous swamp emitting foul-smelling bubbles of gas from thick chocolaty mud, but the reality was very different. In spite of the town having both *monte* and *grotto* in its name, she found herself out of the hills and back down on the flat once more.

The little town appeared to be composed mainly of a grid of straight modern roads lined with trees and gardens, with meticulously pruned bushes and colourful plants on all sides. Two things were immediately obvious to Jane: almost every other building appeared to be a hotel and virtually all the people she saw walking along the pavements were well into their seventies, eighties or even older. Clearly, in spite of Flora's reservations, this was where mature Italians came to take the waters, and the luxury hotels offered accommodation as well as all manner of spa treatments.

After pointing out the ruins of the Roman baths built two thousand years earlier, Veronica explained what awaited them today. She was looking and sounding increasingly buoyant these days and this was good to see.

'We're booked in for the day, and you can choose whatever treatment appeals to you. I'm going to have a mud session first. It's warm volcanic mud and it's supposed to be very good for the skin as well as for muscle aches and pains. The pools are naturally warm water at, if I remember rightly, thirty-seven degrees. It really is like a warm bath. You can have a massage, a sauna and goodness knows what else. Just go wherever you like and we can meet for lunch at one. The food here's excellent.'

There was one big question that Jane had been agonising over ever since hearing they were coming to a spa. 'What's the dress code? It's my first time at a spa. I've brought a costume and a bikini and I'm wearing clean underwear, but do we just wander about like that or do we stay as we are or are we expected to strip off...?'

Veronica can't have missed the insecurity in her voice and actually giggled. 'Don't worry, Jane, it's all in the best possible taste, I assure you. First we take showers – hygiene here is all important – and then we change into costumes. You girls should probably wear bikinis as that way you expose more skin to the mud and the water, although I'm far too old for that, so I'll be a bit more covered up. We leave our clothes in lockers and they provide us with robes to wear for walking around and when we have lunch. You'll love it, I'm sure.'

'So we don't have to strip off?' She still wasn't sure, but Beatrice provided clarification and reassurance – up to a point.

'I've been here a few times and it's absolutely fine. If you go for the mud treatment, it's best to strip off. Don't worry, it's all very private. If you do decide to keep your clothes on, just look out. I tried it wearing a blue and white bikini once and the mud turned it green and brown and the colour never washed out.'

What, Jane wondered to herself, would mud that noxious do to the skin? Still, this wasn't in the same league as defusing a landmine, so she kept her doubts to herself and hoped for the best.

The spa Veronica had booked was part of a huge modern-looking hotel, five or six storeys high, surrounded by spectacularly beautiful gardens. Ancient olive trees and cypresses dotted the well-kept lawns and huge rosemary bushes in flower added their scent to the aromas of lavender and roses. Discreetly concealed sprinklers ensured that the grass was even greener than in her parents' garden back in rainy England and the overall impression was charming. They were met by a lady in a white coat as they walked into the marble-clad lobby and she escorted them through to the spa where they changed. Following her employer's advice, Jane put on her bikini although she knew this would now expose the lacework of scars across her thighs and abdomen caused by the blast. Still, she told herself as she slipped the gown provided by the spa over the top, she would probably spend most of her time wrapped in this and when she did take it off she would be under water or covered in mud, so the pale patches probably weren't going to be too obvious.

Little Linda had no doubts about her priorities and she and her mum headed straight outside to the huge open air swimming pool and Jane went with them. The water was crystal clear, with no detectable trace of sulphur, and as Veronica had said, it was like swimming in a warm bath. Certainly, it was a far cry from the cold lake up at the villa.

From there, Jane followed Diana to the mud bath area where they stripped off and lay, face down, while female staff in pristine white coats smothered them in warm mud that rapidly dried out against their bodies. After a few minutes they were instructed to turn over and the process was repeated on their fronts. After a while the dry mud was washed off and by the time Jane emerged she could feel her whole body tingling. After showering thoroughly, she returned to the pool and floated idly about, feeling remarkably calm and peaceful. The woman who had looked after her in the mud department had told her that the treatment was reputed to have a beneficial effect on the nerves and was excellent at combating stress. Lying back in the water, Jane couldn't help but agree. She hadn't felt so relaxed for ages. When she finally found the energy to climb out of the water and stretch out on a sunbed under a parasol, she was joined by Diana.

'Hi, Jane, well, what do you think of it so far?'

'I feel amazingly relaxed.' She turned her head towards Diana and smiled. 'And as far as I can see, my skin's still the same colour it was when I went into the mud bath. I was worried I might turn green.'

'Jane... I couldn't help noticing the scars on your body...' Diana sounded tentative. 'Was that something that happened to you in the army? You don't mind me asking, do you?'

Jane's state of relaxation dissolved in an instant and she lay there, wondering how to respond. She knew the time had been fast approaching when she would have to tell Veronica and, by extension, her family what had happened before her departure from the army, but this didn't make it any easier. In the end, she decided to fudge the issue.

'Of course I don't mind. I was caught up in an explosion, but the medics managed to sort it all out and there were no lasting problems.' Unless she counted two years of pain and depression and the loss of the man she had loved.

'How awful for you. But you're really all right now?'

'I'm fine, thanks.' Whether it was the mud bath, the Italian air or maybe even a man with a pair of deep blue eyes, up in the hills, she realised that she meant what she said, so she gave Diana a little smile and reached over to squeeze her hand. 'Seriously, I'm okay, but thanks for asking.' She very nearly turned the question back on Diana and asked about her brother but stopped herself in time. If he didn't want to talk about whatever it was that had happened, it would be unfair to ask his sister. Hopefully in the fullness of time he would tell her and, if he didn't want to talk about it, that was his business.

Lunch, as Veronica had predicted, was excellent. It took the form of a cold buffet and it comprised everything from crayfish to roast beef, pomegranates to artichokes, as well as a whole selection of pulses, yoghurts and nuts – presumably for those with specific dietary requirements. Jane helped herself to a gorgeous-looking mixed salad and a slice of cold salmon and sat down with the others. She smiled as she saw that Linda had helped herself to seemingly everything on offer and her head was barely visible behind the mountain of food on her plate. Jane looked over and commented.

'I bet Dino wishes he was here, Linda, don't you? I can just see him chewing his way through a joint of roast beef.'

The little girl's face popped up from behind her food and they had to wait several seconds for her to answer, as her mouth was clearly full and her cheeks bulging. Finally, she swallowed and responded.

'Maybe we could take him home some food. He'd love that.'

'That's a good idea; we could ask for a doggy bag.' Somehow, Jane felt sure there was going to be a load of food left over on Linda's plate. She saw the little girl's eyes light up.

'Doggy bag: what a super word.' They were speaking English almost all the time now and Linda's fluency was increasing daily, together with the breadth of her vocabulary. She turned towards her mother. 'Can we ask for a doggy bag, Mummy?'

Beatrice shook her head. 'I don't think we should. Your uncle's very particular about what Dino eats.'

Seeing as David had been mentioned, Jane tried a bit more digging. 'It's a pity he didn't come with us. There are men as well as women here, after all. Has he ever tried it?'

Beatrice answered for all of them. 'He came a few times when he was much younger but he's never been keen. Nowadays, of course, it's all we can do to get him out of the house and into the garden, let alone into a public place like this.'

'Although he did come to Venice with me the other day.'

'Only because he had chronic toothache.' Veronica looked up from her plate, that same air of regret all too clear on her face. 'Otherwise, he just sits about at home.'

'Not really just sitting about.' Diana leapt to his defence. 'He's published one book and he told me he's halfway into the next one. He spends most of his time at the computer – when he isn't running.'

'Those damn computers.' Veronica sounded resigned rather than infuriated. 'It's all too easy to cut yourself off from real life, real people.' She looked around the table with an unexpectedly forceful expression on her face. 'Mind you, God knows that's what I've been doing and I can't even blame it on a computer. But I tell you this, if *I* can start getting up and about, then so can he. Listen, it's up to all of us to get him away from his computer and out into the open air and the real world again.'

'Amen to that.' Diana was nodding her head equally forcefully. 'Like you say, if you can do it, so can he. I say we make it our mission this summer to get him to change.'

Her sister was quick to agree. 'I'm up for it. We all have our problems. Goodness knows I've had mine.' She glanced across at her mother and smiled. 'Seeing you looking so much brighter has cheered me no end. Just being here today with you is wonderful. A year ago, a few months ago, you wouldn't have dreamt of it, but now here you are. If you can do it, so can David.' She held up her glass in front of her. 'I say we attack him from all sides.'

They all clinked their glasses together in agreement and Veronica looked across the table at Jane. 'And that includes you, if you feel up to it, Jane. I'm sure your shared experiences will mean he listens to you as much as, or even more than, he listens to any of us. If you can help put a smile back on his face, we'll be eternally grateful.'

'I promise I'll do everything I can.' Jane contemplated the task ahead and could see the first hurdle all too clearly. Of course, it was the same hurdle she had been facing herself. 'First things first, we need to get him talking.'

Chapter 20

A few days later she had a surprise visitor. It was David and he came around after lunch with an unexpected invitation.

'Hi, Jane. I need a decent walk and I was thinking about climbing over the hill behind us to see if the hot spring in the next valley's still going. I haven't been up there since I was a boy but I just feel like taking a look. If you're interested, I thought you might like to come along too. The scenery's great.'

Jane was genuinely taken aback. Not only was he sounding more communicative, he was actually asking for her company. She wondered what might have brought about this thawing in his attitude. Did it have something to do with the pact they had all sworn around the lunch table at the spa? Had the others been at him?

'That sounds lovely. Thank you so much. I'll just have to check with your mum to see if she needs me here, but that sounds great. What about Diana or Beatrice? Are they coming too?'

He shook his shaggy head. 'No, they've both gone off to Mantua to see your boyfriend.'

In spite of herself, Jane felt her cheeks flush. 'Paolo's not my boyfriend. I don't have a boyfriend.' For some reason she felt it was important that David knew this.

'Ah… right.'

Jane hurried across to the villa to ask if Veronica could do without her for a few hours. When she told her employer what she was thinking of doing – and with whom – she saw her face light up.

'I'm so pleased.' She gave Jane a wink and lowered her voice. 'I bet Diana or Beatrice put him up to it. They've been bullying him constantly for the past few days.'

'So why didn't they get him to go out with them today?'

Veronica shot her a sceptical look. 'To a costume museum? Really? Even when he was his old self you wouldn't have caught him dead in a place like that. No, it's like you said, we really need to get him talking and we all agree you might just be the one to get through to him.' Her smile faded. 'It's been three years, Jane. He can't go on like this forever. He's still a young man. He needs to come out of his shell and start living again. What happened, happened. It's time he got over it. Besides, talking might just be good for you, too.'

As a result, Jane was feeling quite a weight of responsibility on her shoulders ten minutes later when she picked up her little backpack and went across to his house to meet up with David. They chatted a bit as they walked, but she made no attempt to draw him on anything intimate. If this invitation really was a sign of thawing, then the first move would have to come from him. And just what had his mother meant when she had said 'what happened, happened'?

A gate in the fence indicated the edge of the estate and she turned towards him. 'Which way now?'

He pointed towards a narrow path that disappeared upwards into the trees.

'A fairly tough climb, I'm afraid. But at least we're doing it on a sunny day and only carrying a few pounds on our backs. Imagine doing it in the winter snow, with full pack, rations and ammunition.'

This was another surprise. This was the first time he had mentioned the army to her and she did her best to keep the conversation going. 'Reminds me of my basic training in the Brecon Beacons.' She decided to risk a direct question. 'Did you end up there as well?'

To her surprise, he answered straightaway. 'The Beacons? I think I knew almost every blade of grass and every rock by the end of it.'

'I spent a total of five days there and I've never been so happy to leave a place in my life.' She shuddered at the memory. 'I was expected to carry exactly the same weight as a man your size. I had blisters on my blisters, and my shoulders were black and blue from the webbing.'

His eyes smiled at her. 'Five days? You got off lightly. I must have spent more like five weeks up there on and off.'

'So not just during officer training?'

'No, I was stationed not far from there and we had a whole series of training ops in that area. Wales is a lovely place but I'd happily never see the Beacons again.'

She followed him up the tortuous path, reflecting on what he had just told her. If he had spent so much time on operations in that area, maybe his base had been in the nearby city of Hereford. This historic old city was known to all in the British armed forces not because it was the repository of the famous *Mappa Mundi*, but as the home of the SAS. Had he maybe been in UK Special Forces? She almost asked him but decided against it – for now.

'Well, I'm glad I never have to go through that again. For now, lead on, captain.' She said it as a joke but then she remembered the photo in his mother's bedroom and added a disingenuous, 'I'm just guessing. What was your rank?'

He was already turning away as she spoke but she heard his answer, delivered in a neutral tone.

'Right first time, I was a captain… just like you were.'

On the way up the path she mulled over the fact that he had clearly been talking to somebody or they had been talking to him about her. Did this signify simple curiosity, or maybe something more. Either way, at least he was talking.

It took half an hour of hard scrambling up what was no more than a goat track to get to the top of the hill. Just as they got there, Dino suddenly erupted into paroxysms of barking and shot off sideways into the undergrowth. David stopped so quickly that Jane almost bumped into the back of him.

'He's spotted a squirrel. I recognise that bark. I'd better go and find him. He's been known to run miles following the damn things. Why don't you wait for us here?'

Jane was happy to leave them to their squirrel hunt while she sat down on a rock and wiped the perspiration off her forehead. From up here the view was almost due north over another couple of hills towards the distant Alps with the highest peaks clad in eternal snows. On a hot day like today it was incongruous to think that the snow up there would never melt. She took a couple of photos and settled down to wait for David's return, pulling out a bottle of water from her pack and drinking gratefully. A few minutes later she was joined by the Labrador who arrived looking jubilant, his pink tongue hanging out as he panted excitedly and did his best to climb onto her lap.

'Hi there, Dino. Hunt over? Mr Squirrel got away, right?' She fended him off gently and then glanced around for any sign of his master and, not seeing or hearing him, she raised her voice and called out. 'David, he's come back. Dino's here.'

She had to repeat herself in her parade ground voice before there was a distant shout in response, and then a good five minutes later he reappeared.

'Bloody dog. He's got a real fixation with squirrels.' He wagged his finger at the Labrador and adopted a stern tone. 'No more running after squirrels, right?'

The dog, unrepentant, jumped up at him to be petted and then settled down alongside them both as his master pointed to a clearing in the trees below them in the next valley.

'That's the place. I don't know much about it except that there used to be a pool with a hot spring alongside it. The locals say the Romans built the pool but there's no way of knowing now. There are all sorts of legends about the waters having healing properties but when we were kids we often used to come over here for a swim and I didn't notice anything special.'

'It would be great if it really did have the ability to heal.' She very nearly added 'both of us' but decided that would sound too personal.

He glanced across at her and for a moment she had the feeling he might be thinking the same thing, but he, too, didn't comment. 'The main reason we kids came here was that the water was a damn sight warmer than our lake. Shall we go?'

Jane got up and together they made their way down through the dense forest. The vestigial path they had been following had disappeared and they were soon clambering over fallen trees and between mossy boulders as they headed for the ruins. It was hard work but it was fun and she felt that selfsame lightening in her mood she had felt back on top of Monte Venda. There was something so wonderful about being able to get back to nature, far away from modern civilisation with all its horrors. Scrambling down the hillside, she found herself wondering if David felt the same way and whether his newfound communicativeness would mark the beginning of his return to the happy outgoing man he allegedly used to be. She hoped so for his sake. And maybe for hers too.

The hot spring looked far from attractive. It was surrounded by stinging nettles and a chaos of brambles, and it was a struggle to get close enough for her to dip her fingers in the water. It wasn't hot by any means but, as he had said, it was definitely warmer than the lake. A dead rat floating in the water didn't add to its attraction so she hastily shelved the idea she had been harbouring of splashing the water all over her face or even sipping a mouthful. Salmonella or worse definitely wouldn't help her return to health and happiness.

They retraced their steps out of the brambles and she sat down on a boulder for a rest while he wandered off, leaving the dog sprawled at her feet, tongue hanging out. As he revived his childhood memories, she watched his athletic figure moving about in the undergrowth and was unable suppress the feeling of attraction this produced in her. There could be no doubt about it: something was happening to her and, although puzzling, it wasn't necessarily bad.

David took a few photos and by the time he sat down alongside her, she could sense he was still in his more communicative mood. She was about to capitalise on this to see if she could get him talking about himself when he pointed towards her leg, just below the line of her shorts.

'Looks like you've cut yourself. Sorry, I should have warned you to wear long trousers.'

She looked down and saw a little trickle of drying blood on her thigh. Removing a tissue from her pocket, she dabbed away the blood and was quick to reassure him with a smile.

'It's just a scratch. Probably those brambles.' What he said next wiped the smile off her face in an instant.

'It's certainly far less serious than that nasty scar on your thigh.' He must have seen the shocked expression on her face and hastened to explain. 'I'm sorry, it's just that I noticed it that first day when we met down by the lake.'

Instinctively, she reached for the scar at the top of her leg and pressed her free hand against it, shielding it, although it was well hidden beneath her shorts. Her brain was still processing the fact that in the very few seconds she and he had been together that day at the lake he had noticed the scar and had remembered. She took a deep breath and did her best to provide an upbeat reply.

'In a different league altogether. I wouldn't like another one of those.' But her afternoon of surprises didn't end there.

'You're a very brave woman, Captain Reed. They don't hand out Conspicuous Gallantry Crosses to just anybody.'

Jane was flabbergasted. 'You know about that? I've hardly told a soul. But how…?'

'Regimental records and my inquisitive nature.' She looked up from her feet and got the distinct impression the eyes behind his sunglasses were smiling at her. 'You gave me all the clues I needed: your regiment, the fact that you left two years ago, that leg wound and, of course, I already had your name. I read all about your career as an outstanding officer and the medal citation told me what happened in Fallujah that day. If you hadn't defused the IED before the bomb exploded, a whole heap of people in the hospital would have lost their lives. I hope you don't mind me being nosey. I've got so used to online research it just sort of happened.'

She genuinely didn't know what to say so she burrowed in her bag for a bottle of water. The dog looked up with interest and by the time she had filled his water bowl and then swallowed some herself, a full minute had passed and she had been able to formulate a response. Although her initial reaction had been to feel almost offended that David had started digging into her background, she knew he had every right to do so and she felt sure there had been no malice in his actions. In fact it maybe indicated an unexpected interest in her. She had been readying herself to tell them all about Fallujah any day now so he had only really brought forward the inevitable. She took a deep breath before speaking.

'Of course I don't mind. Apart from anything else, I work for your mother and it's only right you should all know the truth about me. In fact, now that my secret's out in the open, it's probably for the best. She knows I was wounded and I've been putting off telling her the full story because I'm still coming to terms with it myself.'

'Listen, Jane, I haven't said a thing to her or to anybody so it's not out in the open. I promise to keep it to myself. Nobody needs to know a thing.' He sounded concerned, apologetic, caring even.

'Thanks. I owe it to your mother to tell her myself, and I'll do that as soon as I see her next – this evening if possible.'

He stayed silent for a while, and when he started speaking again, his tone was far warmer than she had ever heard from him before. 'It must have been tough. I don't just mean because of your injuries. The girls told me the guy who died might have been more to you than just a comrade in arms.'

Once again Jane took her time before answering. Of course it was inevitable that Diana and Beatrice would have told their brother what they had learned, and he was too smart not to put two and two together. When she did answer, she was gratified to hear her voice sounding fairly firm. 'Yes, he was, and yes, it's been tough.' She surprised herself by managing to look David straight in the eye, if only for a couple of seconds. 'But as Beatrice told me just the other day, life goes on. I know that. And one thing I can say is that since coming over here to work for your mother, I've been feeling a whole lot more positive. I still have my moments, but I definitely feel I'm improving.'

'If there's anything I can do to help, just say the word.' His tone was still supportive and sympathetic; so sympathetic in fact that she decided to turn the spotlight back on him.

'There is one thing, if you really mean that. You could tell me what happened to you. I get the feeling we have more in common than I know, and not just that you were wounded as well.' Seeing the surprise on his face she was quick to explain. 'Your mum mentioned that, but that's all she told me. I would really like to help you, just like you've so kindly offered to do for me.' She risked raising her eyes in his direction once more, expecting to see the shutters come down, but this time he did at least make an effort.

'It's a long, sad story, Jane. Like you said the other day: my departure from the regiment wasn't exactly the way I would have planned it. And just like you, it's something I've been keeping to myself for a long time now. So long, in fact, that it's probably best left that way. Thanks for the offer of help, but I'm afraid it's too late for that. What's done's done, and I'm a lost cause.'

Jane couldn't help reaching across to catch hold of his hand. He didn't resist. 'Nobody's a lost cause, David. Believe me. Talking will help, I'm sure.' She squeezed his fingers and then hastily withdrew her hand again. 'Anyway, the offer's there. Any time.'

'Thanks, Jane, but you're the last person I would want to tell.'

What, she asked herself, did he mean by that?

Chapter 21

That evening Jane went over to Veronica's house to see if she could spare a few minutes. She found her sitting on the terrace in the shade with her mother-in-law alongside her. Jane hesitated for a moment before deciding that she might as well tell her story to both of them. She settled down opposite them, looking out at the lengthening shadows, and made a start.

'David and I have been talking today.' She immediately saw a spark of interest in both sets of eyes. 'The bad news is that we mainly talked about me, not him. It appears he's checked up on my military record and he knows all about what happened to me. I've been meaning to tell you for days now, so that's why I'm here.'

Veronica gave her a gentle smile. 'Tell me as much or as little as you feel happy revealing. Hopefully you and I will be together for a long time to come so don't feel you have to rush. I can wait. I already know you well enough to know you can't have done anything bad, so take your time.'

Jane gave her a grateful look and embarked on her tale. She left nothing out, even going into detail about how she had had no choice but to defuse the landmine and that the man dealing with the unexploded bomb alongside her had been very dear to her. She told them about the explosion, the awful aftermath, the long weeks and months of rehabilitation and the lasting effects on her psyche. All the way through, Veronica and Flora listened intently and made no comment. It was only when Jane finally came to the end that her employer spoke up.

'Thank you, Jane. To be perfectly honest I already knew most of that. It was good to hear it from your perspective though.'

'You knew? Did David tell you?'

Veronica smiled. 'I've known since before your interview in London. The moment Gordon sent me your CV, I felt sure you were going to be perfect for the job, so I asked a friend for a reference. Does the name General Sir Alexander Greene-Finch mean anything to you?'

Jane's eyes opened wide with amazement. 'You know him? He's the Chief of the General Staff, the head of the armed forces!'

The smile only broadened. 'I've known Alex since university. To be totally honest, I had a bit of a crush on him for a while. Anyway, when I heard you'd been in the army I called him and asked him about you.'

Jane was speechless. Veronica had approached the CGS about her? 'And he spoke to you about me?'

'This may come as a surprise to you but he already knew all about you.' Ignoring Jane's look of incredulity, Veronica continued. 'He told me you were one of his finest officers and a very brave young woman.'

'Wow!' Jane's mind boggled. The CGS? Of course, the medal for gallantry would have had to be authorised at the highest level but even so...

'But you're all right again now?' Flora sounded genuinely concerned and Jane was touched.

'I'm fine, thanks. I'm running again; I feel fit, and all my aches and pains have left me.'

'Lucky you.' Flora grimaced. 'With me it's a question of which bits don't hurt.'

'And yet you ride your bike and walk all over the place. I'm massively impressed.'

'Thank you, my dear, but tell me, are you feeling better deep down inside? So often it's not so much the physical injuries that take the longest to heal.'

'I'll be completely honest with you and say that although I'm probably not completely back to a hundred percent normal, I do feel miles better and happier. And being here has been really helpful, as have all of you.'

Veronica gave her a big smile. 'That's so good to hear and thank you for telling us your story. Now, I think a drink might be in order, don't you? Why don't we open a bottle of champagne? I've got a bit of news of my own to celebrate. There should be a couple of bottles in the wine fridge in the corner of the living room. Let me…'

Jane jumped to her feet. 'You stay there, Veronica. Leave it to me. In the corner, you say?'

'It's a fridge disguised as a bookcase. Don't worry, it isn't too hard to find. The top shelf's all Dickens. Bring a bottle. Glasses are in the dresser alongside.'

Jane located the fridge with ease and took out a bottle of champagne from half a dozen others. Picking up three crystal flutes, she went back outside and set them on a low table. By the time she had opened the bottle, poured wine into each glass and handed them out, she had recovered at least some of her composure and was able to address Veronica in normal tones.

'So all this time you've known what happened to me. Why didn't you say?'

'I knew you'd tell me when you felt the time was right. I could see that you were still grieving. Like I've told you before, I know a thing or two about grief so I left it up to you. I'm the only one who knew and I chose to keep it that way until you felt comfortable telling me.'

Beside her, Flora raised her glass and clinked it against Jane's. 'Thank you for taking me into your confidence, Jane.'

Jane took a sip and as the wine trickled down her throat she gradually began to relax again and glanced across at Veronica. 'And you didn't say anything to David? Even though he used to be in the army and was injured himself?'

'I didn't say a word to anybody.' Veronica set her glass back down on the table again. 'So tell me, if David hadn't forced your hand, when do you think you would have felt like talking about what happened to you? I sensed you were drawing close to opening up.'

'You're right – it would have been any day now, really. I knew I owed it to you to tell you the full story but I've been terrified of ending up in tears. I've been feeling so much more relaxed over these past few weeks and it might not surprise you to know that this is just about the first time I've spoken about this stuff without welling up. I honestly can't thank you enough for helping me on my road to recovery. I owe you a lot, Veronica.'

Veronica gave her an affectionate glance. 'You owe me nothing. If anything, I'm the one who should be thanking you. You may not realise, but since you've come into my life, you've been a ray of sunshine. I can honestly say I feel happier now than I have done for years. Thank *you*.'

Jane was about to ask what she had meant about good news of her own when there was the sound of footsteps and Diana arrived, closely followed by Beatrice carrying a sleepy-looking Linda. Diana glanced at the bottle on the table and raised her eyebrows. 'Are you celebrating? What's brought this on?'

'I'll tell you in a minute. But first, how did your visit to the Costume Museum go?'

Diana came over and perched on the arm of the chair between her mother and her grandmother while Beatrice sat in the next armchair. Linda gave a weary wave and settled on her lap, snuggling down with a muffled yawn.

Diana was the first to reply. 'It was great. They have a terrific selection of clothes and some of the stuff has given me ideas for my autumn collection.' She glanced over at Jane and smiled. 'What Paolo doesn't know about fashion isn't worth knowing.' Her smile turned into a cheeky grin. 'And he isn't even gay.' She winked at her sister. 'Did you know that, Bee?'

Beatrice flushed momentarily but recovered. 'You'd be surprised what I know, little sister.'

They were both looking cheerful and Jane took that as a good omen for Beatrice if she really was thinking of trying to rekindle her romance with Paolo. As far as she herself was concerned, she didn't mind in the slightest and she realised that it wasn't because of poor Mark or of her professed lack of interest in finding herself a man. It was because her affections – like it or lump it – now appeared to be directed elsewhere. Somehow the troubled man hidden beneath the unruly thatch of hair had established himself inside her head, maybe even her heart. This real-isation was so striking, she swallowed half a glass of wine in one go and very nearly erupted into a fit of coughing as a result. Mercifully Veronica stepped in before Jane had to do any talking.

'I'm glad you both had a good time. Anyway, there's a reason for the champagne. Jane and I've been talking, but

I have some news of my own. Diana, be a dear and go and call your brother, would you? He needs to hear this as well.'

Jane and Beatrice exchanged quizzical looks as Diana shot off to call David. Beatrice glanced back at her mother and did a bit of prodding. 'Good news or bad? Since you're drinking champagne, I'm assuming it's good.'

'Definitely good.' Veronica smiled. 'Only a few months ago this probably wouldn't have interested me in the slightest but now I'm actually rather excited. Now, why doesn't one of you go and get three more glasses and pour some champagne for all of us?'

Jane jumped to her feet and indicated for Beatrice and her sleepy daughter to stay put while she went to get the glasses. When Diana reappeared with her brother and his dog, Veronica wasted no time passing on news of the unexpected phone call she had received an hour earlier.

'It was Eleanor, my agent in London. It appears that a major film company is interested in turning one of my books, *Love Letter from Vienna*, into a big budget movie. The director and a bunch of Hollywood bigwigs are coming over in September for the Venice Film Festival and they want to meet me. Eleanor says it isn't a done deal yet, but it sounds extremely promising.' She picked up her glass and looked around with a grin. 'It might be tempting fate to bring out the champagne so early, but here's hoping. So, cheers everybody.'

While Flora reached across to kiss her daughter-in-law on the cheeks, Diana went over to hug her mother and David was close behind. Beatrice, under the weight of a sleepy little girl had to settle for blowing her kisses. Dino, caught up in the excitement of the moment, decided it would be a good idea to climb onto Veronica's lap to add his congratulations but was dissuaded by his master as Jane looked on and giggled.

'Do you feel up to meeting this director and a whole bunch of other people?' There was disbelief in Diana's voice.

Veronica's expression became more serious. 'This'll be a big step for me, I admit, but it's time I tried to get back to normal life again. I've been moping around for too long.' For a fraction of a second her eyes met Jane's. 'For now I've said I'll be delighted to meet them. I can always back out at the last minute if I don't feel up to it and, if I do change my mind, there'll always be my agent and one of you can take my place alongside her.'

Jane saw Diana, Beatrice and David exchange glances. Somehow she had a feeling David would be even less willing than his mother to socialise with a load of strangers. Diana looked excited, but awed. Beatrice, on the other hand, with her TV experience, looked unperturbed.

'Don't worry, Mamma, you can do it. I'll be with you all the way, holding your hand.'

'And if they start giving you any trouble, I'll be happy to come along and frighten the life out of them.' Flora looked as if she meant it. 'I know how to handle men.' Jane stifled a giggle. One thing was for sure: she had little doubt that this spirited old lady would be more than a match for a bunch of Hollywood execs.

She also hastened to encourage her employer. 'You'll be fine, Veronica. I'm sure you'll enjoy the experience. Do you think they'll want you to write the screenplay?'

'That's what I asked Eleanor. I've no experience of writing screenplays but I wouldn't want a bunch of anonymous writers in Hollywood to change the book out of all recognition.' She looked up with a smile. 'Eleanor agrees and she told me we need to fight for "full creative control and final approval of the script". It promises to be an exciting meeting.'

'When's the Film Festival?'

'The first two weeks of September. It takes place at the Palazzo del Cinema over on the Lido. So this means we'd better head back to Venice at the end of August.' She glanced across at Jane and explained. 'If it's hot I often stay on up here until well into September, but not this year by the sound of it.'

Jane hadn't yet visited the Lido, the long island that separated Venice from the open sea, but she vowed to remedy this once they returned to the city and, while she was at it, to check out the Palazzo del Cinema. She glanced across at Diana. 'When are you heading back to New York? You'll still be here, won't you?'

Diana nodded. 'My flight's booked for the seventeenth but I can always change it. It'll be fun to mix with a few Hollywood celebs.'

From the expression on his face, Jane definitely got the impression that David didn't share his sister's idea of fun.

–

Later that evening, Jane thought she might take a leaf out of David's book and check *him* out online. Getting into the regimental records of the Rifles wasn't difficult, but her search only revealed what she already knew: Captain D.C. Cooper had left the regiment just over three years earlier. No detail was given, although there didn't appear to be any question of incompetence or what was usually referred to euphemistically as 'conduct unbecoming an officer and a gentleman'. Surprisingly, in view of what his mother had said, there was no mention of wounds either. He had just left, for whatever reason; presumably because his initial term had finished. What was also interesting was that Veronica had said he had been back in Italy for two years now since his father's death. So what had he been doing and where had he been for the missing year?

Thought of David reminded Jane of her moment of epiphany when she had realised that this unhappy man now risked replacing Mark in her affections, whether or not he had any interest in being there. Was it because David, too, had been a soldier, or was there more to it than that? She had never before subscribed to the notion of love at first sight, but she had to admit that in David's case that look into his eyes as they bobbed up and down in the lake had been electric. She had enjoyed being with him on their walk today and she knew there was a spark of something there, even if it was only on her part.

She was sitting, deep in her thoughts, when her phone rang. It was her mum. They had a long chat, during which Jane passed on the news that she had finally opened up to her employer about the circumstances surrounding her departure from the army, and her mum expressed satisfaction. For some reason, however, Jane decided not to mention that David had been the catalyst, or that she found him appealing. There would be time to let her in on that secret once she had had a real chance to digest the possible ramifications of this attraction. Apart from anything else, his mother was her employer, after all, and the last thing she wanted was to screw up what was turning into a wonderful job. Her mum then reminded her of something she had completely forgotten.

'What are you doing for your birthday? Anything planned?'

Instinctively, Jane glanced at the date on her phone. Today was the twenty-first of July and her birthday was on the seventh of August, little over two weeks away. She hadn't felt like celebrating her birthdays over the past couple of years but, as her mother helpfully reminded her, this one would be special.

'You *are* going to be thirty, after all. You need to celebrate.'

Turning thirty didn't feel much like something that deserved to be celebrated but, grudgingly, Jane had to accept that maybe she should at least mark the occasion in some way. She was still thinking about it when her mum made a suggestion.

'Your father and I were talking and we wondered how you would feel if we popped across to see you for a few days. That way we could celebrate with you and then go off and have a bit of a holiday.'

Jane and her parents had always been close and she had no hesitation. 'I'd love to see you both. That's a super idea and there's bags of room here for you to stay.' Her mind was racing. 'Maybe we could all go out for dinner that night or something.'

They left it that her dad would look into flights and Jane settled down after the call to think about how she should celebrate the fact that in two weeks' time she would be entering her fourth decade of existence.

Chapter 22

Over the course of the next week Jane worked for Veronica, paying bills, politely declining requests for interviews and fielding a host of emails from her agent, Eleanor, in London about the prospective Hollywood deal. At the same time she continued to plough through the hundreds and hundreds of unanswered letters and emails from fervent Veronica Leonard fans. She had taken the decision early on to do her best to try to answer each and every one personally – apart from the handful of abusive or bonkers ones – but she had underestimated the work this would involve. Still, she stuck to her guns and tried to knock off at least a dozen a day and the pile was gradually shrinking. In her free time she planned out her book, ran and walked, often with Dino for company, her mind occupied by two main thoughts: her birthday and David.

As far as David was concerned, she hardly saw anything of him. On a couple of occasions she almost went over to his house to see him on some pretext or other, but chickened out at the last minute. She spotted him out running a few times and considered joining him but decided there was no point in flogging a dead horse. If he wasn't interested, he wasn't interested.

As for her birthday, an idea came to her one afternoon when she was out for a walk in the woods with Beatrice and the dog. Veronica was looking after Linda, and Diana had gone to Padua to see some friends. They were talking about the events leading up to Beatrice's divorce and Jane had a moment of inspiration when the subject came around to Paolo. It was quite clear that Beatrice was genuinely interested in him but felt she couldn't make the first move, so Jane suddenly hit on a cunning plan to give her a helping hand, while celebrating her own birthday at the same time.

'Beatrice, my folks are coming over quite soon and I was thinking about having a little party.' She decided not to mention that it would be her birthday in case people might feel obliged to give her presents. 'What if I were to invite Paolo along? That way you could spend some quality time with him and hopefully find out if he feels like picking things up with you again, if that's what you want. For what it's worth, I think he's a good guy, and the fact that you have little Linda wouldn't be an obstacle, I'm sure.'

'That would be amazing…' Beatrice hesitated uncertainly. 'But what about you? Won't he be coming here expecting to spend an intimate evening with you?'

Jane gave her a wink. 'Hardly an intimate evening with my parents, Maria and Alvise, and your sister, mum and brother if they feel like it. Hopefully Silvana and Grazia and some of the others from Padua might like to come too.' She was grinning by now. 'No, I'll spell it out to him that it's just a group of friends getting together. What do you think?'

'I think it's a brilliant idea. By the way, leave David to me. I'll make sure he can't say no.'

'I think you might have a struggle on your hands.'

'He'll do it for me. I'm his big sister, after all; I know how to handle him. Just you wait and see. Now, what can I do to help?'

Within twenty-four hours, the plan had taken shape. Jane's parents would be arriving on Friday the fifth and driving themselves up to the villa in a rental car. The three of them would spend Saturday together and then, with her mum's help, Jane would lay on a buffet supper in her house on the Sunday night. If the weather remained fine, people could spill out of the living room onto the grass. Beatrice was true to her word and surprised Jane by reporting that she had managed to twist her brother's arm into agreeing to come. Along with him would be Veronica, Flora and Luciana, Maria and Alvise. Jane had to be gently firm in turning down all the offers of help from the kindly housekeeper because she wanted her to be able to relax as a guest for a change. Making up the numbers were a bunch of Diana's friends that Jane had got to know over the past few weeks.

The Padua crowd also promised to bring 'music'. Diego, one of the men, claimed to be a part-time DJ and Jane hoped his idea of music wouldn't prove too overpowering for her parents, Veronica or the two elderly ladies. She also stipulated that Dino was invited. He was, after all, one of her very best friends by now. When she called Paolo with the invitation, he accepted straightaway. To be on the safe side, she spelt out to him as clearly as she could what sort of evening this would be and the fact that Veronica and her whole family would be there – including Beatrice – and he sounded delighted at the prospect.

One afternoon, a few days before the arrival of her parents, she was surprised – and delighted – to receive a visit from David. His hair was plastered down on his head and his beard was still soaked, as was the bouncy Labrador at his side, but the bouncy Labrador wasn't wearing a wet T-shirt that stuck to his body like David's did. Jane had to struggle not to give a little growl of attraction. It was no good; she was definitely hooked.

'Ciao, Jane, we've just been for a swim.'

'You don't say!' She repressed a giggle at this statement of the obvious. 'Well, it's always good to see you, wet or dry. It's almost six. Why don't you and your four-legged friend go round to the back of the house and you can both sit and drip on the grass while I open a bottle of wine?'

'I don't want to put you to any trouble. I just came to say thank you for the invitation to your little party.'

'I gather your sister has bullied you into coming.'

The blue eyes smiled. 'She can be very persuasive.' Then he said something that came as a considerable surprise to Jane. 'I would have come for your sake anyway, but I haven't been in the mood for socialising for quite a while now.'

So, he would have come for her sake. That sounded promising, but she didn't comment.

'That's good news. Now, have you got time for a drink? Go on round and sit yourselves down. I'll organise wine for us and something for our canine friend.'

She closed the front door and went through to open the French windows before hurrying back to the kitchen to grab a bottle of Prosecco from the fridge and two glasses. By the time she got back out to the garden David was sitting on the fine old wooden bench out on the back lawn, looking down over the town. Beside him, panting like a steam train was his dog with David wisely hanging onto his collar to stop him rushing into the house and soaking everything. Jane set the bottle and glasses down on the low table.

'Here, if you'd like to do the honours, I'll go and get something for Dino.'

Leaving him to open the wine she went back inside, filled a bowl with water and dug out a dog biscuit for Dino. She also prepared a plateful of grissini along with some local ham and cheese as nibbles for David and herself. After giving the dog his food and drink, she sat down in her turn. Resisting the temptation to take a seat on the bench beside David, she pulled up a folding chair and positioned herself directly opposite him, the plate of food on the table between them.

'You really shouldn't have gone to all this trouble...' He sounded genuinely uncomfortable, but she waved away his objections and accepted a glass of wine from him.

She took a sip of wine and decided to engage him in conversation in the hope that he might loosen up a bit more. For starters, she relayed the contents of an email Veronica had received earlier today. 'Has your mum told you that the Hollywood people she'll be meeting in September might even include a couple of Hollywood A-listers they want to star in it?'

'Sounds like they mean business. I wonder who they'll cast. I'm delighted for her. I've always thought her books would make great movies. By the way, you and I don't talk that often but I've been meaning to thank you for everything you've done for her. The girls and I agree that Mum's come on remarkably since your arrival. We really are grateful to you.'

'I'm just doing my job, but she's a lovely lady, very kind and generous and remarkably easy-going. I like her a lot and I'm as pleased as you are that even in the short time

I've known her I've seen a real improvement in her mood. Here's hoping the next step will be the return of her muse. It must be burning her up not being able to write.' She took a deep breath and risked getting personal. 'Now all I need is to see you looking and sounding more cheerful and I'll be really happy.' She took another mouthful of Prosecco and waited for him to tell her to mind her own business.

But he didn't. Instead, he surprised her with what looked like a little smile. 'But I am.' Evidently sensing her scepticism he explained. 'You haven't known me long but believe me, I've been in a really bad place for the last few years.'

'I had gathered that from what your mum said.'

'What you're seeing now is the new cheerful me.' It looked as though the eyes were grinning now. 'The fact that I'm actually sitting here drinking wine and chatting to a beautiful woman still comes as a surprise to me. I've hardly spoken to anybody for ages, unless it was for my research.'

She decided to let the 'beautiful woman' comment pass, but she could feel her cheeks reacting to the compliment all the same. Instead, she had another go at finding out just what had happened to make him so morose. 'So why the unhappiness? Was it what happened to you in the army? Did something bad happen? You were wounded, after all.' This time she felt sure he was going to tell her to keep her nose out of his affairs but, again, she was wrong.

'A number of bad things happened; one in particular.' The light went out of his eyes in an instant and he lapsed into silence while she searched desperately for a way to loosen his tongue. To give herself time, she reached over, picked up the bottle and topped up their glasses. She set the bottle back down again and decided she had nothing to lose by taking the plunge.

'Can I ask you something? Don't answer if you don't want to, but were you in the SAS?'

He raised his eyes very slowly until he was looking straight at her. To her relief she saw that he was smiling again, albeit wryly. 'It was when I told you I'd been stationed not far from the Beacons, wasn't it? You don't miss a thing, do you? Anyway, yes, I was stationed in Hereford and I did two years in the regiment.'

'Active service?'

'Some of the time. Partly in Afghanistan, partly in Iraq.' He still had that same inscrutable half-smile in his eyes. 'And before you ask, yes, I know Fallujah.'

'How did you find life in the SAS? I know a few guys who've been involved in special ops and they said it gave them the most amazing adrenalin rush.'

'More than defusing a landmine? I don't think so. But yes, I did get a kick out of it in a masochistic sort of way right up until the last few months.'

'And then?' She did her best to prompt him as gently as possible. 'Was it then that things changed?'

She saw him nod his head. 'They changed.' He hesitated for a few seconds. 'Or, rather, I changed.'

She waited in vain for him to say more, but all he did was slowly shake his head.

'I've been trying hard to put it behind me. Sooner or later, I'll manage.' He drained his glass of wine and stood up. 'Now I'd better get back.'

She stood up as well. 'Well, just remember I'm here if you need a shoulder to lean on. Any time.'

'Thanks.' He hesitated for a few moments. 'And I really am a whole lot more cheerful than I have been... honest.'

Chapter 23

Jane's parents arrived on Friday evening and she was delighted to see them. But not as delighted as they appeared to be at the sight of her. Her mother in particular was almost beside herself with joy.

'You're looking so much better – not just because you've got a bit of sun on your skin but you look so much happier, so much more serene. The dark rings under your eyes have disappeared and there's a spring in your step that hasn't been there for a long time. We've been praying that you'd be able to sort yourself out and it looks as though that what's happened.'

Even her father – normally fairly taciturn as far as personal matters were concerned – joined in. 'You've been so awfully dejected for ages now and suddenly you look transformed. You can't imagine how happy that makes us.'

'I can honestly say I *am* feeling a lot brighter. Yes, I still have my bad moments, but they're getting fewer and fewer. The really good news is that I haven't had a seriously bad dream since I arrived over here in Italy. Like I say, I'm not there yet, but I'm getting there. Even I can feel it.'

She and her parents had a quiet dinner together at her house on Friday night and then on Saturday she took them down to Padua. She gave them a tour in the morning followed by a lunchtime pizza and then a circuit of the Colli in the afternoon, taking in a stop in Arquà Petrarca. It was less crowded than the last time and they managed to get close enough to the tomb of the great poet: a Roman-style pink marble sarcophagus on pillars in the main square. Interestingly, Jane's phone told them that in 2004 the tomb had been opened and it was discovered that, while the body probably belonged to Petrarch, the skull belonged to a woman who had died over a century earlier. The mystery of Petrarch's skull continued to puzzle academics but didn't appear to trouble the swarm of visitors around his grave.

It was another fine, sunny day and when they got back to the villa Jane got a text message from Diana asking if they would like to come over for tea with the family. When they went across to the main house, they found Veronica, Flora, Luciana, Beatrice and Diana sitting outside on the back lawn with a familiar black form stretched out at their feet, apparently unconcerned that Linda and her teddy were sprawled all over him, playing. When he spotted them, Dino jumped to his feet and ran across to greet them effusively, starting with Jane. Veronica was quick to remind him of his manners.

'Dino, don't jump all over the guests.' She rose to her feet and greeted them in her turn before inviting them to sit down and accept a slice of sponge cake – freshly baked by Maria this afternoon – and some tea. They were soon chatting freely and Jane found herself the subject of much of the conversation. It came as something of a relief when Dino's master appeared. Jane had already warned her parents that he looked more than a little unkempt but she hadn't mentioned to them that, in spite of his appearance, she felt a definite connection with him.

'Sorry I'm a bit late. I got caught up with a seminar on the internet.' He walked across and introduced himself, shaking hands politely. 'Good afternoon. I'm David; Beatrice and Diana's brother. I'm pleased to meet you, Mr and Mrs Reed.' He sounded very formal and Jane could see he was uncomfortable in a social gathering like this.

The conversation continued and by the end Jane had the impression that Veronica and her parents were getting along fine, and even David had been cajoled into taking part – mostly in the guise of history guru, talking about the First World War. When they returned to the summer house later on, her mother waited until the door had closed behind them before turning towards Jane and cutting to the chase with the same unerring knack for putting her on the spot she had demonstrated on numerous occasions all the way through Jane's childhood and adolescence.

'You like David, don't you?'

At first Jane attempted to play down any feelings she might have been developing for him, but her mother wasn't going to take no for an answer.

'I could see the way you were looking at him. You definitely like him.'

Probably because he could see Jane's embarrassment, her father then intervened. 'Well, what's not to like? He's clearly bright, comes from a good family and I suppose the only question is what he looks like underneath all that hair. He certainly looks fit enough.'

Jane shot him a grateful glance but then admitted defeat. 'Yes, you're right, I do like him.' She caught her mother's eye. 'Considering I came over here certain that I'd never look at another man again, it's unexpected, but I can't help it. There's something almost magnetic about him, his eyes in particular.' She toyed with the idea of showing them the photo of him in uniform on her phone but decided that might look too much like she was stalking the poor man.

Her mother reached out and caught hold of both her hands. 'Well, I for one, am delighted for you. We all know how close you were to Mark and how awful these past two years have been for you but you've got to move on with your life. Whether anything happens between you and David is unimportant. What matters is that you look so much more relaxed and there's a smile on your face that wasn't there before. Whether it's anything to do with David is up to you to decide, but something, or someone, here is doing you good.'

The party the next evening went well. Jane and her mother had decided to make it a help-yourself buffet and they spent the afternoon preparing all manner of dishes from nibbles to hot food. Because they were in Italy, they decided to make it an all-English affair and Jane had bought a big piece of beef from the butcher further along the valley, which they roasted together with potatoes and her mum's homemade Yorkshire puddings. Just to make sure that everybody got a truly authentic English meal, Jane made a big pot of her speciality chicken tikka masala and a heap of rice. This raised more than a few eyebrows, but she was able to tell everybody that this Indian dish had become one of the most popular in England and it appeared to be met with approval. The only concession she made to being in Italy was that she bought a load of wonderful meringue ice cream from the shop in the village which made the best ice cream she had ever tasted. She served this with a fresh fruit salad containing everything from strawberries to white flesh peaches.

Diego's disco turned out to be really rather good, once Jane had explained to him that there was no need for the noise levels to set the glasses in the kitchen jingling. He produced an eclectic mix ranging from Sixties classics like the Rolling Stones and the Supremes all the way up to Italian pop which allowed those who felt in the mood to get up and dance. Among these was little Linda who appeared to be loving her first party with grown-ups and a certain ninety-five-year-old who even got up and danced with her. Jane watched in awe before returning to running around, serving food and collecting dirty dishes while her father acted as barman, dispensing Prosecco, red wine and beer, along with non-alcoholic drinks. She barely had time to exchange a few words with Paolo when he arrived but she was gratified to see that Beatrice had taken him under her wing. When the time came for an overtired Linda to be put to bed, Jane noticed that Paolo went with them. It looked as if her plan was working out.

Dino the dog wandered about from group to group, tail wagging hopefully, doing his unsuccessful best to look as though nobody fed him. His master arrived late and surprised Jane with a birthday present. Nobody was supposed to know it was her birthday and she wondered how he had found out. He didn't hand it to her and she only discovered it as she was clearing up the dessert dishes later. Taking it out to the kitchen she opened it and found a copy of his book on the origins of the First World War with a dedication inside. This read: *To my good friend Jane. David.*

She stood there and looked at it for a few moments, digesting his choice of words. He had included the adjective *good* in front of *friend*, which he didn't need to do, but there was no disguising the fact that it couldn't be described in any way as intimate. Hearing approaching footsteps she closed it again and set it down on top of the fridge. What had she been expecting? A declaration of undying love? Hardly.

The party broke up at midnight and the guests gradually went their separate ways. Jane was standing outside the front door watching Diego load his disco gear into the boot of his car, when she felt a tap on her shoulder and turned to find it was Paolo. There was a funny expression on his face – almost of embarrassment.

'Hi, Jane. Thanks for inviting me. It was good to meet your parents. Sorry we haven't had much chance to talk.' He hesitated and the uncomfortable expression became more pronounced. 'I wanted to ask you something: would it be all right with you if I asked Beatrice out one of these days? I mean… you and I are just good friends, aren't we? That's what you want, isn't it?' He sounded really awkward and her heart went out to him.

'Of course it's all right, Paolo. Yes, you and I are good friends.' She couldn't help noticing that these were the very same words David had used in his book dedication and the parallels were unmistakable. Clearly, David's feelings towards her were similar to her own feelings for Paolo. 'I hope we remain very good friends and I do hope you and Beatrice enjoy being back together.'

An expression of relief flooded across his face. 'Thanks, Jane. The thing is, it's clear you have somebody else on your mind.' He reached over and kissed her on the cheeks. 'Thanks again for a lovely evening and I hope it works out for you and David.'

And he disappeared into the darkness, leaving her feeling like a freshly landed fish on the deck of a boat, flailing about helplessly. Her mother had seen it, and now even Paolo had seen it. Was she really so transparent? And if they could see it, did that mean that David had also noticed the attraction she felt for him? Her thoughts were interrupted by the man himself.

'Ciao, Jane. I'm just going for a walk around the perimeter with Dino and I wondered if you might feel like keeping me company?'

Jane spun round as he emerged from the doorway behind her. 'Hi, David. Yes, of course. I'd like that. Just let me put on some sensible shoes.' She disappeared back inside and pulled on her trainers. Her parents had already gone up to bed so she closed the French windows before coming back out again. She found David and Dino waiting for her and they set off side by side in the darkness. As the lights of the house receded into the distance behind them, her night vision improved and she found she could make out the path quite clearly. It was another cloudless sky and although the moon had not yet risen, the starlight was strong enough to cast shadows. Up here away from the pollution down on the industrial plains, the air was clear and the deep velvet of the sky above their heads was filled with pinpricks of light from far distant galaxies. It was a breathtaking view.

'Did they teach you how to navigate by the stars?' His voice almost made her jump. 'There's the Great Bear and Orion's Belt, so the north must be...' He let the question hang in the air and she smiled as she supplied the answer.

'That way.' She stopped and pointed confidently towards the north, pleased to find that this memory from her military past didn't produce a wave of nostalgia.

'Correct. Well done, Captain Reed.'

'It's an amazingly clear night, isn't it?'

'It's a beautiful night.'

His voice sounded so soft and tender, she very nearly reached over and caught hold of his arm but restrained herself. If they really were just 'good friends' she didn't want to put him into an awkward situation; not least as he was the son of her employer and this could potentially scupper her job. For his part, he made no move.

They circled the estate side by side and she thanked him warmly for her present. 'But I was deliberately not telling anybody that today's my birthday. I didn't want people to think they had to give me anything. How did you know?'

'Army records are pretty detailed.' From his voice, she was pretty sure he was smiling. 'But don't worry, your secret's safe with me. By the way, I thought you were younger. You look it.'

She almost told him he would look a lot younger without all the hair but stopped short. How he chose to look was his affair, not hers. Instead, she changed the subject to Flora.

'It looked as though your grandma enjoyed herself. Dancing at ninety-five takes some doing.'

'She's a tough old bird.' She could hear the affection in his voice. 'Has she told you how she met my grandfather?'

'No. How did it happen?'

'He came through the roof of the orangery.'

'He did what?'

'He was piloting a Lancaster bomber that got hit by anti-aircraft fire and the crew had to bale out. Those old parachutes were notoriously difficult to steer and he landed in her father's sub-tropical garden.'

'Wow. And he wasn't hurt?'

'Not as badly as the pineapple plant he landed on from what she says. The thing is, this was in December 1944 and, although the Italians had signed the armistice, the

Germans were still occupying northern Italy, but at great risk to himself and the family, my great-grandfather took him in and hid him until the German capitulation in early May 1945.'

'And that's how she met him and fell in love with him. How romantic.'

'And dangerous. If they'd been caught, the family would have been shot or shipped off to a camp. It's a frightening thought.'

'It is indeed. I'm beginning to see how come your grandma's such a strong character. It must run in the family.'

'I hope you're right...'

What exactly did he mean by that?

They carried on walking, chatting sporadically about trivialities, occasionally interrupted by the dog emerging from the shadows, his eyes glowing a ghostly green in the starlight. Then, when they finally returned to her door, there was an uncomfortable moment as she stopped and turned towards him, their faces barely a few feet apart. For a second or two she wondered if he might be thinking of kissing her and she was almost on the verge of throwing caution to the winds and kissing him when she saw him take two steps back.

'Thanks again for tonight. I enjoyed myself far more than I was expecting to do.'

She had to make a conscious effort to calm her swirling emotions before answering. 'And thank you for my present. I look forward to reading it.'

'Don't feel you have to. It's just a token. Ciao.'

He and the dog turned away and she was left wondering at his choice of words – a token of what?

Chapter 24

A few days later, after her parents had gone off, Jane borrowed Dino and headed once more into the woods. Beatrice had returned to work in Rome, leaving Linda with her grandmother and great-grandmother for a few more weeks' holiday, and Diana – who had eagerly stepped into the role of surrogate mother – had volunteered to look after the little girl at the villa for the day. David was tied up as usual but Jane always enjoyed the dog's company and this left her to her thoughts. She had made a start on her book and a quiet walk on her own would give her time to think things through.

All was going well until Dino spotted a squirrel. One minute he was trotting happily along in front of her on a narrow path through the ferns and moss, the next he had charged off into the trees and all she could hear was furious barking, fast receding into the distance. She shouted his name but with no result, so she set off after him, determined not to let him out of earshot. The last thing she wanted was to lose David's lovely dog.

Running through the jumbled mix of rocks, brambles, fallen branches and massive ants' nests built of dead leaves and pine needles, she knew she had to be very careful. It would be easy to trip and break an ankle or worse. She ran for quite some time until she was streaming with sweat, still just about able to hear the dog ahead of her, before the barking suddenly stopped dead. Either he had caught the squirrel or he had given up. She hoped it was the latter and she renewed her shouts to him, even managing to produce a few piercing whistles like her father had taught her. She carried on in the direction of the last barking she had heard and was beginning to get really worried that she might have lost him when she was relieved to hear a muffled woof and a whining noise from just up ahead.

'Dino, Dino, is that you?'

The sound came again and this time the whine sounded more sinister, almost as if he were in pain. Terrified that he might have managed to injure himself, she followed the sounds until she came to an outcrop of rock surrounded by a jumble of boulders and realised that the noise was coming from the middle of them. She scrambled gingerly over the slippery moss-covered rocks and suddenly discovered what had happened. Between two huge boulders was a crevice, little wider than her shoulders, that disappeared into darkness below. From the depths came the sound of whining.

'Dino, is that you down there?'

The answer was an uncharacteristic yelp from below her feet, but it was unmistakably him. Sliding cautiously forward until she could peer into the fissure, she pulled out her phone and turned on the torch. By leaning forward she was able to see that the rock face, covered with a slippery coating of moss and lichen, sloped not quite vertically down into a cave. Inside it, three or four metres down, was the Labrador, his eyes shining back up at her in the torchlight. She was relieved to see him moving about normally so she flicked off the torch so as not to dazzle him and made comforting noises while debating what to do.

First things first, she called his master, praying that that there was a good signal and that he would respond. The sound of his voice came as a great relief.

'Jane, hi. All well?'

As succinctly as possible she gave him a report of the situation and explained as well as she could just where they were. He listened intently before answering.

'I'm pretty sure I know where you are. I'll come straight over.'

'If you bring some rope and a sheet or something to make a harness, we should hopefully be able to pull him out.'

'All right, but you just be careful. I wouldn't want anything to happen to you.'

'Neither would I, but I'll be fine. Ciao.'

She lay there for almost twenty minutes, making encouraging noises to the dog. During this time she found herself thinking of all sort of things. She thought of Mark, but this time not so much with sadness as with gentle nostalgia. She also thought of Beatrice and Paolo. They had gone out twice before Beatrice's return to Rome and appeared to be picking up where they had left off fifteen years ago. She thought of her parents who had stayed for the weekend before heading south to visit Ravenna, Bologna and Florence. It had been good to see them again and to hear how pleased they were to find her looking happier. And they were right about that. Since coming to Italy, something fundamental had changed inside her head and her heart – whether due to David or not – and she knew it had marked a turning point in her rehabilitation.

She was still lying there, her head now filled with thoughts of David as she tried, yet again, to come to terms with her growing attraction towards him, and debated whether there was any chance he might feel the same way about her, when she heard shouts. Although he was far away, she immediately recognised his voice, so she stood up and shouted back, hoping the dog wouldn't start jumping about and hurt himself as he reacted to the arrival of his master. She heard crashing as David came running up through the undergrowth towards her and she guided him with shouts and waves until he emerged from the ferns at the base of the mass of boulders and started to scramble towards her.

She pointed towards the backpack on his shoulder. 'Rope?' He nodded. 'Something to make a harness?' He nodded again so she laid out the plan she had been hatching. 'I reckon if you go up on the rocks above me and let me have the harness and the end of the rope, you can lower me into the cave. It's not quite vertical but the rock's wet and slimy so there'll be virtually no grip at all. Once I'm in there I can tie Dino into the harness and you can pull him out, followed by me.' She shot him an encouraging smile. 'Sound like a plan?'

'Sounds good, but just you be careful.'

He nodded, pulled out an old sheet and handed it to her before turning away. She watched as he clambered up the rocky outcrop above her and made the rope fast. He then braced himself against a massive boulder with the rope running over his shoulder and through his hands and called down to her, 'Tie yourself on and I'll lower you down. I just wish it could be me in your place.'

She wrapped the old sheet around her waist, gave him an answering wave of the hand, and did as instructed. Once the rope was securely fastened around her, she gripped it tightly and started to slide down into the cave. The fissure at the top was so narrow she felt sure David would never have managed to squeeze his broad shoulders through, but with a bit of wriggling, she succeeded. As he lowered her into the darkness, she could hear excited yapping from the dog below and the sound of his paws scrabbling at the rocky walls. She kept talking to him as calmly and comfortingly as possible until she felt paws scrabbling at her legs and then her feet touched the floor of the cave.

She gave two sharp tugs on the rope to tell David she had arrived, untied it from around her body and then pulled out her phone and turned the torch back on. She set it carefully on top of a nearby rock and bent down to stroke the dog, calming him until she could fashion a sort of huge nappy out of the sheet David had brought. With this cradling the dog's tummy, she tied it onto the end of the rope and gave it two more tugs. The rope tightened and the dog was lifted off the ground, giving a plaintive whine, but she stroked him gently until he was lifted out of her reach. The harness worked well and a few moments later she saw his paws disappear into the daylight. While she waited for David to release the dog and drop the rope back into the cave, she took a good look around.

The first thing she saw was a skeleton of a young deer, complete with short antlers. The unfortunate animal must have done the same thing as Dino but hadn't had somebody to rescue it. Alongside it was another, far more sinister, skeleton – this time of a snake. Although there was nothing left of it but bones, it gave her the creeps and she was relieved when she heard David's voice echoing down into the cave.

'Tie yourself on and try to scramble up the rock. I should just about be able to lift you but if you could help I'd be grateful.'

'I'm not that heavy, you know!' She smiled to herself as she tied a good strong knot. 'Okay, all tied on. Let's do this.'

The rope tightened and she began to climb the rock wall. With his help from above it wasn't too hard, although she was constantly slipping and sliding on the slimy surface and bumping her elbows as she did so. She had one bad moment when a small chunk of the rock wall broke off beneath her foot and caused her to fall sharply forward and bang her knee on the rock face, sending a stab of pain up her leg. It took over a minute of wriggling for her to squeeze through the narrow opening into the daylight and it was with an immense sense of relief that she emerged into the open, stepped onto a boulder, untied the rope and looked up at David.

There was sweat running down his face and she realised she was drenched as well. In spite of it, he was smiling broadly and she smiled back.

'See… I'm not that heavy, am I?'

'Absolutely not. I'm sure Dino weighs twice as much as you.' The blue eyes sparkled. 'Funny how my arms ache all the same…' His tone became more serious. 'Thanks, Jane. Really, thank you.'

He rolled up the rope and they clambered back down over the rocks onto the forest floor where she found the dog tied to a tree. Before untying him, David wagged a stern finger at him.

'You are a very bad dog. Leave the squirrels alone in future. No more squirrels, got that?'

The dog had the decency to hang his head for a few moments, but as soon as he was untied he jumped up at his master to be petted. Suppressing a sigh of frustration, David led them off downhill until they reached a rough track. Jane was delighted to see the Labrador trotting along normally, apparently unhurt by his slide into the cave. In contrast, her cut and bruised knee was causing her quite a bit of discomfort. In consequence she was happy to find David's Land Rover parked in the middle of the track. The idea of walking home really didn't appeal.

Looking down at her leg, she saw blood running from the cut on her knee so she slowed. 'I think I'd better clean this up.'

'I've got a first aid kit in the car. You stay here. I'll get it.'

She sat down on a fallen tree trunk and Dino the dog came over, rested his heavy head on her thigh and looked up with adoring eyes as if to say 'Thank you'. She tousled his ears affectionately.

Seconds later, David returned with the medical pack and knelt in front of her. Ignoring her protests that she could do it herself, he set about cleaning and disinfecting the wound, swatting away his dog's attempts to help. The stinging of the antiseptic was a small price to pay for feeling his hands on her bare skin, and she felt herself relax into a dreamy state.

'I don't know what to say, Jane. Thank you so much for rescuing this monster.' David stuck a dressing over the wound and straightened his back. Quite spontaneously, she reached down towards him.

'Thank you, doctor. Come and sit beside me, would you? I feel a bit weary all of a sudden.'

She caught hold of his hands and pulled him onto the log beside her. His arm stretched around her shoulders and clasped her tightly. A wave of happiness washed over her and she buried her face against his chest. A moment later she felt a big hairy paw land on her thigh and then another. The next thing she knew, an equally hairy face was nuzzling hers as the dog emitted little affectionate whimpers.

'Dino, get off her.' She heard David's voice as if from inside cotton wool.

'He's fine, David. Let him be.' She wrapped her free arm around his waist and clung there for quite some time, enjoying the feel of him and the silent, peaceful surroundings. She could hear his heart beating against her cheek and it gradually began to slow just as hers did. Finally she straightened up and found herself looking at him from close range. Even through the mass of hair she could see a gentle smile on his face and she released her hold on him, reached up, and kissed the only part of him she could see – his lips. It was only a fleeting touch but she knew she would remember it for the rest of her life.

'Thanks for looking after me.'

'Thank *you*, Jane. From the bottom of my heart, thank you. I don't know how to thank you enough. He's my best buddy. It would have been awful if anything had happened to him.'

She jumped at the opportunity. 'If you really want to thank me, all I want is to hear what happened to make you leave the army, but only if you're ready, of course.'

His eyes blinked several times, but then there was the slightest hint of a resigned nod of the head.

'I owe you that and a whole lot more.'

She waited for him to speak, wondering what he was about to reveal.

'You know I was in the SAS.' Not waiting for her response, he continued. 'It was the very last op I did. It was only a couple of months before the end of my term and it was as a result of what happened that I decided not to reenlist. I knew I had to get out and give up on the idea of a career in the army.'

He was still sitting on the tree trunk beside her, but his eyes were staring out over the trees on the far side of the road. He was speaking to her but he could have been addressing the dog, the sky or the Land Rover. His tone was deadpan, emotionless.

'It was in Afghanistan. I can't tell you where, but it doesn't matter. We were part of a mixed team of special forces from three different countries. The commander was a big guy – I can't tell you his name or even his nationality – and he was one of those larger-than-life characters that war throws up from time to time. We moved in at night on foot over the mountains. It was a long, hard climb and an even hairier descent next morning. The plan was to attack a Taliban stronghold, a major collecting point for drugs to go out and for arms to come into the country. The word was that they had a big shipment about to be collected and it was our mission to destroy it and the gang handling it.'

There was a long pause and she was just about to prompt him when he started again, his voice still low and expressionless.

'The moment we started the attack, suddenly all hell was let loose. We found out later that the enemy had been tipped off in advance and we'd walked into an ambush. A heavy machine gun on a rooftop cut through our guys and the man beside me was killed outright. After a fire-fight lasting well over an hour we pulled back. Of the twenty-four men in the group, three were dead and five seriously wounded. We needed to call in air support and then medevac for the injured, but the commander – let's call him Major Tom – was hell-bent on earning himself a silver star or whatever his country handed out for these things. He ordered us to regroup and then led us back up the hill in a suicidal second attack. Two more men were killed and Major Tom himself was badly injured.'

'But you were unhurt?'

'A few scratches, nothing serious.' He sounded miles away. 'Those of us who were still alive fell back to a defensive position and I took command. Major Tom was bleeding badly but he grabbed me and told me to attack again.' David suddenly turned towards Jane and she found herself staring into his eyes. 'I refused. I told the surviving guys to stay put and called in helicopter evacuation for the wounded instead. Major Tom's last words to me were that he would see me court-martialled for disobeying orders.'

'How many of you made it out safely?'

'Five men died in the action and two others died of their wounds before the chopper reached us. Major Tom – although, like I say, that wasn't his real name – died in the helicopter. As soon as it became clear that they'd been expecting us, it was lunacy to go ahead with the second assault, let alone a third, without air support but that's the kind of guy he was: death or glory. Well, he got death.' His voice tailed off, but he rallied. 'Six more guys were seriously wounded but survived. That left just ten of us.'

'And your mission?'

'With the help of a drone attack, we managed to get the job done, but it was tough.'

'And that's when you were wounded?'

'Yes.' This was followed by a long silence before he added, 'Walking wounded. I got off better than most.'

Jane was dying to find out more about the extent of his wounds but it was clear he didn't want to talk about them, so she just did her best to sound encouraging. 'But why leave the army? These things happen. You can't win all the time.'

'One simple reason: I disobeyed a direct order and Major Tom was right. That would have been a court-martial offence if anybody else had heard it. Luckily for me, nobody did – or at least the ones nearby claimed not to have heard a thing. The army isn't designed for people who decide to pick and choose which orders to obey. But the fact is, if the circumstances were to be repeated, I would absolutely do the same thing all over again. A hundred years ago, after the defeat at Caporetto, not that far to the northeast of here, the Italian High Command ordered hundreds and hundreds of summary executions of men who did what I had just done. No, I knew I had to get out, so I did.'

'But surely that's the end of it now. You did the right thing.' She laid a supportive hand on his arm and gave it a little squeeze. 'Now you need to get on with your life. That's what everybody's been telling *me* to do, after all.'

'Ah, but you left a hero. I left under a cloud – at least inside my head. If Major Tom had survived, all I would have got would have been a dishonourable discharge.'

'I think you're wrong. We live in different times now. The days of the Charge of the Light Brigade are long gone. The lives of our troops are far more valuable now. If anything, Major Tom deserved to be put on trial for sacrificing his men in such a foolhardy manner. From what you've told me, any tribunal would have sided with you in taking the decision to save the lives of the last of your men.'

'And myself, don't forget. No, I'm sure Major Tom would have slanted it so as to show that I was just thinking about saving my own skin.'

'I still think you're wrong.'

'Who knows? But there was more to it than that.'

'Such as…?'

'It's complicated. I'll tell you some other time.'

She tried a few more times to make him see sense, but he remained adamant that he had left the army before the army kicked him out. In the end, all she could do was to sit quietly alongside him, still gripping his arm, contemplating the horror of the events that had taken place in an anonymous Afghan valley three years earlier. War, as she knew full well, was indeed a terrible thing.

Chapter 25

She didn't see David again for several days but she knew she wanted to, and she wondered whether he might be deliberately avoiding her after his confession. There was no sign of him until one morning she spotted him out for a run. Quickly changing into her running gear, she headed out to join him as he came past her door a second time. Falling into step alongside him, she dissuaded the dog from bouncing up at her in effusive greeting and looked across at his master. 'Hi, David.'

'Hi, Jane. How's the sore knee?'

'A lot better. The main thing is I can move it perfectly well.'

'I'm glad. I told the countryside wardens about the cave Dino found and they're going to put a grill across the entrance to stop any more animals or humans from falling in.'

'Good idea.'

He was running strongly, but she was feeling a lot fitter these days and found it easy to keep up with him. They ran in silence for at least half a lap of the perimeter before he slowed slightly and turned towards her. It was clear he had something on his mind.

'That stuff I told you the other day, I'd rather you kept it just between the two of us if you don't mind.'

'You haven't told your mum or your sisters?'

'I've told them there was a firefight and a number of men died, but I've never told a soul about disobeying orders before.' He looked across at her. 'You could shop me to the military authorities if you felt like it.'

'Don't be ridiculous. The more I think about it, the more convinced I am that you did what any sane person would have done.' She slowed to walking pace and put a hand on his arm. 'It's what I would have done.'

'Thanks for that, but will you promise me to keep it to yourself?'

'I won't breathe a word to anybody, but for what it's worth, I still think you did the right thing.' Another thought occurred to her. 'Tell me something: after you left the army, where did you go? Your mum said you came back to Italy when your dad died two years ago. Where did you spend the previous year? Somewhere exotic?'

'Not exactly exotic. I spent a bit of time in and out of hospital at first.'

'In hospital? I thought you said you just picked up a few scratches and a light wound.'

'A bit more than that, but it's all healed up. I'm going to need another operation some time soon, but I don't know when yet. In fact, I've got an appointment with a specialist tomorrow.' He caught her eye. 'But I got away with my life and that's more than can be said for many of the other guys. Anyway, after I came out of hospital, I didn't feel like seeing anybody so I rented a little house in northern France and spent day after day trudging over the battlefields of the First World War, come rain or shine. The result was my first book. It's about the three hundred and six British and Commonwealth soldiers executed by firing squad for desertion or cowardice during that war. Ninety percent of them were poor devils suffering from shellshock, what we now call PTSD. The authorities back then refused to accept that it was a thing.'

He caught her eye for a moment.

'Of course you know all about PTSD. Anyway, I never even tried to get the book published. It's a grim read, I freely admit that. I was in a bad place when I wrote it and, looking back, it was probably more a way of letting off steam than anything else. It was good practice for the book I subsequently wrote and published, the one I gave you.'

By mutual consent they speeded up again and completed another two circuits of the estate before Jane felt she had done enough. When they got back, she was about to invite him in for a coffee when he surprised her by asking first. 'Why don't you go and change and give me time to do the same, and then you come across to my place? I make pretty good coffee, I promise.'

She smiled back at him. 'It's a date.'

Twenty minutes later, freshly showered and changed, she went over to his house, tapped on the door and heard his voice from inside.

'It's open, come on in.'

She walked in to a boisterous greeting from the Labrador and a friendly welcome from his master. Whether it was the result of opening up to her about what had happened or something else, there was no doubt that he was looking and sounding noticeably more cheerful compared to when she had first seen him just over a month ago. Now, if only she could persuade him to go to a barber…

This was the first time she had been inside his house and she immediately fell in love with it. It was far older than the villa and far less ostentatious. The floors were ancient terracotta, worn down by the passage of count-less feet, while the ceiling was supported by rough-hewn tree trunks. The modern kitchen units somehow comple-mented the historic feel of the place and she imagined it in midwinter with an open fire blazing in the hearth and the dog snoozing on the floor in front of it. Unlike the villa, this place felt like a home.

'What can I get you? This machine does a great cappuccino, or there's tea of course.'

'To be honest, I think I'd prefer tea, if that's all right.'

She stood and watched as he made the tea. He had changed into shorts and a fresh T-shirt and he looked good. She subjected him to a close, if surreptitious, inspection and could see no trace of a wound but she knew she couldn't ask for details. Maybe it was something of a more intimate nature. Her deliberations were interrupted by the arrival of a mug of tea.

'Here you go. I must confess that I hardly drank tea before enlisting, but after years in the British Army I'm totally addicted now. Shall we sit outside?'

Together they walked through his large living room and out of a door set in a huge glazed archway. The sun was on the other side of the house and it was refreshing to sit in the shady garden. Dino obviously agreed as he was soon stretched out at their feet, snoring peacefully. Gradually they started to reminisce about their time in the army. For her it wasn't just the shade that was refreshing. Being able to talk freely about her military career for the first time in two years produced a considerable release of pent-up emotion. From time to time she glanced across at him and got the impression it might be having a cathartic effect on him as well. Finally he made a suggestion that was as welcome as it was unexpected.

'You know I said I have to go down to Venice tomorrow to see the specialist? Hopefully, he'll tell me when the next operation will be. Well, I was wondering if you might like to come with me. The appointment's at eleven, and I thought that afterwards maybe I could offer you lunch in a little place I know to say thank you for saving Dino. What do you think? Fancy a trip to Venice? I can promise you a great meal and I need to say thank you properly.'

Jane would dearly have liked to know more about the nature of the operation he was to have but she could tell he didn't want to talk about it, but this sounded like the closest thing to a date he had proposed so far and she had no hesitation in saying yes. 'There's no need for thanks. You did all the heavy lifting.' She grinned at him. 'Not that I'm saying I'm heavy, of course. I'd love to come down to Venice with you, and lunch would be great. I'd just better check with your mum whether she needs me tomorrow.'

'I think I spotted her in the garden as we were running.' He stood up and peered through the trees. 'Yes, I think she's still there. Come on, let's go and see what she says.'

He led the way down to the rear garden of the villa. Maria was in the process of serving tea to her employer who was sitting in one of the wicker armchairs with a book. David went over and explained what he was proposing, ending with the words, 'Jane wanted to be sure you could do without her for a day.'

Veronica looked up with a broad smile. 'Of course. That sounds like a wonderful idea, although the middle of August means it's going to be terribly busy down there.'

'We'll use the boat so we should be able to keep away from the crowds. I thought I'd take Jane to Burano for lunch – you know, *Da Marcello*.'

Veronica sighed. '*Da Marcello* – what a super little restaurant. I haven't been there since before your father died. Maybe when we're back in Venice in the autumn I might go there again.'

Jane and David exchanged looks. This was most encouraging. Veronica was actually contemplating a trip to a restaurant. Things were looking up and David obviously agreed.

'You're very welcome to come with us tomorrow.'

'Oh, dear Lord, no, not in July. The people, the heat, the insects... No, you two go and enjoy yourselves and then come back and tell me all about it. If Marcello's cooking's still as good as ever then I promise I'll let you take me there when it gets a bit cooler.' She glanced across at Jane. 'This reminds me of something I've been meaning to say, Jane. When's the wedding you're going to in Bath? This weekend, isn't it?'

'It's on Saturday. My flight's on Friday afternoon.'

'And what are you going to wear?'

'I bought a dress when I was last in Venice with David. It's nothing special, but it should do.'

'Why don't you go and put it on?'

'What, now?'

'Yes, if you don't mind. I'd be interested to see it.'

Jane nodded and hurried back to her house, slipped out of her shorts and top and into the dress. It looked fairly good, although her everyday sandals didn't do it justice. Maybe she should invest in a pair of smart shoes while she was in Venice tomorrow. One thing was for sure: nice as they were, if she were to wear her new really high heels for a full day she would end up lame. Back outside again she found herself standing in front of mother and son, feeling as if she were on the catwalk. Probably noting her discomfort, David was the first to react.

'That looks lovely, Jane.'

She shot him a grateful look and waited for his mother's judgment. When it came, it was less effusive, but was followed by a tantalising offer.

'David's right, you do look good, but with your long legs and those cheekbones you'd look good in anything. I was just wondering, seeing as you're going down to Venice in the morning, if you'd like to wear something from my collection.'

'That's amazingly generous, but I couldn't possibly turn up at the wedding dressed in something a film star would wear without the bride attacking me with an axe. It's her day, not mine and the last thing I'd want to do would be to spoil it.'

Veronica burst out laughing. 'You're so considerate. But I've got all sorts of dresses, not just ball gowns. Let me think…'

Jane sat down and waited for her decision. The idea of borrowing another piece of cinema history was very appealing but the last thing she wanted to do was to upstage the bride. Finally Veronica came up with a solution. 'I've got it: Audrey Hepburn. It might be a bit of a squeeze – she really was wafer thin – but how about that chic black dress she wore in *Breakfast at Tiffany's*? Now, before you ask, I haven't got the original. Believe it or not, it was sold a few years ago for over half a million dollars. No, but this is by the same designer, Givenchy, and it's the exact same style but it's knee-length, not a long gown like the one in the movie. To the best of my knowledge, Hepburn never wore my one, but it's a lovely dress, and not in the least bit risqué or flashy so you don't need to worry about being assaulted by the bride.' She grinned at Jane. 'This one's not black but a very subtle cornflower blue colour which, unless I'm very much mistaken, should match your eyes perfectly.'

'But it must be worth a fortune. What if I damage it or if my bag gets lost at the airport or if somebody spills…?'

Veronica held up a calming hand. 'Don't worry about it. Honestly. It's only a dress.'

'Only a dress…' Jane felt almost overcome. 'I don't know how to thank you.'

'No thanks necessary. Now, let me explain where you'll find it…'

Chapter 26

Next day's drive to Venice contained far fewer awkward silences than the previous one. Jane and David chatted about all sorts – mostly their shared experiences in the army – and he even laughed out loud on a number of occasions. Jane was delighted for him and pleased for herself at being able to open up to somebody at last. The fact that he had also been in the army and been wounded formed a real bond between them and she found her feelings for him increasing as he became more and more communicative.

When they got to Venice after another long slow crawl in heavy traffic over the last few kilometres, it was a relief to get into the launch. It was very hot today – the temperature was already over thirty and it was barely mid-morning – and the slight breeze as they motored down the Grand Canal was most welcome. This time David just dropped her at the palazzo landing stage and carried on down the canal to his appointment with the specialist. Jane stood on the landing stage and watched him head around the bend of the canal, wondering what the specialist was going to say and just how serious the operation he would have to have might prove to be.

After he had disappeared from sight, she told herself worrying about it wouldn't help so she unlocked the door, turned off the alarm and took a good look around, picking up the mail from the doormat and checking that all was well. After that, she hurried upstairs to her employer's dress collection.

Following Veronica's directions, she easily located the dress. Slipping it out of its protective covering she felt that same sense of awe she had felt when she had handled the Ingrid Bergman dress. This, too, was silk, and as she held it up against her body she saw what Veronica had meant by it maybe being a tight fit. Although she was all alone in the house it felt somehow improper to strip off here, but rather than waste time running upstairs to her apartment, she decided to change down here, not least as the room boasted no fewer than three full length mirrors. Although the dress was a bit fiddly to get into, she was very pleased to find that it did in fact fit, and she could even breathe. She checked herself out in the mirror and had to admit that Veronica had got it dead right once again. It could have been made for her and the colour was a perfect match for her eyes.

She felt sure it would look even better with heels, so she decided to head out to look for a new pair of shoes, with a bit of heel but not so high that they would cripple her if she wore them all day long. Very carefully, she removed the dress and hooked it into a special suit bag for carrying, vaguely wondering if she should look for a hat as well but dismissed the thought. She had never been very keen on hats and had no idea what sort of thing people were wearing these days and so decided to stick with her initial decision and go bare-headed.

Back outside again, she found the crowds as thick as ever, but the shop where she had bought her original shoes was only a couple of hundred yards away and she managed to get there without too much trouble. There was no point searching for shoes to match a dress she would never wear again, so she opted for a pair of stylish, nude pumps with just enough heel to look good but not enough to stop her walking normally – or as normally as possible. They weren't cheap but she was spending so little of her generous pay at the moment that she was easily able to afford them. Armed with her purchases, she stopped off for a cold drink at her favourite cafe by the Rialto bridge and was cheered to receive a warm welcome from the owner who recognised and remembered her. This gave her a little glow of satisfaction and a feeling of homecoming. Yes, she really was settling into life in Italy.

At midday she was on the landing stage waiting for David and the moment she climbed into the launch, she queried how the appointment with the surgeon had gone. His answer was heartening.

'He says he's very happy with everything and the op's going to be next week.'

Restraining the urge to ask him to explain exactly what this was going to involve, all she could do was wish him well.

He took her through a maze of narrow canals in order to show her a bit of 'alternative Venice' as they weaved their way through to the eastern side of the city. It was fascinating to run close alongside Renaissance buildings, past hidden squares almost devoid of people, and to squeeze underneath humpback bridges. Some were barely wider than the boat and once or twice she had serious doubts as to whether they would be able to fit, but they did. When they finally got out of the houses and into the open waters of the lagoon, they headed east, past the island of San Michele. High red brick walls punctuated by white arches surrounded the island, and dark green fingers of cypress trees rose up beyond the walls. Back in Venice behind them David pointed out the hospital where he would have his operation, right on the water's edge. Over to the left of them was the airport where a regular procession of aircraft from all over the world were delivering yet more tourists to this unique city. Jane gazed at the views in fascination but couldn't help returning her attention to her companion from time to time. It was nice being with him – more than nice.

It took almost half an hour to get to Burano, which was a considerably smaller island than Murano, and Jane was immediately fascinated by the brightly coloured houses lining the narrow canal that ran through the middle of it. There was every colour of the rainbow – and a few more – and the whole place had a far more relaxed feel to it than the claustrophobic streets and alleys of Venice. The restaurant was close to a wonderful old bell tower, not dissimilar to the bell tower in St Mark's square, but with the difference that this one was leaning sideways at an alarming angle. David told her it had been like this for hundreds of years and everybody was hoping it would keep standing.

Trattoria Da Marcello was down a narrow alley and from the outside it was unprepossessing, with peeling plaster on the walls and a gaudy fly curtain at the entrance. Inside however, the narrow hallway opened into a large dining area with arched doors at the far end leading onto a brick-paved courtyard garden dotted with lemon and orange trees in massive terracotta pots. David was welcomed as an old friend by Marcello – once the portly restaurateur had recognised him beneath his mass of hair – and received an affectionate hug. When David introduced Jane, she found herself on the receiving end of an appraising look and a broad smile from Marcello before he showed them to their seats and she couldn't help wondering if David had brought other women here. Their table was over to one side of the courtyard, shaded from the sun by the surrounding high walls and the branches of a lone palm tree that rose up even higher than the houses.

After Marcello had left them, David looked across and she could see his eyes smiling. 'I should have checked. You do like fish, don't you?'

'I love fish and any kind of seafood – big, small, hot, cold, prawns, lobster, crab, mussels – you name it, I love it all.'

'Excellent. My father told me – and I've since confirmed it time and time again – that Marcello does the best seafood in Venice. Hopefully we're in for a treat.'

'Today's already a treat. Being ferried around Venice by my own personal boatman is more than most people ever experience but, tell me something: Marcello didn't recognise you at first. Does that mean you haven't been here since you decided to go all bohemian?'

He nodded. 'It must be four years now. I was still in the army when I last came here.'

She did her best to keep the conversation upbeat. 'Well, if the food's as good as you say, you must have incredible willpower to be able to stay away for so long.'

'The fact of the matter is that I've hardly been out for ages.'

'That would appear to be something you and your mum have in common.' She paused for a few moments. 'Mind you, I'm a fine one to talk…'

'But you're doing better now, aren't you? And, with your help, Mum's really perked up. Did you hear what she said about maybe coming here? That's real progress.'

'If this is your first time back here in four years, then the same applies to you.'

The bright blue eyes smiled again. 'And for the same reason. It's your influence. Since meeting you I feel so much more cheerful.' She could see him grinning now. 'It may not look like it to you but, trust me, I do.'

At that moment Marcello appeared with a carafe of water, two glasses of Prosecco and a saucer of plump mussels and shelled prawns surrounding a little pot of what looked like green wasabi sauce. 'Now what can I get you to eat?'

He rattled off a list of fish – the names of most of which Jane didn't recognise – and she was delighted to go with David's suggestion that they opt for the mixed seafood antipasti, followed by *fritto misto*. Marcello was keen to persuade them to have a risotto before the fried fish but Jane shook her head and told him she wouldn't be able to do it justice. He went off to get them a bottle of good Valdobbiadene Prosecco and she settled back to enjoy the meal, the surroundings, and the company. And today David really was good company.

They talked about the army but they also talked about his books and hers, their respective families, their hobbies, interests, but not relationships. Neither of them spoke about their wounds and he made no mention of any women in his life. For her part, she made no reference to Mark or the handful of other men she had dated before Mark. Still, she found him remarkably easy to talk to and he was definitely more communicative than he had been so far. The meal flashed by and she barely registered the exceptional quality of the cuisine. The *fritto misto* in particular was excellent and in among the lightly fried fish, octopus and prawns, there were bright yellow courgette flowers and slices of green and red peppers which gave the whole dish a fascinating look and taste.

By the time they asked for coffee, she felt she knew him a whole lot better – although just why he had decided to bury himself in his research and look like a hippy still remained a mystery.

After a long, lazy lunch lasting almost two hours, they set off in the launch once more. On the way back across the lagoon, she asked if it might be possible to visit the island of San Michele and he said he was happy to oblige. He told her the island had been transformed into a huge cemetery a couple of hundred years earlier on the orders of Napoleon, with a number of famous people including Ezra Pound and Igor Stravinsky buried there. When they reached the landing stage, he dropped her off and said he would wait with the boat in case he got moved on. Evidently parking problems in Venice weren't restricted to roads and cars. She told him she wouldn't be long and walked in past the imposing white marble façade of the church of San Michele in Isola.

In sharp contrast to Venice itself, there was an air of peace and tranquillity on the cemetery island. She could hear little noise apart from a distant aircraft, a handful of squabbling seagulls and the crunch of her feet in the grit as she walked down the narrow alleys flanked by cypress trees, towards the red brick chapel in the centre. All around were graves ranging from simple crosses set in the ground to marble-clad tombs and elaborate private chapels belonging to old Venetian families. Most of the handful of people she saw were carrying bunches of flowers and there were flowers on many of the graves, with bees and small birds flitting among them.

Inevitably, as she wandered through the cemetery, her mind turned to Mark. He had been interested in history and she felt sure he would have loved this city and this little island. Somehow, although she was surrounded by the dead, this wasn't a sad place, but rather a place of reminiscence and reflection. She sat down for a few minutes on a bench shaded from the full strength of the sun by a tall cypress tree and let her mind roam, doing her best to banish the bad and trying to remember the good times she and Mark had enjoyed together.

She was resting there, her head full of memories, when her eyes were caught by the sight of a little feather blown across the gravel by the breeze. It wheeled and turned, caught for a few moments on a fallen twig before moving on. Finally, as it reached the far side of the alley, a stronger gust lifted it skywards and she watched as it floated ever upwards until it disappeared into the burning sun.

A single tear ran down her cheek, but she made no move to wipe it away. Just like the feather, Mark had gone and she was left here to continue with her life. She savoured the months she had spent with him but she now knew that the moment to move on had arrived. By the time the breeze and the heat had dried the tear on her cheek, she felt the beginnings of a smile forming on her face. She didn't know what the future might hold for her, but she knew she was not only ready for it, she was looking forward to it.

Chapter 27

The night before her flight to the UK, David surprised her and the rest of the inhabitants of the villa by announcing that he was going to do a barbecue and they were all invited. Because of Linda he made it an early evening event, and the setting sun was still warm on Jane's back as she walked up past the villa to his house. The shade provided by the ancient trees surrounding it came as a welcome relief from the August heat. Following her nose, she walked around to the side of the house and found David already busy at the grill. By his side, predictably, was his dog. Dino wagged his tail when she appeared but the enchanting aroma of grilling meat kept his nose firmly pointed at the main attraction.

David looked up and she saw his eyes smiling. 'Ciao, Jane. Help yourself to a drink. I daren't take my eyes off the meat or we'll be eating cinders.'

She shot him a big smile. 'What about you? Can I get you a drink while I'm at it?'

'There's cold beer in the fridge in the kitchen. If you don't mind, I'd love one.'

By the time Jane came out with two bottles of beer, the others had arrived and Maria ignored David and Jane's protests and insisted on taking over as waitress, pouring Prosecco for the grown-ups and her own home-made lemonade for Linda and herself. Jane went over to join the group and stood with them, looking out over the village and onwards down the valley. Today the plains beyond were almost completely shrouded in heat haze and she felt sure the temperature and humidity down there must be uncomfortably high. Beside her, Diana was thinking the same thing.

'I was talking to Silvana this afternoon. It's thirty-six degrees in Vicenza today.' She glanced at Jane. 'Was it terribly hot in Iraq?'

'The summer months were absolutely boiling.' She was delighted to be able to talk increasingly freely about this now. 'One time I had to reprimand a couple of my men for frying bacon and eggs on the bonnet of their Land Rover – that's how hot it was. Trouble is, it ruins the paintwork.'

'*My men?*' Diana giggled. 'What was it like being in command of a bunch of hunky men? It must have felt strange.'

Jane grinned. 'They weren't all hunky by any means but, yes, it was a bit weird at first but I soon got used to it – and them to me.'

'David, did you ever get bossed about by a woman?' Diana went over to see how the food was coming on and Jane went with her.

'Apart from Mum, Nonna, Maria, and you and your sister, you mean? No, I don't think that ever happened.' He flicked that little internal switch and addressed Maria in Italian. 'I'm just saying how you used to boss me about.'

Maria smiled back at him. 'And I still do. Now concentrate on what you're doing and look out for those sausages or they'll burn.'

He glanced back at Diana and Jane and winked. 'See what I mean.'

He didn't burn the sausages and the meal was excellent. It was all very simple – meat, spicy sausages, grilled cheese and salad – but it was exactly what they needed on a sultry evening like this. They ate seated around a long table made from a pair of diagonal slices taken from what must have been a massive tree trunk. It was mounted on hefty trestles and positioned beneath two chestnut trees, from where there was an unimpeded view across the hills. It was a delightful evening in good company, and it would have been very peaceful if a pair of red squirrels hadn't chosen to put in an appearance in the branches high above them just as the sun went down.

The humans were all instantly deafened by Dino's furious barking as he scrabbled ineffectively at the tree trunk in a vain attempt to climb up and see the squirrels off, and it was only when David handed him the T-bone from the grilled steak to eat that he finally subsided. While the charming little animals continued to play in the branches above, sinister growls came from under the table, accompanied by even more sinister cracking and crunching sounds as the dog took out his pent-up aggression on the bone.

Silence once more descended on the table and Jane heard David give a heartfelt sigh. 'Thank the Lord for that; a bit of peace and quiet.' He disappeared into the kitchen and reappeared with three candles which he lit and set on the table. There wasn't a breath of wind and they didn't even flicker. A few minutes later he returned to the kitchen and brought out a strawberry tart and a big tub of ice cream. As he served dessert, he explained that he had got both from the shop in the village.

'I'm all right at grilling meat and that sort of thing, but I've never tried baking.' He switched seamlessly into

Italian. 'You're the best baker I know, Maria. Maybe I should ask you to teach me. What about you, Jane? What are you like in the kitchen?'

'Sponge cake and chocolate brownies are about my limit. Maybe we should both take lessons from Maria.' She was delighted to see him looking and sounding so relaxed and communicative. Maybe he had been telling the truth when he had told her he was coming out of whatever had been troubling him. She certainly hoped so.

When the meal came to an end and he and Maria served coffees and teas, Diana groaned theatrically and glanced down at Linda whose eyes were closing. 'This little one needs to go to bed, so I think I'll head back to the villa as well. It's the heat, saps your strength... mind you, the Prosecco probably doesn't help.'

Luciana pulled herself to her feet and reached for her sticks and Flora followed. 'We'll come with you. I'm asleep on my feet.'

Veronica was following suit when a thought struck her. 'Jane, what time are you off in the morning?'

'The flight's late afternoon. I'll head off after lunch. In fact, I was going to ask if somebody could give me a lift.'

She saw David look up, but Veronica beat him to it with a sensible suggestion. 'Just take one of the cars and leave it at the airport. If you take the Fiat, that leaves the Mercedes and David's got his car as well. Just take it.'

David looked almost disappointed and Jane wondered if he had been about to offer to take her. Certainly, another hour of his company would have been nice, but the car suggestion was eminently sensible so she thanked Veronica and accepted the kind offer.

After the others, including Maria and Alvise, had started to leave, Flora hung back and caught Jane by the arm. Lowering her voice, she glanced over to where David was clearing up the dirty dishes. 'Why don't you stay and give David a hand? I'm sure he'd like that.' She accompanied this with a little wink before turning and following the others.

She left Jane feeling nonplussed. First her mum, then Paolo and now Flora appeared to have worked out that she was falling for David. Was she really that transparent?

'Jane, help me finish this bottle of Prosecco, will you? It's a shame to see it go to waste.'

David's voice roused her from her daze and she turned back towards him.

'I shouldn't, really. I've drunk quite enough this evening as it is. But a little drop more won't hurt. And let me give you a hand with the dishes.'

Despite his objections, she helped him collect all the dishes and take them back inside. He refused to let her start washing them, objecting there was a dishwasher for that very purpose, and dragged her back outside again. He poured the last of the wine into two glasses and they walked over to the top of the field and sat down on the tinder-dry grass. She deliberately sat down close enough to him to be able to feel his warmth through her shoulder, and it felt good. A few moments later a black shadow wandered up and plonked himself down at their feet, stretching out with a deep sigh. David leant forward and ruffled the dog's ears before turning his attention to Jane.

'Cheers. Hope you enjoyed the barbecue. It looks as though Dino did.'

She clinked her glass against his. 'I enjoyed every minute of it. You live in such a wonderful place and I love your family.' She took a sip of wine and decided that he sounded relaxed enough for a few questions. 'So, what's the plan? Do you intend to spend the rest of your life locked away up here like a hermit or are you going to re-join the outside world?'

He didn't reply immediately and she let her eyes roam down the valley, past the lights of the village towards the flickering orange glow of streetlights down on the plains. In many ways, being up here really was like being marooned on an island, separated from reality, and she could well understand why he had chosen it as a place of refuge.

'I honestly don't know.' He sounded distant, pensive. This was followed by a long, but not awkward, silence before he spoke again. 'It depends on so many things, starting with the operation next week.'

'Is it a big operation? Should I be worried for you?'

'That's very sweet of you, but it isn't life-threatening. I should be out again in a matter of days.'

Yet again, she struggled to repress the urge to ask him exactly what it would entail but his reticence to talk about it stopped her. The fear that had been plaguing her returned to the forefront of her mind. What if he had been injured somewhere particularly intimate and personal? It was a scary thought but this would explain his depression and his reticence to talk about it. She took another, bigger, mouthful of wine before replying.

'That's good to hear. So, assuming all goes well – and I'm sure it will – what's the plan? Will you come down to meet the Hollywood delegation with your mum in early September? Come to think of it, that's barely ten days or so from now. I'm sure she'd be grateful for the support.'

'I'm sure she would. I will try, honestly. It all depends how things go...'

He lapsed into silence and she didn't press him any further. Instead, she turned the conversation to Saturday's wedding and told him the names of some of the people she expected to see there. He even recognised a few of them and asked to be remembered to them. She took this as another good sign. Even though he had opted to use a pseudonym for his writing and had locked himself away in isolation, it now appeared that he was at least prepared to reveal his existence – albeit three years on.

Sitting there alongside him like this, she realised without a shadow of a doubt that she was falling for him hook, line and sinker. If he were to take her in his arms and kiss her, she knew that not only would she not resist, she would relish the idea. But he didn't. She could hear warmth in his voice and his interest at what they were talking about, but it didn't go any further. She still remembered the feel of that fleeting kiss she had given him after Dino's rescue and considered proving that she was a modern woman who was prepared to make the first move. However, she immediately discarded the idea because of the possible complications this might create for her and her job if he didn't react the way she hoped. Finally, unable to put up with the suspense any longer, she decided to go off home and stood up. He immediately followed suit.

'Going? Dino and I'll walk you to your door.' Hearing his name, the dog opened his eyes, stood up, and shook himself.

Together, they walked back down past the villa and across the grass to the summer house. When they reached the door, there was a part of her that came very close indeed to asking him to come in, but once again she held back and this time she realised it was for two reasons and, interestingly, she could honestly say that Mark was no longer one of them. The main reason for saying nothing was of course the fact that she worked for his mother and a false move now could screw up what had become a most enjoyable job, and the second was the Labrador who was standing staring at her as if to say, 'I'll be watching you'.

She was still mulling these thoughts over in her head when David threw her into total confusion by leaning towards her and kissing her softly, but tenderly, on the lips. She found it the most natural thing in the world to reach up with her hands and catch hold of his head and pull him tightly towards her, savouring the feel of him in her arms. She kissed him back and melted against him. Even the mass of hair rubbing all over her face didn't spoil the excitement and enjoyment she felt. Finally, he had reacted as she had been hoping.

Then, as if he had had a change of heart, he stepped back and caught hold of her hands. This time when he spoke, his tone was hushed, his demeanour more low-key.

'I'm sorry, that was a mistake. This can't go anywhere. I shouldn't have kissed you. Please excuse me. Forget that happened.' The words came out in a rush.

She recoiled in shock and her response was immediate and heartfelt. 'I'm sorry, David, but I can't forget what just happened. It was magical. I wanted that kiss to last forever.'

She saw him shake his head and the moonlight glint in his eyes. 'I'm really sorry, Jane, but it's best if I leave you now. I hope you enjoy the wedding. I'll see you when you get back.'

And, with that, he and his dog disappeared into the night, leaving her feeling more confused than she had ever been.

Chapter 28

All the way to the airport next day and throughout the whole flight, there was only one thought in her head. It was those four words he had murmured: 'This can't go anywhere'. What did they mean? Why couldn't things develop between them? The way he had behaved, it had almost sounded as though he was being prevented from getting closer to her by something or somebody beyond his control? Was there somebody else? There had been regret in his tone – of that she felt sure. But why?

It was early evening by the time she got to Heathrow airport and met up with her parents. In the car they told her about the touring holiday they had had in Tuscany and further south after their weekend with her, and she told them more about life in the hills and Dino's brush with disaster in the cave. It was only when they had finished dinner and she was in the kitchen helping her mum with the dishes that she decided to tell her all about David. She left nothing out, telling her how her feelings for him had been deepening almost on a daily basis, culminating in the barbecue and his inexplicable behaviour at the end of the evening. Her mother listened intently right to the bitter end before commenting.

'You say he sounded regretful? So you think he maybe wanted things to get more serious but he was somehow being prevented from doing so?'

Jane nodded despondently. 'I'm afraid that's the way it sounded to me.'

'And what do you think might be holding him back? Is there another woman involved?'

'I don't think so...' Jane hesitated, racking her brains yet again. 'He's never so much as hinted, and I'm pretty close to the rest of his family now – I would have thought they might have mentioned something.'

'Mind you, even with that beard and all the hair, he's a very good-looking man – and very wealthy, don't forget. It seems very unlikely he should be all alone. Are you sure there isn't someone?'

Jane shook her head in frustration. 'I honestly don't know for sure, but my gut feeling is no. We all live fairly close to each other up there in the hills. I'm sure I would have noticed if a strange woman had appeared, and he definitely hardly ever leaves the estate. No, I don't think it's that.'

'Maybe there was a woman but she's gone. Could it be he's in the same state you've been in for the last two years, grieving for his lost love?'

This scenario too had crossed Jane's mind more than once but all she could do was give a frustrated sigh. 'I suppose anything's possible...'

'Or is it maybe because you work for his mother? You know, sort of an *Upstairs Downstairs* thing where he can't get involved with a servant?' Catching Jane's eye, she clarified. 'I don't mean that they think of you as a servant – what I mean is an employee.'

'I don't think it can be that either. Like I say, the family seem to have accepted me as one of their own. His mum's often told me to try to talk to him, and his grandma even winked at me last night and told me to stay behind with him after they'd all gone. No, I don't think it can be that.'

'That leaves his mysterious wound. I mean...' Her mother was sounding unusually uncomfortable. 'If he was hurt... you know... down there, maybe he feels he isn't a proper man any longer and it wouldn't be fair to you.'

Jane had done an awful lot of thinking about this very same thing and she had come to a conclusion quite early on. 'It wouldn't matter to me. There's more to a relationship than sex. I could live with it, if that's what's holding him back.'

'It's not just sex. That would probably mean no children...'

Jane shook her head decisively. 'Honestly, I could cope. It would be disappointing, but I could handle it.'

'Fair enough, then that leaves us with the whole gold digger thing. Weren't you telling me his sister was complaining that she can't tell whether men are interested in her for her, or for her money? Maybe it's the same for him. It's no coincidence that rich people often marry rich people – look at film stars for instance. Maybe he's afraid you're only interested in him for his money.'

'I've been wondering about that, too. It would be awful if it's true, but he's never struck me as somebody with much interest in money. Of course, he's mega-rich, the whole family is. The palazzo in Venice alone must be worth millions, but I really don't think he's that into money. He drives around in a battered old Land Rover; I've hardly seen him in anything but scruffy shorts and old T-shirts, and he doesn't appear to have any expensive hobbies like yachts or racing cars or anything like that. But yes, I have been wondering if that might be it. Of course, these days there are prenups. If he was worried that I just might be out for his money, he could always get me to sign something, couldn't he?' She gave a frustrated sigh. 'It's so baffling. I'd almost prefer it if he just said he wasn't interested and to leave it at that.'

Her mother caught her eye and gave her a wry smile. 'You wouldn't really, though, would you?'

Jane dropped her eyes. 'No...'

'Well, you're just going to have to sit down and talk to him, aren't you? When are you flying back to Italy?'

'Sunday evening. I should be home late that night.'

'Then go and see him first thing on Monday morning and have it out with him. That way you should at least get some sort of closure.' She took off her apron and hung it over the back of a chair before catching hold of Jane's arm and leading her towards the lounge. 'Now, tell me about the wedding tomorrow. Who's getting married and where?'

—

Jane travelled down to Bath by train next day and took a taxi to the old pub a few miles outside the city where she had booked a room. This was conveniently near the converted medieval barn where Fergus and Virginia's wedding was due to take place. It was in a typical Somerset village, complete with thatched cottages, village green and a stream with ducks bobbing up and down in the clear water. It could have come straight off a Visit Britain poster. She could well understand why they had chosen this spot and she had to admit that somewhere in the fantasy perfect wedding scenario she had been imagining since she was a teenager, a place like this had figured highly.

Her single room at the Boar's Head was unexpectedly large and she had ample space to get ready and change. After squeezing into the Audrey Hepburn look-alike dress, she set about doing her hair. It took a while, but she managed to curl it up on her head in a reasonable facsimile of the updo the hairstylist in Venice had created for her before the charity auction. She had kept the chopsticks and now inserted them in pretty much the same spots as he had done, hoping that it would all hold together. Finally stepping into her new shoes, she checked herself out in the mirror. She had to admit that she looked all right, and immediately found herself wishing that David were here to see her.

Needless to say, thought of David took her mind back to all the questions that had been flying around in her head and she was so caught up in her thoughts as she emerged from her room for the short walk up to the old barn at a quarter to four, that she didn't immediately recognise the army officer waiting at the bottom of the stairs in his full-dress uniform.

'Jane, hi… blimey… you look fantastic. Wow.' He sounded gobsmacked.

She blinked a couple of times and emerged from her reverie. 'Tommy, how amazing to see you again!' In fact, it wasn't amazing to see him at all. Captain Tom Cruise – he always insisted on specifying that he wasn't the film actor, although at six foot six and with freckles and carrot-coloured hair there was little chance of confusion – had been a close friend of Fergus as well as of Mark and her. He looked very smart in his formal uniform and she couldn't miss the fresh major's crowns. She pointed at them. 'Looks like you're going up in the world. Congratulations.'

'What, oh yes, that.' He was still looking stunned. Finally his face burst into a broad smile. 'Jane, you can't imagine how happy I am to see you and to see you looking so good.' He sounded quite overcome and she realised that the last time they had met, she had been in a hospital bed, hooked up to a drip and swathed in bandages. She went across and kissed him warmly on the cheeks.

'And I'm feeling good, too. Where's Margie?' Tommy and Margie had been married for some years now.

'She couldn't come. She's just had baby number two. I mean literally the day before yesterday.'

'Congratulations to you both. Another boy?'

'No, a girl this time – Eloise.'

'Lovely name. And Margie didn't mind you leaving her all on her own?'

'Her mum's with her, and her sister, and little Donny.' He grimaced. 'He's teething. To be honest, I was quite glad to get away. Besides, I promised Fergus and Ginny I'd take you under my wing in case you were... you know, still a bit under the weather.'

This even managed to bring a hint of a smile to Jane's face. 'A bit under the weather' was a very English way of describing what she had been through. Still, she told herself, she was coming out of it now. She could feel that. She caught hold of his arm and let her smile broaden. 'That's very sweet of you, but I'm a lot better now. Come on, lead the way. It all kicks off at four, doesn't it?'

Together they walked out of the pub and up the road to the old barn. It was a gorgeous day with warm sunshine – not suffocating Venetian sunshine, but pleasant English summer sun with just enough freshness in the air to make it feel agreeable. When they reached the old barn, they found a gaggle of people outside on the carefully mown

248

lawn, enjoying the sunny afternoon. Among these, Jane recognised a number of familiar faces, many of them in dress uniform. For a moment she felt a stab of regret that she was no longer part of that community but she didn't have much time for regrets as a succession of people came over to greet her and tell her how good she was looking. Of course, in comparison to the bomb-blasted wreck she had been, they were right – but she felt sure the Audrey Hepburn dress probably deserved most of the credit.

The ceremony took place in the lovely old tithe barn with magnificent oak beams spanning the vaulted ceiling and ancient flagstones on the floor. The walls were lined with pictures and mirrors and the whole place smelt of lavender and roses. The bride looked stunning, as did the groom in his finest uniform, and Jane felt sure there was no risk of Virginia feeling outgunned by the film star dress and so was able to relax. The service was quite short, but during it, Jane couldn't help thinking of Mark and how, if things had been different, it might have been him and her walking up the aisle today. She allowed herself a few moments of melancholia before taking a deep breath and counting her blessings. She was alive, fully restored to fitness and health, and gainfully occupied with a job she loved, working with people she liked a lot. And then there was David...

Or was there?

The happy couple emerged from the barn after the ceremony and walked out under the swords of an honour guard of fellow officers while the guests showered them with rose petals. All in all it was faultless. Out in the sunshine, waiters and waitresses served champagne and canapés as the newly-weds circulated among the guests. When Fergus and Virginia reached Jane, they looked genuinely delighted to see her. She and Mark had often spent time with them as a couple and Jane knew them as well as any of her former colleagues and liked them both. She gave them hugs and was quick to admire the bride's dress.

'You look absolutely super, Ginny. I love the dress. It's gorgeous.'

'Thanks, Jane, and you're looking ever so good… and happy.' Virginia leant towards her. 'We've both been very worried about you after what happened.'

Jane was relieved to find she was able to respond without too much emotion in her voice. 'I'm so fortunate to have very good friends like you two, and I know it's been a worrying time for everybody but, honestly and truly, I'm much better now.' She took a deep breath. 'I still think of Mark, but the hurt's died down. I've accepted that life has to go on and I've found myself a super job over in Venice.' She gave them a brief account of what she had been doing for the past couple of months and read pleasure on their faces. In return she heard what had happened to the battalion during the intervening years: who had been promoted, who had left, and new faces who had joined. By the time the bride and groom moved on, she had caught up with the news and felt sure the happy couple had been relieved to find her looking and sounding upbeat – which she was, give or take the unknown quantity that was David.

After a while they all slowly made their way across the lawn to a large marquee. A quick look at the seating plan revealed that she and Tommy would be sitting with Jack and Denise, another couple from their regiment, and four other people whose names she didn't recognise. What she did recognise, however, was the uniform that the dark-haired army major opposite her was wearing. After they'd all sat down and introduced themselves, she took the opportunity to check her facts.

'Am I right in thinking you're in the Rifles? I recognise the insignia.'

He nodded. 'That's me. Are you military too?'

She sensed a sharp intake of breath from Tommy beside her, but gave the major a smile and a nod, and felt Tommy relax. 'Yes, I was a captain in the Sappers until a couple of years ago, but I left.' She didn't go into detail and he didn't ask.

They chatted amiably in general terms about military matters until two of the wives decided it was time to change the subject. Jane couldn't blame them. When military personnel got together it was instinctive to talk shop and it could be pretty boring for outsiders. A few minutes later the best man stood up and proceeded to reveal as many embarrassing moments from Fergus's past as he could fit into the allocated time. It was a most amusing speech and he had everybody laughing – even a red-faced Fergus.

After a starter of cold salmon salad which was very nice but not a patch on the fish she had enjoyed at Marcello's restaurant in Burano, there was a far more serious, but mercifully relatively short, speech from the father of the bride. The main course was roast lamb with all the trimmings and fresh mint sauce, and it was accompanied by a choice of white or red wine and jugs of water. Jane tried the wine, rather liked the red, but decided to pace herself and mostly drank water. The last thing she wanted was to get sloshed and maybe descend into a morbid state of regret for what might have been.

Finally, while the bridegroom thanked everybody and gave his speech, dessert was served. This was summer pudding with clotted cream and it was definitely the star of the show as far as Jane was concerned. She resolved to buy a big pot of clotted cream to give to Veronica as a little taste of home when she returned to Italy.

Once the meal was over, the tables were cleared to one side to reveal the dance floor. The band struck up and they all stood and watched the newly-weds have their first dance together as man and wife. Jane looked on and was genuinely happy for them. Other couples then joined them on the floor but Jane decided to look for a seat and found the Rifles major sitting on his own. She gave him an enquiring look.

'Not dancing? Mind if I join you?'

He pulled out a chair and waved her down. 'Help yourself, please. I pulled my Achilles a few weeks back so I'm just a bystander. My wife's gone off to dance with some chap. What about you? Has Tom deserted you?'

Jane smiled. 'Seeing as I'm on my own, he's been looking after me, but I've told him to go and have some fun.' She checked they weren't being overheard. Now that she had the major alone, she had a question to ask.

'Can I ask how long you've been in the Rifles?'

'Almost ten years now.'

'Tell me, did you ever come across a friend of mine, David Cooper?'

He immediately nodded his head. 'I certainly did. We served in Afghanistan together for a year or so. You heard he left the army? A shame; he was a good soldier.'

'Were you in Special Forces with him?'

'No, he went on to the SAS but I stayed put. I know my limitations and, besides, I'm a family man. My wife would have divorced me.'

Jane smiled back at him. 'I can well imagine.' She did a bit more digging. 'It was such a pity about him being wounded, wasn't it?'

He nodded grimly. 'I heard something about that but at least he got out with his life.'

Jane cursed silently. It looked like this man wasn't going to be able to shed much light on David's mystery wound. Nevertheless, she had one more go. 'Did you hear how it happened?'

'I heard some stuff, but you know the SAS, they tend to keep things very much under wraps. I know the operation went badly wrong and there were fatalities. It must have been a bad business.' He raised himself in his seat and looked around, searching the faces in the crowd. 'I can't see him at the moment, but I thought I spotted Taffy earlier. Do you know him?' Seeing Jane shake her head, he explained. 'As far as I know, he's still in the SAS. He'd know all about it, if you can persuade him to tell you. If I see him, I'll send him your way.'

At that moment Tommy reappeared and refused to take no for an answer as he dragged Jane onto the dance floor. The rest of the evening flew by and Jane found herself dancing with a long line of men, from the bride's seriously drunk uncle to a very precocious twelve-year-old boy who actually grabbed her bum at one point. All in all, she had a very good time and by the end, standing outside and waving farewell to the newly-weds as they left in a stylish vintage Rolls Royce, Jane was feeling happy with just one regret, but that regret was soon to be satisfied.

Chapter 29

She was standing on the lawn, savouring the smell of freshly mown grass and the warm summer evening when the Rifles major came looking for her accompanied by his wife. With them was a tall, hard-looking man in his thirties wearing the uniform of a captain in the Welsh Guards.

'Jane, this is Taffy. I told him you're a friend of Dave Cooper. Now, I'm afraid we're off. We have to drive back to Aldershot. It was really good to meet you. Do say a big hello to Dave when you see him. Wish him all the best from us. Bye.' Jane thanked him warmly and shook hands with them before he and his wife headed for the car park.

Jane watched as they disappeared down the drive before addressing the tall man. 'Hi, there. Thanks for coming to see me. I hope I'm not dragging you away from anything. It's just that I'd really appreciate it if you could spare me a few minutes.' She breathed deeply and took the plunge. 'I gather you're in the SAS. I know it's something you guys don't like to talk about, but it's important to me.'

His response was a guarded nod. 'Yes.'

'I'm Jane Reed. I used to be in the Sappers but I'm out now.'

He nodded again. 'I know.' His face was still expressionless, his eyes hard. There was no doubt this was the face of a man who had seen and done things that others had not. In a way, she felt a bond with him. She, too, had seen and done her fair share of scary stuff.

'The thing is, Taffy… can I call you Taffy?' He nodded yet again so she continued. 'I was wondering if you knew my friend.'

'Dave Cooper? Yes, I know him well… I knew him very well.' His Welsh accent was soft, although his tone was still guarded.

This was sounding promising. 'That's good. The thing is, I wanted to ask…'

At that moment Tommy arrived to say he was heading back to the Boar's Head, and she was on the point of telling him she would come along later when the tall Welshman did it for her.

'That's where I'm staying, too. You and I can walk back together if you like, Jane.'

Jane shot him a grateful look and gave Tommy a warm hug, thanking him for looking after her. 'Give my love to Margie and good luck with the new baby.'

He glanced across at the Welshman and then gave Jane a lurid wink before heading off down the road. After he had gone, she turned to Taffy again.

'Fancy a nightcap? I think they're still serving drinks over in the marquee.'

They walked back to the tent and for old time's sake she ordered two pints of bitter. They sat down at the far end, away from the band, and she held up her glass towards him.

'Cheers, Taffy. Thanks for sparing the time to talk. Listen, I'd better lay my cards on the table here. I work for David's mother and I see a lot of him. Over the past few weeks, I've found myself getting ever closer to him but I can tell he's still got serious hang-ups and I feel sure it's all to do with his final mission, the one in which he was wounded. He's told me a lot about it but I still can't get to the root of the problem. I don't suppose you can shed any light on what happened, can you?'

The Welshman took a long draught of beer and she could almost hear the cogs turning inside his head. She took a sip of her own beer and realised this was probably a mistake after champagne and red wine, so she set it down again and waited for him to respond. It was a full minute before he spoke.

'We don't talk about ops.' There was a longer silence and she was on the point of trying again when he spoke. 'I heard you won a CGC. Is that true?'

'Who told you that?'

'Fergus did. He spoke very highly of you.'

Now it was her turn to nod. 'Well, it's true. Nothing spectacular; I used to be in bomb disposal.'

He gave a non-committal grunt but she sensed he must have reached some sort of conclusion. 'You say you know Dave well and you like him. What did he tell you about that final op?'

'He went into a fair amount of detail but obviously he couldn't tell me much, for the same reason I quite understand that you can't either. Let's just say I know it was Afghanistan, I know they walked into an ambush and a lot of men died.'

He stared at her impassively for another minute before speaking. '*We* walked into an ambush.' The stress on the pronoun was unmistakable.

'You were there?'

'I was there.'

'Can you tell me what happened? I give you my word it won't go beyond the two of us.'

He didn't answer directly. 'Did he tell you about the guy leading the mission?' Clearly he was fishing to see just how much information David had felt he could trust her with.

'He said he was a big guy, larger than life. He called him Major Tom – although he said that wasn't his real name.'

For a second, a hint of a smile passed over the hard face. 'We called him a whole lot worse than that. Did Dave tell you what a crazy bastard he was?'

Jane nodded. 'Completely reckless. Two assaults, even though it was clear you'd walked into a trap. The guy sounds mental.'

'Did Dave tell you I almost shot him myself?'

Jane looked up in amazement. 'No, he didn't say anything like that.'

'I even had him lined up in my sights at one point. He was intent on getting us all killed.' He took another big mouthful of beer. 'Anyway, I didn't, but I came close. I'm afraid my training just wouldn't let me do something like that. As it turned out, an enemy sniper did it for me a few minutes later.'

'David said that after Major Tom was wounded, he took over. He called in a medevac chopper before completing the mission with the help of a drone strike.' She saw Taffy nod and decided the moment had come to ask the big question. 'David told me he was wounded in that final assault. Did you see what happened?'

'Yes, I saw it happen. He was hit by a burst of machine gun fire.' His voice was low, his tone sombre.

Jane listened in horror. 'And the burst from the machine gun…?' She held her breath, anxious to hear what the answer would be but dreading it at the same time. When it came, it was delivered in deadpan tones that only accentuated the horror of the words.

'The machine gun ripped the side of his face open.'

A long pause then ensued as Jane struggled to take in the ramifications of what she had just heard. Suddenly the mass of facial hair was explained. It wasn't just because he didn't care about his appearance. The hair was camouflage. Beneath it, his face had been torn apart. She found herself thinking of the photograph of the handsome, confident young officer that was now hidden amongst the other photos on her phone. Now his time in hospital, his retreat into isolation, his lack of interest in his appearance, in people and in life, all made sense. She had been blown up in an explosion but had had the good fortune to emerge almost as good as new. From what she had just learnt, such would never be the case for Captain D.C. Cooper and she felt an overwhelming urge to break down and cry.

'Jane...' The big Welshman must have sensed her anguish. 'You look as though that came as a shock. But surely, if you know him and you're close to him, you must have known about that?' He sounded remarkably caring for a hard man.

She took a couple of deep breaths and looked up. She could feel the tears in the corners of her eyes but she refused to let them run. Clearing her throat, she explained to Taffy about David's mass of hair that did a wonderful job of hiding any deformity. She told him how sad she felt, now that she knew the full truth of what had happened and of the consequences of such life-changing disfigurement for him. She read compassion in those hard eyes and received an unexpectedly tender piece of advice from him.

'You need to know something, Jane. Dave saved my life that day. He saved all our lives – and he still got the job done. The regiment don't do medals but if ever a man deserved one it was Dave out there in the back of beyond. He led from the front and he knew exactly what to do. Now, by the sound of it, he's the one who needs saving and he needs all the help he can get. You're a very brave woman – your record speaks for itself – and you're going to need all your courage if you want to help him. It's going to be tough but, believe me, he's worth it.' She saw him study her for a few moments before adding, 'But you already know that, don't you?'

She felt her cheeks flush and just nodded her head.

She saw him reach into his pocket and pull out the order of service for today's wedding. He tore off the back page, produced a pen and scribbled a few lines before taking the piece of card and folding it carefully in half and half again. Finally he pushed it across the table to her.

'When you see him next, would you give him this? It's just a short message asking him to give me a call. I've put my number on there.' He caught her eye. 'And would you do me another favour? Take my number and save it on your phone. Let me know how it all pans out, will you? I've tried to contact him but he seems to have disappeared off the radar.'

'The other members of his family told me he's cut himself off from everybody over the past few years, but maybe that's beginning to change. Of course I'll give him your message. Thank you so much for talking to me and I promise I'll do whatever I can to help your friend.' Her voice was hoarse, but she held herself together.

To her surprise his face cracked into a real genuine smile. 'I know you will. Somehow I have a feeling he's fallen on his feet with you. It was a chance in a million that he found you. If anybody can help him, I feel sure it's you.'

'I do so hope you're right. Thanks again, Taffy, and I promise I won't tell a soul. Now at least I have a clear idea of what happened.' She took the piece of card, tucked it into her purse and then stood up. 'I promise I'll keep you informed. Now, I'm beginning to feel tired. I think it's time I went to bed.'

He swallowed the rest of his pint and stood up. 'I'll walk you.'

They walked back to the pub in silence and when they reached the bottom of the stairs, she gave the big man a hug and thanked him for his frankness. He gave her a glimmer of a smile in return and headed for the bar, while she went up to her room.

In spite of her fatigue, the first thing she did was to sit down in the seclusion of her room and open Taffy's note to David. She read it with tears in her eyes. It wasn't long, but the message was deeply moving. Somehow, the impassive Welshman had managed to understand how deeply she felt about his wounded former comrade in arms, and his own affection for David was clear to see.

> *Dave, I've met and talked to Jane. You're very lucky to have her. With her help you can do anything. I know you can. Don't let her go.*
>
> *Call me. It'll be good to talk. We all love you, man, and we miss you.*
>
> *Taff*

Here, away from prying eyes, she finally let the tears flow. It had been an emotional day and a cathartic evening. She knew she would carry out her promise to deliver the note to David and do all she could to help him, but she could only hope his reaction would be positive – particularly to the Welshman's apparent assumption that they were a couple. Taffy had scribbled his number across the bottom of the card and she immediately copied it onto her phone. One thing was for sure – he would be one of the first to hear if things worked out between her and David.

Of course that still remained to be seen…

Chapter 30

It was almost midnight on Sunday by the time she got back up to the Colli Euganei. She had spent an enjoyable, if anticlimactic, day visiting two old university friends in Bath before heading for the airport, and this had had the great advantage of preventing her from obsessing over David. It was only as she sat waiting for her flight that her thoughts, inevitably, had returned to him yet again.

The mystery of those four little words was now revealed – or at least she thought she might now know what had been holding him back. Knowing that he would be disfigured for the rest of his life, he had been deliberately distancing himself from her to save either of them getting too badly hurt when she realised the true nature of his injuries and inevitably – or so he thought – dumped him as a result. Putting herself in his place, she could imagine how his brain would have been working. He was no longer the handsome young man he had once been and, in his mind, there would be no way she would want him in such a disfigured state. And yet, she knew full well, as far as she was concerned, that was rubbish.

The story Taffy had told had, if anything, only served to increase her feelings for David. So he was scarred... so what? She had her own fair share of physical and mental scars, even if she had been lucky enough not to have them across her face. She knew, and she resolved to make it her mission to ensure that he knew, that these things were only superficial. The David she was falling in love with – and she found herself prepared to use that word, at least inside her own head – might look like a caveman, but his hirsute appearance hadn't put her off, so what difference did it make if there were scars below? What mattered was the man beneath the skin and everything she had heard about him this weekend only made her love him more. Far from only trying to save his own skin, he was a hero, and even a battle-hardened warrior like Taffy had said so.

As she drove in through the gates and up the drive, she looked across at David's house but there were no lights to be seen. The villa was similarly dark, so she headed back to the summer house and decided that her confrontation with him would have to wait until the morning.

Next morning, as she was making herself a cup of coffee and checking through the latest emails and messages to her employer, she heard a familiar scratching sound outside her door and opened it to find a very happy Labrador clearly overjoyed to see her again. She was equally delighted to see him and crouched down on the doormat to cuddle him while, at the same time, looking around for any sign of his master, but there was none. Accompanied by the dog she went back into the kitchen, gave him a biscuit and finished making her coffee. She was sitting at the computer, nibbling a biscuit – not the canine variety – and sipping her cappuccino, when running footsteps had her looking hopefully at the open door. A second later little Linda came rushing in, arms extended in greeting.

'Jane, *bentornata*. You're back!' It was a lovely mixture of the two languages and it brought a broad smile to Jane's face.

She jumped to her feet, caught hold of the little girl's arms and swung her around in a big circle before setting her down and hugging her. It really was good to see her again.

'*Ciao, bella*. I hope you've been good while I was away because I've brought you a present from England.' She had a thought. 'You've been to England, haven't you?'

'I've been lots of times. I've been to London, to Cambridge…' – she paused for thought – '…to Paris.'

Ignoring her little guest's haziness as far as geographical matters were concerned, Jane went over to the worktop and produced the package she had bought in Bath the day before. The other package, containing clotted cream, strawberry jam and scones for Veronica, was safely in the fridge. Hopefully a Devonshire cream tea bought in Somerset would come as a pleasant surprise to her employer.

'Here, this is for you.'

The little girl took the package from her and tore the paper off eagerly to reveal a Paddington Bear bag with three English story books inside. Jane watched Linda flicking through them and went on to explain. 'I thought you might find the bag useful for carrying all your bits and pieces around.' Linda had a habit of leaving her possessions – from sunglasses to crayons – lying all over the estate and many of them ended up being chewed to pieces by the Labrador. 'You can even put Teddy in there if you like, and the books are for you to read with your mummy or your Auntie Diana or with me.'

Linda came over and gave Jane a big hug, thanking her most politely. The dog, not to be outdone, followed her and stood up on his back legs, pawing both of them while his tail wagged furiously.

At ten o'clock they went over to the villa where Linda went off to 'help' Maria in the kitchen while Jane had her regular morning session with her boss – now brought forward from its original midday time slot as Veronica's sleep pattern improved – and she gave her the food parcel from the UK, which was gratefully received.

'Jane, how lovely of you. Clotted cream's one thing we never find over here. Mind you, it's probably just as well, or I'd have blocked arteries by now if it were available. I love the stuff. Diana's still in bed but we must have mid-morning cream tea when she wakes up.' She indicated a chair alongside her. 'Sit down and tell me how it went. I hope the bride didn't attack you with an axe after all.' She almost giggled and Jane couldn't miss just how much brighter she was looking and sounding these days.

'It was a lovely wedding.' Jane went on to tell her all about the old tithe barn, the little village, the pub, and the compliments she had received on her appearance in the Audrey Hepburn dress. For now, she made no mention of the fact that she had met and talked to Taffy, or of what she had learned from him about David. At the end of her account, she decided to mention him as casually as she could. 'I met a load of old army colleagues and some of them knew David and asked me to say hi to him. I'll go over and see him later to tell him.'

Veronica looked up and shook her head. 'I'm afraid you've missed him. There was a call from the hospital yesterday. They want him there this afternoon for a series of tests and the operation's going to be tomorrow. He left an hour ago. Alvise has given him a lift down to Venice. He said there's stuff he has to do first – like having a shave and a haircut for example. That's good news, isn't it?' She was putting a brave face on it but Jane could see she was worried for her son.

Of course, Jane now knew why he would have to have at least a shave, if not a full haircut, before the surgeons could work on him but, for the moment, she made no comment. Instead, she did her best to reassure Veronica that he was in good hands, although the disappointment that she wasn't going to be able to see him and talk to him for some days was intense. 'I'm sure it'll all go well. He told me the hospital's very good. How long is he likely to be kept in?'

'He didn't know for sure. Hopefully only a day or two. He's hoping he'll be out well before the end of the week.'

'That sounds good. Not least as there's an email just arrived for you this morning saying that the Hollywood film people want to meet you on Friday. Apparently the Venice film festival starts this weekend. Hopefully David will feel up to keeping you company.' Although she had a feeling that he was unlikely to put in a public appearance with fresh scars on his face and without his hairy camouflage.

Veronica looked up in consternation. 'Friday? I hadn't realised it would be so soon.' A look of anxiety swept over her, and Jane leapt in to provide more reassurance.

'It'll be fine. They ask if they can meet up with you in the morning. I was thinking – why don't you invite them to the palazzo? It's a wonderful environment and it'll feel more comfortable to you if you're on your own turf.'

Veronica looked slightly reassured by the suggestion. 'That's a good idea. Even if David can't make it, Diana's going to be around and, of course, you'll be here. I'll phone Beatrice to see if she can come up as well.'

'I already texted her and she said she'll definitely be here. She says she'll try to come up on Thursday night and then she'll take Linda back to Rome on Monday as school will be starting soon.' She checked her iPad. 'I told your agent, too, and she says she'll be flying in on Thursday afternoon. I'll get Alvise to pick her up from the airport and I'll ask Maria to get a guestroom ready for her.'

'Thank you so much, Jane. I don't know what I'd do without you.'

'I was wondering if it might be a good idea to offer to run the Hollywood folk across to Marcello's restaurant in Burano for lunch on Friday after the meeting. They're visitors to Venice so we might as well give them a bit of a tour.'

'That's a wonderful idea. Will you set that up?'

'Of course. Now, coming back to David, what about visiting him in hospital? I'd really like to see him. If it's all right with you, maybe we could take it in turns?' This would give her the chance to see him alone and Jane knew this was something she needed to do.

Veronica nodded. 'Of course, that's a good idea. Can you check to see what visiting hours are, please? From what they told him he'll be having tests and so on today, so maybe I'll just call him tonight. Hopefully the operation's still on for tomorrow morning, and then once he's had it, we can take it in turns like you say, depending on what he and the medics tell us. In the meantime, we really need to start thinking about moving back down to Venice so as to be near him and to get ready for the film people. What day is it today… Monday? God, that gives us so little time. I'll talk to Maria and see what she says, but I'd like us to move back tomorrow if possible or Wednesday at the latest so we can get ready. I'll go and see her now.'

Later that morning Jane was back in her kitchen, checking to see how many people there would be in the Hollywood party so she could book Marcello's restaurant for Friday lunch, when there was a tap at the door. She was surprised to see that it was Signora Flora, today wearing a remarkably stylish pair of yoga pants and a Christian Dior T-shirt accompanied as always by her leopard-print ballerinas. Jane gave her a welcoming smile.

'Hello, good morning. How nice to see you.' And unexpected. This was the first time Flora had visited Jane in the summer house.

'Ciao, Jane, I was wondering how the wedding went? Was it nice to be back in England?'

Jane invited her in and told her about her weekend – but without mentioning what Taffy had told her – while she made coffee for them both. After Flora had oohed and aahed over the old barn and the picture-postcard village, she brought up a subject much nearer to home that sent a rush of colour to Jane's cheeks.

'Feel like telling me how it went with David last Friday night?' Seeing Jane's discomfiture, she extended a hand and patted her arm. 'Sorry for being nosey, but the thing is, I'm convinced the two of you are made for each other.'

Jane took a gulp of boiling hot coffee and very nearly had to spit it out again. Nursing a scalded tongue, she swallowed cautiously and did her best to reply in measured tones. 'For what it's worth, I'd love to think you might be right.'

'So…?'

Jane collected herself and decided to tell the truth. 'On Friday night it went wonderfully well for about twenty seconds and then it didn't.'

'I'm afraid you're going to have to explain.'

So Jane did. She told Flora what David had done that fateful night and then what he had said. Reading sympathy on the elderly lady's face, she decided to open up fully and went on to tell her what she had learned at the wedding about his injuries, ending with the conclusion she had drawn. 'I have a feeling he deliberately didn't want to take things further because he was afraid I wouldn't want him once I found out he'd been disfigured. It's awful to think he might believe I could be so superficial, but I can't think of any other reason for him to behave like that.'

Flora reached forward with both hands and caught hold of Jane's on the table. 'Oh, Jane, I'm so sorry for you. The thing is, he's been burned before.'

'Now you're the one who has to explain.'

'Have you ever heard of Scarlett?'

'Scarlett O'Hara, *Gone with the Wind*?'

'This is a different Scarlett; still American, but very much twenty-first century. She comes from one of Boston's oldest and wealthiest families, and she and David were together for two or three years. There was talk of engagement and marriage.'

'*Was* talk…?'

Flora nodded. 'It all broke up three years ago.'

'I'm sorry.' Jane didn't know what else to say. Her brain was desperately trying to work out where this might be leading.

'Nothing to be sorry about if you ask me. If you'll pardon my language, she was a cow' She let out a hiss of exasperation. 'Anyway… the thing is, she dropped him like a hot potato after he was wounded. You see, appearance was everything to Scarlett. Apart from all her designer clothes, between you and me she must have spent a fortune on surgical enhancement. Mind you, not as bad as her mother – they say that woman's had so many nips and tucks, when she winks her eye, her leg lifts.'

In spite of the circumstances, Jane almost laughed. 'So you're saying that this Scarlett dumped David because she couldn't stomach being associated with somebody who had been scarred?'

'Exactly. Can you imagine the effect it had on him? There he was, lying in hospital, fearing for his looks, if not his life, and the woman who might have been his future wife takes one look at him and says, "Sorry, darling, but I'm off. You're on your own." Talk about kicking a man when he's down!'

Jane sat back and digested what she had just heard. Just like her mother had said the other night, David had quite possibly hooked up with a very wealthy woman so as to rule out the chances of a gold-digger being after him for his money rather than himself, only for her to turn her back on him in his hour of need. It was disgusting, but it helped to explain his reaction on Friday night. Once bitten, twice shy. He had stepped back after that kiss because he had been afraid of falling into the same trap once more. She took a tentative sip of coffee and ran her other hand through her hair in frustration.

'Wow, what a cow indeed! And where is she now?'

'Diana tells me she's just about to marry the owner of a chain of casinos in Las Vegas, according to *Hello!* magazine. Sounds like a match made in heaven.'

'Poor David, talk about a double whammy. Little wonder he decided to drop out and take refuge up here. After what he's been through, it's a wonder he's still sane.'

'It's been hard, all right. That's why I'm so pleased to see the way he's come on over the past few weeks and I know it's down to you. He's clearly attracted to you.

You've had a tough time as well and you can understand what he's been through far better than most people. It's like I said; I'm convinced you're made for each other.'

'I hope you're right.' Jane gave Flora a nervous smile. 'And you wouldn't object if he was?'

'Object? I can't think of a better partner for him. Of course I give you both my blessing, but first, you need to have a serious talk with him – sooner rather than later.'

'That's lovely to hear, thank you so much, and thanks for telling me this. Now all I've got to do is convince him that I'm a different kind of woman from Scarlett.'

'He already knows that, I'm sure.'

–

Jane spent the rest of the day making arrangements for the Hollywood people as well as working through more of the fan letters. The bag was beginning to lighten now and she reckoned she should have dealt with them all by the end of September. David was never far from her thoughts, and after a late snack lunch, she tried phoning him to wish him well but received the *we have been unable to connect you* message. Presumably he was already in the hospital and her heart went out to him.

Later on that afternoon she took Dino for a vigorous walk up the hill behind the villa and they both sat down for a well-earned rest when they reached the top. It was another scorcher of a day and she could feel her heart pounding. At her feet, the dog was panting like a steam train. She looked down at him affectionately and rubbed his tummy with her foot as she addressed him.

'Looks like you're going to have to come back to Venice with us until your master returns. That means you won't have all this space to run around in.'

He stretched and grunted happily while the realisation dawned on her that as soon as David was well enough, he would no doubt return to his house up here while she and his mother would take up full time residence an hour and a half away in Venice. It was a sobering thought. She had got so used to seeing him and his lovely dog on a regular basis up here that it was going to be grim to be separated from them.

She wondered if it might be possible for her to come up at weekends – maybe using the excuse of taking Dino for walks in the woods – and stay in the little house. The moment this occurred to her it simultaneously crossed her mind that she hadn't seen any radiators in the little summer house. Maybe the reason it had been given that name was because it was only for summer use and she wouldn't be able to stay there in the colder months. For a few moments she had an alluring image of sharing a house – and a bed – with David before reality once more descended on her. She had yet to find out whether he saw the relationship developing or whether he still intended to keep his distance, even though she now knew and didn't care about the nature of his wounds. She wasn't another Scarlett and she knew she would do all she could to prove that to him.

She pulled out her phone and tried calling him again, and this time was delighted to hear it ring and then to hear him answer.

'Jane, hi, how did the weekend go?' He sounded surprisingly cheerful for somebody about to go under the knife. Just hearing his voice sent a surge of emotion running through her, and she had to make a conscious effort not to purr with pleasure over the phone.

'Hi, David, it's great to hear your voice. Where are you?'

'Sitting in a hospital corridor, waiting for an X-ray. How was the wedding?'

'It was lovely and I met a number of people who know you and who asked me to say hi to you.' She reeled off the names of everybody she could remember, but avoided mentioning Taffy or what he had told her or, indeed, that he had written the note. This would be something for when she and David were face to face and alone. She told him all about the wedding reception and gave him the good news that she had been able to handle the host of memories her reunion with old friends and comrades had thrown up, without drama. He sounded relieved and delighted for her and gave her his own news: the operation was scheduled for the following morning and he promised to contact her afterwards to tell her how it had gone. There was just one awkward moment when she told him she intended to come and see him after his operation. The news was greeted by stony silence but, fortunately, at that moment he was called for his X-ray and he just bade her a hasty goodbye.

She sat there looking blankly at the screen for a few moments, wondering if he would refuse to let her see him. After what she had learnt from Flora, she knew she was going to have to tread softly but that, as she reminded herself, was something she had been trained to do. She hoped she would be able to live up to Taffy's and Flora's expectations – and her own.

Chapter 31

Jane received a text from David just after lunch next day reading simply:

> All done. Op went well. Talk tomorrow or the next day.

She shot him off an equally short reply:

> Great news. Look forward to talking. x

Just to be sure, she went up to the villa to check that he had also been in touch with his mother. She found Veronica in the back garden with Alvise, moving the furniture about.

'Hi, Veronica, have you heard from David?'

Her employer straightened up and nodded. 'Yes, he phoned a few minutes ago. He says the op went well. He sounded a bit dozy but that was probably just the anaesthetic. The specialist has told him they need to keep him in for a few days as the dressings need changing regularly. I told him we'll leave him in peace today and start going to see him tomorrow evening. If we all move back to Venice tomorrow morning, it's just a short walk across town to the hospital and it simplifies things. All right with you?'

'Fine by me.' Jane glanced at the wicker armchairs. 'Would you like me to help with moving these?'

'No thanks, there's no weight to them, and I need a bit of exercise. It gets wet and very cold up here in the autumn and winter so we bring them in. Tomorrow morning, as we've got Linda and Diana and her monster suitcase to think of, I was wondering if you wouldn't mind setting off first and driving them along with Maria down to Venice, while Alvise and I close up here. Then if you can come back up to collect me and the dog, Alvise can bring the last of the stuff in the Fiat. All right with you?'

'No problem, although I have to say I'll be sorry to leave.' Jane glanced out over the tree-covered hills and the regular rows of the vines below. 'It's a gorgeous place and it's had a really positive effect on me – and on you, right?'

'My husband used to call these the healing hills. Any time one of the family caught a bad cold or felt under the weather he'd pack us in the car and come up here. It never failed. But don't worry about going back down to Venice. Don't forget we're going back to one of the most beautiful and fascinating cities in the world. There'll be operas, ballets, exhibitions, shows, balls and, of course, the *Festival del Cinema*.' She caught Jane's eye. 'And this autumn I intend to get out and about and start enjoying life again. I hope you feel the same way.'

'I really do. The healing hills have done us both good.'

Early next morning, Jane crammed the Mercedes full of bags and cases and drove Diana, Maria and Linda down to Venice. Inside the air-conditioned vehicle they were very comfortable but when they arrived at Venice and opened the doors, the heat was still intense – maybe not as bad as a month earlier, but still hot and very humid. They started unloading the bags and it was only then that it occurred to Jane that somebody was going to have to drive the launch along the Grand Canal and the only boat she had ever piloted had been a pedalo one summer in Greece. She queried how they were going to manage, and Diana then revealed that her brother wasn't the only one who had grown up messing about in boats.

'I'll drive. It'll be fun. It'll be my first time out on the water this year. I'm looking forward to it.'

After they had loaded all the bags into the boat, Diana started the engine. Although Jane offered to go with them, Maria and Diana told her they could cope with unloading the luggage when they reached the palazzo, so Jane returned to the car and drove back up to the villa to collect Veronica and Dino. An hour or so later, just as she was starting the climb into the hills, her phone started ringing and she felt a little thrill when she saw who the caller was. She pulled into a convenient lay-by and answered.

'Hi, David, how're you feeling?'

'I feel fine, thanks.' His voice sounded strong and she rejoiced. 'It's all a bit sore but no big deal. Are you guys moving back down to Venice today?'

'Yes, I was just saying to your mum yesterday how I'll miss being up at the villa. I've loved being in the hills.' She hesitated and then decided to go for it. 'And I've loved being with you and Dino. I'm going to miss you.'

'And I'm going to miss you, too.' There was definitely a wistful note in his voice, and now would have been a good time for him to add something along the lines of 'but I'll come down to Venice to see you as often as I can' or even 'you can always come and stay with me,' but he didn't. Nevertheless, she ploughed on.

'I can come to see you later today – if you like. Your mum's planning on coming to the hospital this evening and I thought I might come with her if that's okay.'

There was a definite delay before he replied. 'I'll check with the medics but it should be fine, even if it's just a quick chat through a glass screen. They're very wary of infection at the moment so I'm being kept closeted away until it all heals up.'

'Just seeing you will be great.'

'Just don't expect too much.' The insecurity in his voice was palpable.

She decided to throw caution to the wind. 'Taffy told me what happened to you. So what? I can't wait to see you.'

She had to wait some time for his reply. 'You saw Taffy and he told you?' His voice was hoarse.

'He told me everything. Like I say, I can't wait to see you. Believe me.'

At least, she thought to herself, she should be able to see him this evening and talk to him, although she had been hoping for a hug at the very least. The bad news was that it sounded as though the serious conversation she needed to have with him about where they went from here might have to be delayed still further. It was frustrating in the extreme, but there was nothing she could do about it for now.

'Well, if you're sure…' He was still sounding tentative.

'Of course I'm sure.' She adopted a less serious tone. 'You're not the only person around here to be injured in the line of duty, Captain Cooper. Just you remember that.'

'Yes, but…'

'Yes, but nothing.' Aware of his continued discomfort, she changed the subject slightly. 'Your mum's looking forward to seeing you again as well.'

'I'm delighted she's prepared to get out of the house, even if it's just for a short walk through the town.' He sounded brighter. 'She's been stuck at home for so long. I look forward to seeing her.' Now would have been a good time to add the words 'and you' but he didn't.

Back at the villa, she found Alvise in the final throes of loading the Fiat. She spotted several boxes of fat red tomatoes, freshly picked pears, and a crate of wine in the boot, alongside a number of jars containing porcini mushrooms, artichoke hearts and olives. He saw her looking and grinned.

'You can't beat home produce. There's more wine, fruit and vegetables and a big bag of polenta flour stuffed in behind the front seats. All you need to take are Her Ladyship's bags and the dog. You should have plenty of room in the big car.'

'Would you prefer to take the Mercedes? I'm just as happy driving the Fiat if you like.'

He shook his head. 'No, you go with Her Ladyship. That way you can speak English together. Maria's convinced it's been speaking English with you and the girls which has brought her out of her shell. Personally, I think it's your influence, rather than the language but, whatever it's been, it's worked. She's so much more cheerful nowadays.'

'Long may it continue. Now all she's got to do is to start writing again.'

Flora and Luciana came along to see them off and there was a definite sparkle in Flora's eyes as she gave Jane a hug and kiss on the cheeks. Jane was sorry to leave her but promised to come back and see her again as soon as she could. Whether this would be with David remained to be seen. She and Veronica chatted almost all the way back to Venice, and the change compared to the first few times she had met her was palpable. Mind you, Jane told herself, Veronica wasn't the only one. She, too, was feeling much more cheerful than even just a couple of months earlier – or, at least, she would be once she had had the chance to talk to David properly.

After calling ahead, they found Diana waiting for them with the boat when they arrived in Venice. By the time they had unloaded the bags and the dog and Jane had squeezed the car into the garage, Alvise also appeared in the little Fiat and they managed to get everything and everybody into the launch and headed down the Grand Canal to home. Huge banners on some of the bridges announced the *Festival del Cinema* and the crowds in the city didn't appear to have lessened, even though September was just around the corner. Luckily, out here on the water, they could still breathe.

It was past two by the time they arrived at the palazzo and Jane was mightily impressed to find that not only had Maria removed the dustsheets from the furniture and opened up the shutters and windows to air the old building, she had also prepared a meal for them all. Jane joined the family for a late lunch in the dining room looking out over the canal, and she had to admit that the view here onto centuries of history really did take some beating, even if there were no wide-open spaces or wooded hills. Above all, she had a feeling of homecoming and when she went up to her apartment after lunch it felt familiar and welcoming, not least as she was accompanied up the stairs by the Labrador, who immediately stretched out on her floor and was soon snoozing contentedly. She decided to follow his example and lay down on her bed feeling a bit drowsy – as a result of the hours of driving and also probably helped by the glass of wine she had consumed with lunch – and within moments she was asleep.

–

Jane and Veronica managed to avoid the worst of the crowds and got to the hospital surprisingly quickly, finding themselves with fifteen minutes to kill before the agreed time of seven p.m. for their visit to David. Jane suggested stopping for a coffee in a little cafe just along from the hospital and this gave her and Veronica a chance to talk. First, Veronica asked for a progress report on Jane's book and sounded very pleased to hear that it was coming along well. Jane tried to explain what point she had reached.

'You know they say you should write about what you know? Well, I've set the start of the book in London but the main part is going to be here in Venice.'

'That sounds exciting. Let me know if you want me to take a look at the first few chapters for you, or maybe you prefer to wait until you've finished?'

'I'd love you to take a look at what I've done. I'll print out what I've got for you. Thank you so much. And what about you? Still no sign of your muse returning?' To her considerable surprise, she saw a little smile appear on her employer's face.

'I don't want to speak too soon, but I was talking to my mother-in-law last night and then I had an interesting dream. I think it just might add up to the bare bones of a new romance.'

'That's fantastic news. Do you want to tell me about it or do you prefer to keep it to yourself?'

'I need to work out a few more details but then I promise I'll tell you, and you can let me know what you think of the idea. I hope you approve. It might be a bit controversial.'

'That sounds intriguing, and exciting.' Jane almost felt like getting up and giving Veronica a hug. 'That's the best news I've heard for ages. Now all we need is for David to tell us the plastic surgery to his face has been successful, and that'll be that.'

Veronica shot her a whimsical look. 'So you know all about his wound now, do you? Did he tell you, or was it Diana?'

'Neither. It was a chance meeting with a comrade in arms of his at the wedding last Saturday. He gave me the whole story. David had told me some of what happened, but hearing it from a third party was fascinating.' She shrugged apologetically. 'I had to promise I wouldn't repeat what the guy told me – although I must admit I did end up telling your mother-in-law yesterday – but what emerged clearly is that David acquitted himself brilliantly.' She caught Veronica's eye. 'You've raised a very brave man, but also one with considerable respect for the lives of his men. You can be very proud.'

Veronica looked quite overcome for a moment before she started talking, now in a more sombre voice. 'Thank you. I was very much against him joining the army, but he was dead set on it and of course my husband saw it as continuing the family tradition. There have been Coopers in the British Army for almost two centuries. When I heard he'd been seriously wounded, I was devastated. Peter, my husband, was distraught and I often wonder if the cancer that killed him a year later was somehow brought on by what happened to David.'

At that moment a waiter arrived to take their order. After ordering a cappuccino for herself and an espresso for Jane, Veronica carried on, her voice a little stronger now.

'It's only now, looking back, that I realise just how deep into despair I let myself fall.' She looked up and caught Jane's eye. 'And it's you, more than anybody, I have to thank for helping me out of it. Really, Jane, thank you.' Jane was still mumbling a few words in reply when her employer suddenly stunned her. 'David thinks the world of you, you know.'

At first, Jane tried to make light of it. 'For helping you? I was only doing my job and, besides, I like you a lot as well.'

Veronica's face cracked into a gentle smile. 'But not in the same way as David likes you. Tell me, what do you think of him? I promise I won't say a word.'

To Jane's own surprise, she answered immediately and honestly, without any attempt at diplomacy or caution. 'I think I'm falling in love with him... In fact I think I *have* fallen in love with him.' The smile on her employer's face only broadened so she took heart and carried on. 'The thing is, your mother-in-law's been telling me about Scarlett and I'm scared stiff he's going to shut me out for fear of the same thing happening again. And of course, the last thing I would ever want is to compromise my relationship with you if you disapproved.'

'Falling in love with my son is the most wonderful thing you could ever do for me.' Veronica reached over and squeezed Jane's hand tenderly. 'I really mean that.' Her expression then became much less affectionate. 'As for Scarlett, David was a very good soldier but a seriously bad judge of women. We could all see she was wrong for him but he wouldn't see reason – right up to the bitter end.' Shaking her head to clear the sad memories, Veronica began to smile once more. 'I'm delighted his taste in women has improved so spectacularly. I couldn't ask for better.'

Fortunately the waiter returned with their coffees at that moment and Jane's blushes were able to subside before she responded. 'It's not just me. From what I heard at the wedding, his men thought the world of him as well. Special Forces don't do gallantry medals but it sounds as though he's far more deserving of one than I was.' She reached into her bag and brought out Taffy's note. Without a word, she pushed it across the little table to Veronica, who took it, opened it and read it. It took a couple of minutes before she commented and her voice was heavy with emotion.

'That's so good to read. His father would have been immensely proud.' She looked up and Jane could see the tears sparkling in her eyes, but a little smile also appeared. 'I'm pleased to see that this chap shares my feeling that you and David should be together.'

'I just hope David does.'

At exactly seven o'clock they went into the hospital, and after checking in at the front desk, they climbed the stairs to the second floor. All the time Jane was bracing herself for what she was going to see. For days now she had been doing her best not to think of the horrific images she had seen of disfigured soldiers from the First World War – some with no jaw bone or with appalling scarring to their faces. Nevertheless, she had convinced herself that she didn't care what he looked like and she told herself firmly that she had fallen in love with the man beneath the beard – whatever he looked like. But that didn't lessen her anxiety.

A nurse met them and accompanied them to a side room separated from the corridor by a glass screen. In there, propped up on two or three pillows was David and as Jane caught sight of him a massive wave of relief flooded over her and her heart went out to him. He was looking good – in fact far better than she had imagined. All right, he was pale, but of course, she told herself, it was probably because the skin of his face had been buried beneath inches of bushy beard for years now. The hair on his head was now little more than half an inch long and it suited him far better than his unruly thatch. The clean-shaven right side of his face was every bit as handsome as in her photo, while the left side was covered by a white dressing, as was his left ear but the shape of the jawbone beneath didn't look abnormal. Veronica had told her that this would hopefully be the final bout of reconstructive surgery he would undergo and from what Jane could see so far, it looked like it had been successful.

The nurse pointed to a button on the wall below the window which, when pressed, allowed two-way communication. After she had gone off, Jane pressed and held the button and indicated to Veronica that she could speak to him.

'Ciao, David, how're you feeling?'

'Physically fine, thanks, Mum. Just a bit frustrated. I'm hoping they'll let me out before long.' He waved. 'Hi, Jane, thanks for coming.'

That also sounded positive so she waved back and kept it light. 'How much did you have to pay the barber? Removing all that hair can't have been a quick job.'

He smiled and then grimaced. 'Ouch. They tell me it's good to keep my face muscles moving but every time I smile it hurts. As for the barber, I gave him a hefty tip. He deserved it. I imagine he's got enough to stuff a pillow.' It was good to hear him sounding cheerful.

He chatted to them for some minutes until a masked nurse appeared with a tray of food for him and Jane slipped the note from Taffy onto the tray, adding a few words of explanation through the window.

'Your friend Taffy gave me a note for you. I suggest you read it after we've gone.' Hastily changing the subject, she pointed to his tray, on which she could see a bowl of minestrone soup and what looked like a crème caramel. 'How's the food?'

He grimaced. 'I'm on liquids and soft foods only for the time being. The food here's okay but it isn't a patch on Marcello's. Remember the *fritto misto*?' He sounded positively nostalgic.

'How could I forget? It was amazing.' She glanced across at Veronica. 'In fact we're taking the Hollywood people there on Friday.'

She nodded in agreement. 'Yes, indeed. David, do you think you'll be able to make it? The meeting's at home at ten and then we're all going to Burano.'

'I'll do my very best. The medics say it's all healing up fast.'

'I do hope so.' Veronica pointed at the tray of food. 'The nurse said not to make you talk too much so we'll leave you to your meal. You don't want it to get cold. We'll see you tomorrow.'

Jane gave him a big smile and a wave but she felt the same sense of frustration he had mentioned. The sooner she could sit down and have a serious talk with him the better.

Chapter 32

Next day Diana took Jane over to the Lido along with Linda and the dog. Arriving at the island they motored up a narrow canal amid noticeably more modern buildings with cars parked all along the sides of the roads. Coming from the car-free *centro storico*, this was quite a shock to the system. They moored up at a pontoon just behind the Palazzo del Cinema, a modernist building of the Fascist era with flags of all nations along the edges of the flat roof and hung with banners advertising the upcoming event. For now, it was all still closed up and they walked past it and headed for the beach. There were many fine residences with flourishing gardens all around, but most looked as if they dated back a century or two at most, rather than to Renaissance times like the old part of the city they had left behind.

Diana took Dino for a walk while Jane and Linda went for a swim. David was never far from Jane's thoughts and she had just settled back on her sunbed to dry when she received a call from him and her heart leapt. She glanced down at the little girl and mouthed the words 'It's Uncle David'.

'Hi, David, still locked up?'

'Not for much longer. I should be out tomorrow, and apparently I can even start receiving visitors from this evening. I'll be all bandaged up for a while but they tell me they're happy with the progress I'm making.' There was a pause before he spoke again, this time sounding more serious. 'Thanks for bringing me Taff's note. I'm glad you met him. He's one of my closest friends.'

'He told me you saved his life, and the lives of all the others that day.'

'All I did was to call off the attack. Any normal person would have done the same – you said it yourself. I bet Taff didn't tell you he was the guy who carried me off the battlefield under fire.'

'I thought you said you were walking wounded.'

'Well, maybe that was a bit of an understatement, but at least I was conscious.' There was another pause. 'I couldn't help noticing what he said about me and you. I think we'd better have a talk, don't you?'

She was desperately trying to work out from his tone what he might be thinking, but it was hard. All she could do was to agree. 'I'd like that. Listen, I wouldn't want you to think I gave him the wrong idea about you and me. He just must have jumped to conclusions.'

'Don't worry, we can talk about everything this evening. It'll be good to talk.'

'I'm looking forward to it immensely.' And she was – but not without trepidation.

After the call ended she lay back, trying to decide whether he had sounded pleased or not at Taffy's assumption that the two of them had got together. The fact that he had said 'don't worry' and 'it'll be good to talk' was encouraging, although a declaration of undying love would have been preferable. She was still trying to sort things out in her head when she was interrupted by the little girl's voice. She looked across to see Linda peeking into her new Paddington Bear bag at her teddy whose nose was just protruding from inside.

'You're right, Teddy: Jane loves David.'

Jane almost fell off her sunbed. Now even a seven-year-old could see through her. She did her best to sound casual as she joined in the conversation, deliberately addressing her remarks to the bear in the bag.

'What makes you think that, Teddy?'

'That's easy.' Linda answered for her ursine friend. 'Teddy knows everything. Like, for instance...' – she lowered her voice – 'Did you know that Diana's got a pair of bright red knickers? Teddy's seen them.'

Interesting as this might be, it didn't help explain what had given Jane away, so she tried again. 'So how does Teddy know about David and me?'

'Well...' The little girl settled down importantly alongside the teddy in the bag and explained. 'Grandma says so, and Mummy agrees and so does Diana. And of course, Maria was talking about it ages ago.'

Jane shook her head slowly in disbelief. Linda's mother had gone back to Rome weeks ago so if she had talked about it, it must have been common knowledge in the Cooper household for ages. 'And they all said they thought I was in love with David?'

To her amazement, Linda shook her head.

'No, silly. They all said they thought David was in love with you. Now, listening to you on the phone, Teddy knows that you love him back.' For the first time the little girl raised her eyes from the cuddly toy and looked across at Jane. 'And that's good. Teddy and I both think that's good.'

'You do?'

'Of course, because we love you, too.' She said it in such a matter-of-fact, simple way that Jane felt tears rush to her eyes. She reached across and scooped up the little girl and the teddy, pulling them over to her sunbed and hugging them to her.

'And I love you to bits as well, Linda.' She reached into the bag and pulled out the bear. 'And I love you too, Teddy.' And she kissed them both.

Now all that remained to be seen was whether the women in his family had got it right. Did Uncle David really love Auntie Jane?

—

At seven o'clock precisely, Jane and Veronica arrived at the hospital. A nurse told them not to stay too long so Jane insisted that Veronica should go in to see her son on her own first. As his mother went in, Jane looked through the glass and caught David's eye, delighted to see him manage a cautious smile. He raised a hand to give her a little wave. She waved back and then turned away, to give him and his mother some privacy.

She walked along the corridor until she reached a window and looked out across the lagoon. The shadows were lengthening but the sky was still a clear blue. Right below her a vaporetto was just setting off from the *Ospedale* landing stage, heading towards Murano, while a little further out three gondolas were sculling to and fro, and it looked as though these were beginners learning the age-old art. David had told her he had also learned this skill and she wondered if he would ever take her for a romantic ride along the atmospheric canals of Venice in a gondola.

Her thoughts turned to the way her life had changed so radically in the past few months. She had come to Italy in a depressed state, barely able to raise a smile, and since meeting Veronica and her family she had begun to feel the dark clouds begin to clear. Then she had met David up in the hills and her whole world had changed. The more she saw of him – whether in his running shorts with his faithful hound or lying here in hospital – there could be no doubt in her mind that she had found real true love. But what about him?

She now knew without a shadow of a doubt that she wanted to be with him and, if he was willing, to spend the rest of her life with him, but there still remained the question of just how he felt about her. Yes, she felt sure he liked her and she had convinced herself that his hesitation had been as a result of the way his former girlfriend had reacted to his disfigurement. But was that it? Until he and she could have a real talk, the doubt remained that he might not share the same depth of feelings for her as she did for him. The nervous tension coursing through her at the thought of the imminent meeting was all too familiar to her – except this time it wasn't a landmine responsible for it, but a man.

She was still lost in her thoughts when she heard Veronica's voice at her shoulder.

'Your turn. They don't want us to spend much time with him but he's looking and sounding so much better and he's coming out tomorrow. Now, go on in and see him but the nurse said just for a few minutes. I'll wait for you here.'

Jane straightened her shoulders and went back along the corridor. When she reached David's room, she took a deep breath before opening the door, knowing that the whole future direction of her life potentially hung on the events of the next few seconds. That same cautious smile reappeared on his face as he saw her and she drew strength from it.

'Hi, Jane, thanks for coming to see me. Surely you must have better things to do.'

'I can't think of anywhere I'd rather be.' She could hear the emotion in her voice and felt sure he must hear it too. She stood hesitantly in no man's land, partway between the door and the bed, uncertain what to do while all her instincts were screaming at her to go across and hug him tight.

His smile didn't falter. 'I've been thinking about you a lot.'

'Have you? I haven't stopped thinking about you. You can't imagine how happy I am to see you getting better – and you look great.' She was still standing a few feet from him. Then a sudden thought occurred to her. 'I bring greetings from Diana. She told me to give you a kiss from her.'

'That's kind.' He raised a hand in her direction and winked. 'Well, are you going to deliver her message or aren't you?'

His eyes sparkled and she felt another surge of affection for him as she stepped forward. Leaning down, she reached out and caught hold of the sides of his face with her hands, deliberately placing her right hand very softly against the gauze pad on his wounded cheek. She then kissed him equally softly on his good cheek before pulling back a few inches until she was looking deep into his eyes at close range.

'That was from Diana.' She still couldn't be sure what was going through his mind but she decided to go for it anyway. 'This is from me.' And she leant towards him and kissed him on the lips. To her delight she felt his hand reach behind her and stroke her hair, pressing her tighter to him as he kissed her back. Her head started spinning and she came close to collapsing on top of him before an apologetic voice from behind shook her back to reality.

'The doctor said only a few minutes, signora. Tomorrow you can come back again.'

Jane glanced round and gave a little nod of comprehension. Once the nurse had left the room, she returned her attention to David. Before she left, she really had to know.

'David, about you and me…'

She wasn't quite sure how to phrase this. She wanted to tell him how she felt about him, how she had been drawn ever closer to him and how she wanted to spend her whole life with him, but the words failed her. She was still searching for the right thing to say when he reached out and laid a single finger on her lips.

'You and me is the most wonderful thing that's ever happened to me, Jane. If you're sure…' – his other hand waved vaguely towards his scarred cheek – '…if you're sure, I'm sure and I've never been so certain about anything in my life.'

She was almost overwhelmed by the wave of joy that surged through her and it was a real struggle to restrain herself and just kiss him softly once more and then stand up, staring lovingly back at him. Tears ran down her cheek as she managed to produce a reply. 'I'm sure, David. Just like you, I can't imagine anything better.' Realising she really had to leave, she took a big breath and gave him a little wave. 'Ciao, *a domani*.'

'*A domani*, Jane.'

She set off back along the corridor to Veronica, wiping her eyes and blowing her nose on the way, but she could barely contain the bubbles of delight effervescing through her whole body. He felt the same way about her and he was going to be all right! Her life, so sad only a few months ago, was bright and joyful once more. Whether or not she had the healing hills to thank for this monumental shift in her life was unimportant. What counted was that it had happened. When she got back to Veronica, she had a big silly grin on her face and she had a feeling it wasn't going to leave her for a long time. It did not pass unnoticed.

'It's good to see the old David back again, isn't it? How did the reunion go? Was he happy to see you?'

Jane nodded. 'I think he was every bit as happy to see me as I was to see him.'

'And does he feel the same way about you as you do about him?'

'He says he does. I really think he does.'

'That's wonderful.' Veronica gave her a warm smile and an equally warm hug. 'Now, I don't know about you but I'm starving. There's a little *pizzeria* just around the corner from here that was always very good. I haven't had a good pizza for ages and I've not been there since before Peter's death but I think I rather like the idea of going there now. Would you care to join me? Fancy a pizza?'

The restaurant was in a little piazza less than five minutes away from the hospital and they were given a table outside, looking out over a narrow canal that edged the square. After ordering their pizzas and a bottle of Prosecco, Veronica filled the glasses before holding hers up towards Jane.

'Cheers, Jane, thanks for everything.' They clinked their glasses together. 'Welcome to the family.'

It was all Jane could do not to burst into tears, but she managed to hold it together and a big sip of the cold wine helped. She was still composing a response when Veronica's voice interrupted her thoughts.

'I thought you might be interested to hear that I finally started writing a new book this afternoon. Maybe you might like to hear the title I've come up with for it.' She caught Jane's eye and grinned mischievously. 'It's a story of two people, both with tragic backgrounds, who meet up and fall in love.' Her grin expanded even more. 'I need to know what *you* think of it, even though as it says in all my books: "Any resemblance to actual persons, living or dead, is entirely coincidental". I do so hope you approve.'

'How could I not? I'm delighted for you that your muse has returned at long last.' Jane smiled back at her. 'So… what's the title?'

'In view of how lucky these two people are to find each other after so much heartache and pain, I've decided to call the book *A Chance in a Million*.'

Epilogue

The Cooper family party to celebrate *Carnevale* the following February was a glittering event. The whole of the *piano nobile* of the palazzo was hung with bunting and the façade facing the Grand Canal was festooned with coloured lights. A regular string of launches and water taxis disgorged guests in evening finery at the jetty, and Alvise in his smartest uniform greeted them and ushered them into the house. Earlier that day, Jane had helped the others clear much of the furniture from the living room and a string quartet was now playing at the far end, while uniformed waiters and waitresses circulated, dispensing champagne and canapés. Candles strategically positioned around the room reflected in the glass pendants of the chandeliers and the whole place sparkled.

As Venetian carnival tradition dictated, the guests were all masked and dressed in their finest and most extravagant clothes. As Jane helped to greet the new arrivals she immediately recognised the Duchess di Pontegrande by her diamond tiara, even though her face was covered by a glittering silver mask trimmed with lace. Her husband's sinister plague doctor mask with a grotesque hooked nose failed to disguise his mop of grey hair and Jane greeted them both by name. The duchess was moment-arily confused.

'Beatrice, is that you?' Jane was also masked, although her fair hair had been curled up into a precarious swirl and was very different to Beatrice's. She was about to reveal her identity when the duchess realised her mistake. 'But it's Jane, isn't it? Of course it is. Veronica's been telling me your wonderful news. How lovely to see you again and how simply stunning you look. That dress is sublime.' She waved a hand towards her. 'Do, please, spin around for me, just so I can admire you in all your glory, would you?'

Jane did as she was bidden, rather glad that her lacy mask covered her blushes, and was relieved to accomplish a three-sixty spin without toppling off her high heels. She felt the silk dress billow out around her and heard the duchess give a little sigh of admiration.

'Simply gorgeous.' She leant towards Jane and lowered her voice. 'From Veronica's collection, by any chance?'

Jane nodded and added in similarly guarded tones. 'Of course, and I'm still trying to get my head around whose dress this used to be. Feel like hazarding a guess?'

There was a pause as the duchess did some thinking. 'I have a feeling I might have seen Grace Kelly wearing something similar in one of her films. Am I right?'

Jane shook her head. 'It's a bit older than that. Believe it or not, this dress once belonged to Greta Garbo. I'm terrified I'll mess it up.'

'You'll be fine, Jane. Just enjoy the experience. We all need to dress up from time to time and embrace our good fortune to be alive and well and living in this most wonderful of cities. From what Veronica tells me, you're going to need to get used to it, and I'm so happy for you.' The duchess glanced over at her husband. 'And now we really must go and say hello to Veronica and the rest of the family but I look forward to talking to you later on. Come, Sandro, we must move on.'

Her husband's mask prevented him from kissing Jane's hand but she distinctly saw his eyes smile at her before he and the duchess left and heard him murmur under his breath. 'So beautiful. My compliments.'

Jane could still feel her cheeks glowing as the next couple arrived and she welcomed them.

As the evening progressed, she found herself talking to all manner of different people, all masked and all bar a few unknown to her. Flora was there, wearing a ruby red dress with a matching mask that bristled with red and orange feathers, making her look like a delicate little bird of paradise. From the light in her eyes, she was thoroughly enjoying herself.

One tall man looked vaguely familiar beneath his red fox mask that covered most of his face and half his head. He approached her and inclined his head in a little bow.

'Good evening, Jane. It's good to see you again.' His Welsh accent was unmistakable and Jane's surprise was complete.

'Taffy!' She instinctively threw her arms around him and pulled him down so she could kiss him on the cheeks, or as close as she could get with the long nose of the foxy mask in the way. 'I didn't know you were coming.' She heard him chuckle.

'Dave told me he wanted it to be a surprise. I'm delighted to be here and to see you looking like a movie star. Seriously, you look amazing.'

Just then, they were joined by another tall man. This one was wearing a stylish silk evening jacket and a ghostly white mask that merged into a black highwayman's hat on his head.

'Ciao, bella. Greta Garbo, I presume.'

'Paolo! I would never have recognised you underneath that disguise. How did you know about my dress? Did Beatrice tell you?'

'I would love to say I remembered it from an old movie but you're right, I cheated. Bee told me.'

At that moment Beatrice arrived with a visibly excited Linda at her side dressed like a fairy. Since starting her new job as a news anchor on Venice TV in January, Beatrice and Linda had been living at the palazzo, although Jane had a feeling it wouldn't be long before she moved in with Paolo. As Jane introduced them both to Taffy, Beatrice stretched an affectionate arm around Paolo's waist, pointed at Jane with her free hand and glanced down at her daughter.

'Can you guess who this is, Linda?' The little girl didn't hesitate.

'Jane!' And she ran over to wrap herself around Jane's waist.

Jane looked down at her affectionately. 'How did you know it was me?'

'The ring, silly.' Linda reached for Jane's left hand and held it up so that the diamond cluster on the fourth finger sparkled in the candlelight.

The man in the fox mask looked up sharply. 'Dave didn't tell me about that. Does this mean what I think it means?' As Jane nodded, he carried on. 'I couldn't be happier for you… and him.' He surveyed the crowd. 'Where is he anyway? I only arrived in Venice a few hours ago and I haven't seen him yet. I have an urgent question for him.'

'And what's that?' Jane wondered if it might concern her and her new fiancé but in fact it was far more prosaic.

'I need to ask him if he's got any straws. How the hell I'm supposed to have a drink with a six-inch hairy nose sticking out of the middle of my face? Wear a mask, he said... You can buy one when you get to Venice, he said...'

At that moment the musicians reached the end of the piece they had been playing and there was the unmistakable sound of a spoon clinking against a glass. The noise in the room gradually died down and all eyes turned towards the low stage in the corner where the musicians were now taking a well-earned break. Veronica stepped up onto it and waved a welcoming hand towards her guests. As she did so, she removed her mask and the delight on her face was clear to see.

'My friends,' she spoke in Italian. 'Thank you all most warmly for coming. Tonight is a night of celebration for me. I have some big news. First, the film version of *Love Letter from Vienna* will be coming out just before Christmas later this year but, even more importantly, I've just finished writing a new book which should, if all goes well, be appearing on the shelves this summer. I can't tell you how pleased and relieved I am to have got my writing muse back again. I would ask you all to join me in a toast to *A Chance in a Million*. This will be my first book since the death of my beloved Peter and I know it won't be the last.' She held up her champagne glass. '*A Chance in a Million!*'

Jane made a heroic attempt to take a sip of champagne without removing her mask and without bursting out laughing as she watched Taffy turning his head almost upside down so as to do the same. She had just straightened up again when she received a sharp prod to her bottom. Even through the silk of the dress she could feel that this was a cold wet nose and as she looked down, she saw the sparkling eyes of a very happy Labrador at her feet.

'Dino, what are you doing here? You were supposed to be in the kitchen.'

'It's all right. He's with me.'

She raised her eyes to see a now very familiar tall, broad-shouldered figure in an immaculate dinner jacket, wearing a black leather wolf mask that made him look remarkably similar to his four-legged friend at his feet. David stretched a loving arm around her and rubbed the side of his face, the injured side of his face, affectionately against hers before suddenly realising who the man in the fox mask was. He took two steps towards Taffy and the men embraced. In spite of the masks and in spite of the hug lasting barely a couple of seconds, Jane could feel the emotion in the air. As this was the first time they had met up in over three years, Jane could tell how overcome David must be by the memories flooding back into his head, so she stepped in to give him time to recover.

'Taffy has an important question for you.' She caught hold of one of David's hands and gave it an encouraging squeeze. As she did so, they were interrupted by the arrival of the hostess, still beaming with delight.

'I've just had a call from Diana. She sends her love but she's in the middle of her exams.' She gave them a warm smile. 'It's so, so good to know that things are once more going well for the Cooper family.' She turned towards Jane. 'And for you, my darling Jane. We couldn't have done it without you.' She plucked a glass of champagne from a passing waiter and held it up. 'To us. May all our hearts rejoice.'

They all joined in the toast, and as they did so, Jane felt David's lips at her ear.

'To you, Jane. You mended me and I still can't believe it.'

'We mended each other.' She saw his blue eyes sparkle beneath the mask and she reached up to kiss him on the nape of the neck. 'I love you, David Cooper.'

He hesitated for a moment before pulling the mask up until it was sitting on his head, revealing his face with its slightly lopsided look she had come to cherish. He bent towards her and kissed her through the lace of her mask.

'And I love you too, Jane, and I always will.'

There was a movement at their sides and she saw him glance down affectionately.

'We love you, too, Dino, but dogs stay on the floor, not halfway up my leg.'

The dog looked unrepentant and just for a moment it looked as though he winked.

Acknowledgements

Warmest thanks to my lovely editor, Emily Bedford, and everybody at my publishers, Canelo. This is my fourteenth book with Canelo and it has been a most enjoyable journey. Thanks also to the mysterious "Tim from the USA" who took the trouble to contact me with a suggestion which has resulted in the scene where Dino the dog goes AWOL. And finally, thanks to Mariangela who reads all my stuff and comes up with so many good ideas – as well as telling me when she thinks I've got it wrong.